Funny how life worked out...

Fifteen years ago Joe had fantasized about a moment like this. Him and Molly together, under the night sky, puffy snowflakes falling gently around them. He'd dreamed of taking her to a movie, then parking somewhere with her snuggling her head on his shoulder, him putting his arms around her.

Stirring, she lifted her head at the same moment he looked down at her. His chest tightened when he found himself looking directly into her eyes, his mouth less than an inch from hers. Time spun backward and Joe was that unsure boy again, wanting to kiss the most beautiful girl in school.

He could think of a lot of reasons why it was wrong to listen to what his body was telling him to do. To let his body melt into hers. To open her jacket and slide his hands from her slender waist to those magnificent breasts. To kiss her until they were both breathless and fiery with needing each other.

Molly's eyes bore into his, and Joe knew he had a split second to kiss her...or let her get away again.

Margaret St. George

JOE'S GIRL

Harlequin Books

TORONTO • NEW YORK • LONDON
AMSTERDAM • PARIS • SYDNEY • HAMBURG
STOCKHOLM • ATHENS • TOKYO • MILAN
MADRID • WARSAW • BUDAPEST • AUCKLAND

ISBN 0-373-16710-5

JOE'S GIRL

Copyright © 1998 by Margaret St. George.

Chapter One

"Look," Molly said into the telephone, trying not to let her voice reflect her frustration and thinning patience. "All I'm trying to do is find out what my address is. Why is this so difficult?"

The woman at the county clerk's office sighed heavily. "I'm trying to figure it out for you, okay? Tell me again where you live."

Molly leaned against the kitchen wall and stared out the window. This was the third county employee she had talked to, and she was no closer to getting an answer than she had been when she dialed the phone. "All right. Are you looking at a county map?" Her own map was spread across the card table she was using as a temporary kitchen table. "I'm five miles west of Vrain. Turn right on Steamboat Mountain Drive, and right again on County Road 2408. Now. Do you see the private no-name road that cuts off of the county road? I just moved into the first twenty acres along that road. The old Stevens place. So, what's my address?"

"There's no mail delivery out there. Your address will be a post office box."

"I understand that," Molly said, suppressing a scream of exasperation. "But I need a physical address for UPS and FedEx." She waved a hand. "Or suppose I need to call the police or the fire department. Where do I tell them to come?"

She heard a riffling of pages, and then the nasal voice returned. "Hey, I found you. Here it is. Your physical address is 0090 County Road 2406."

Frowning, Molly thought a minute. "That can't be right. The road that runs in front of my house isn't a county road. It's a private road."

"I know. But if you and the others who live along that road ever get together and upgrade the road to county standards, and then if you deed it over to the county, it will be County Road 2406."

Molly pinched her arm to make sure she was awake. She was feeling the way Alice must have felt after she tumbled down the rabbit hole. Drawing a long breath, she tried again.

"But it isn't a county road now. And there's only four parcels of ground along the private road. I can't imagine four families would chip in thousands of dollars to upgrade the road and then deed it over to the county. If that ever happens, it will be years in the future. I need to know what my address is *now*."

"Well, that *is* your address now."

"But I'm looking at a county map, and there's no County Road 2406."

"Of course not. You people haven't deeded it over yet."

"Look," Molly said, speaking through gritted teeth. "Suppose my house catches fire. I call the fire department. Will County Road 2406 show up on the fire department's map?"

"Why would it? County Road 2406 doesn't exist yet."

"That's what I've been trying to tell you!"

"But the fire department will know where you mean."

"Really? How? Are they psychic?" She stopped herself and drew a deep breath. Sarcasm was not going to help. "Okay," she said after a long pause. "I give up. You win. If my house catches fire, I'll just tell the fire department to drive west until they see flames."

"That's the spirit," the county employee said cheerfully. "Is there anything else I can do for you?"

Molly held the phone out in front of her and blinked incredulously before she put it back to her ear. "As a matter of fact, there is. Does it make any difference to you people that the house up the no-name road from me has the same house number that you just assigned to me?"

"Oh." There was the sound of more pages riffling. "I see the problem. We'll have to work on that. By the way, you need to display your house number in four-inch letters before you start your remodel project. That's a county ordinance."

"So I should go out and buy some large house numbers that are the same numbers as the house nearest me and display them on the side of my house."

"See?" the county employee chirped. "That wasn't as difficult as you thought, now was it?"

A battered green pickup turned off the no-name road into her driveway and rattled toward the house. That would be Joe Townsend, her contractor.

"I have to hang up now," Molly said into the phone, "before I start screaming, have a nervous breakdown and say something we'll both regret. I imagine a lot of people have hysterics while talking to you, so I'm sure you'll understand."

She hung up the phone and relieved a bit of frustration by swatting about eight flies on the window while watching Joe Townsend swing out of his pickup and walk toward her front door. Despite a foot of snow on the ground and temperatures in the low twenties, he wasn't wearing a coat or a jacket. He wore cowboy boots, jeans, and a blue-and-black plaid flannel shirt with the sleeves rolled to his elbows. His only concession to a frigid January was a denim vest.

Occasionally life tossed an interesting coincidence across a person's path, and Joe Townsend was definitely an interesting coincidence. Molly had known Joe since the seventh grade. To say that she had known him wasn't quite accurate. She had sat in front of him in several classes, but she'd been aware of him enough to remember him all these years later. She had lost track of Joe in high school, and hadn't thought of him again until three weeks ago, when she discovered they were now both living in Vrain, Colorado. She hadn't hired him because she'd known him way back in middle school, but she'd been secretly glad when his bid was the lowest.

Swatting flies and watching him approach the house, she noticed that his baseball cap was on crooked and he could use a haircut. She also noticed that he was whistling and appeared to be in a good mood. Right now, she would have preferred a mood as black as her own.

"Hi, honey," he called, walking in the front door. "Is the coffee on?"

Turning away from the window, Molly stared at him. "Isn't it customary to knock before you walk in someone's house?"

A dazzling grin lit his tanned face and crinkled his eyes. "Knock on the door of a construction site?" He walked to the coffeepot and opened the cabinet door above it. "Cups up here?"

"Help yourself." Molly smacked another fly, amazed by the number of them, waited a minute, then walked past him to refill her own coffee cup. "This isn't a construction site yet."

"It will be, starting tomorrow morning." He sat down at the card table, glanced at the map spread across it, then raised his coffee cup in a salute before he drank half of it. Molly couldn't believe it. The coffee should have scalded his throat, but he didn't seem to notice. "Not bad, but you can't beat coffee made in a tin pot on top of the stove."

"Listen. I'm in no mood for criticism." She sat down across from him and narrowed her eyes. "If you don't like my coffee, then bring a thermos."

He laughed, a deep rumble that started low in his chest. "Bad morning?"

"You could say that. As a matter of curiosity, what is the address listed on your building permits?"

"Oh-oh-nine-oh County Road 2406."

"I can't stand it." She stared at him, wondering if he remembered her from the seventh and eighth grades. Probably not. He hadn't mentioned it. "That address doesn't exist! That is not a county road out there, it's a private road. And 0090 is the number of the house over there!" She pointed out the window, to the vacant house half a mile farther up the private road.

Joe grinned, and his eyes twinkled. "Will it push you over the edge to hear that the phone company thinks you live on County Road 2401, and the utility company swears you live on County Road 2408?"

Molly exploded. "It isn't a county road!" Standing, she paced across the kitchen's old, cracked linoleum floor and stopped beside an outdated fridge that made clunking noises every few minutes. "I'm sorry. This is my first experience as a homeowner. I had no idea that people went through this kind of craziness merely to find out what their address is." She answered his grin with a weak smile and returned to the card table. "So, you start tomorrow?"

"I'll be here at seven o'clock. The pooches will arrive at seven-thirty."

"Pooches?"

"My crew." He passed her on the way to the coffeepot, poured another cup, then returned to the table. Fascinated, Molly watched him take a swallow. She'd never known anyone who drank scalding coffee.

"Seven o'clock," she repeated. One of the nice things about being unemployed was that she had reverted to the natural rhythms of a night person. Not having to get up early was the only thing she didn't miss from her previous life. Now it appeared she would be returning to the early-morning wake-up calls she had dreaded when she was modeling. In order to be showered and dressed when he arrived, she'd have to get up around six. The thought dismayed her. "Seven," she said again.

"We have to talk about you living here during the project."

"We've already covered that," she said absently, still thinking about having to get up early.

"Honey, the first thing we're going to do is gut this floor to the outside walls and the bearing wall. We're going to pull out the heaters. We're going to cut holes in the outside walls for the new windows. We're going to open both ends of the house. It's going to get damned cold in here."

"You'll have to leave me some heaters in the bedroom, and in the basement, where I've set up my desk."

He nodded, his blue eyes steady on hers. "I'll instruct the electricians to jury-rig a couple of heaters for you. But they aren't going to be very effective against both ends of the house being open to the great outdoors. Plus, tearing out walls and building new ones creates a lot of dust and debris, and knocking down most of a house, then rebuilding it, is going to be noisy. Honey, it would be a hundred times more convenient for everyone if you'd take an apartment for the next four months."

"Look," she said, turning her gaze to the mountain view outside the window. "A lot of things have happened to me during the last year." That had to be the understatement of her life. "I'm still trying to cope with…a lot of changes."

If it hadn't been for two old friends, Darcy Connors and Anne Clancy, helping her—taking over, really—she didn't know how she would have gotten packed or made the move from New York City to Vrain. Her chest constricted painfully at the thought of moving again, this time with no one to take charge. She wasn't ready for another change. Just thinking about finding another place and packing again felt overwhelming.

"This is a rough time for me right now," she explained in a low voice, still gazing out the window. More flies had appeared. Where on earth were they coming from? "I don't want to look for an apartment. I don't want to move again. I don't want to make decisions right now. Can you understand that?" she asked, turning to glance at him.

No, she decided, studying the angles of his strong face.

Joe would not understand. He didn't look like a man who had ever experienced any difficulty making a decision.

"I know a little about what happened to you. It was in the newspapers and the tabloids," he said finally. He leaned forward, resting his forearms on the card table and studying her expression. "Maybe this isn't the best time for you to jump into a big remodel project."

"There isn't much choice, is there? Look around you. No one has lived in this house for fifteen years. And my grandparents didn't maintain it as well as they should have in the years before they died. The place is crumbling." It required all her willpower not to turn her face away from his scrutiny, not to raise her hands to cover the scar on her upper lip and the scar that cut through her left eyebrow.

"May I ask you a personal question?" When she didn't answer, he went ahead anyway. "You seem to have plenty of money. Presumably you can live anywhere you want to. So why come to Vrain? To a house that needs extensive remodeling?"

Because she had known Joe Townsend as an adolescent, she had a tendency to treat him as if they were old acquaintances. But they weren't. And pride wouldn't allow her to admit to a stranger that she'd run away from her life, that she'd fled to the place she thought of as home, although it had never really been her home. But this land and this house had been a refuge when she was a child, and that was what she needed now. A place to hide until the time came—if it ever did—when she felt strong again, when she knew what she would do with the rest of her life.

"The point is," she said, standing and walking to the sink. "I'm here. I may stay for a year or two, or I may not." She shrugged and ran a fingertip over one of the chips in the porcelain. "Fixing my grandparents' house gives me something to do, a sense of feeling as if I'm accomplishing something. Right now I need that."

Joe shrugged shoulders that were disproportionately broad for his wiry frame. "It's your money and your choice. As long as you understand that you'll be living in the middle of a construction zone.'' He cupped his hands around the coffee mug. ''And there will be decisions you'll have to make as we go along.''

The tight feeling returned to her chest. ''Isn't everything decided? On the blueprints?''

''We're doing a custom job here. You can make any changes to the plans that you like.'' He shrugged again. ''Just stay ahead of me, honey. Making changes after something is built and already in place gets expensive.''

''There's something we have to talk about,'' she said sharply. ''My name is not Honey.''

''Oh, hell, I call everyone honey. It doesn't mean anything except I'm not good with names.''

Maybe that was why he didn't remember her. Or maybe middle school was too many years ago. Maybe she hadn't made the impression on him that he had on her. ''Considering how much money I'm going to pay you, and considering that we'll see each other every day for the next four months, it seems to me that you could make an effort to remember my name. Molly Stevens isn't hard to remember.'' In fact, considering the media blitz Apple Cosmetics had created when she was selected as the Apple Girl, she would have guessed that most of America would recognize her name. ''But if you forget, just look at the bottom of the check every week.''

He laughed and stood. ''The reason I came out here today was to take a final walk-through to make sure we're on the same wavelength.'' She moved aside when he came to the sink, rinsed his cup and put it in the dish drainer. ''Basement first,'' he said, striding toward the door. ''Let's see where you set up your desk.''

Silently Molly followed him down the stairs. It was like descending into a cave. Even though it was a walkout basement, the only light in the entire area came through the window of the door leading outside.

Joe snapped on the overhead lights and pulled a crumpled notepad out of the back pocket of his jeans. ''Okay. We're going to finish this area, right?''

"Right." Thirty years ago, Molly's grandfather had framed out two bedrooms and a laundry room, but he'd never finished the project. Wrapping her arms around herself against the chill, Molly turned up the thermostat while Joe inspected the old framing. "I'm going to go crazy down here until we get some more windows in."

Frowning, he glanced at her desk, then examined the rafters above it. "This might not be the best place for a desk. The new wiring is going to come through here. And the plumbing lines." Hooking his thumbs in his back pockets, he rocked back on his heels and examined her desk. "What kind of work will you do here?"

Molly peered out of the window on the door. Once this wall was opened up with a bank of windows, the view would be wonderful. "I've been offered a book contract. I have to deliver the manuscript by the first of July."

"You're writing a book?"

"I haven't started yet, but yes, I'm going to write a book. At least I'm going to try."

"What's it about?"

"My publisher thinks people would be interested in my life." She shrugged uncomfortably. "That's odd, isn't it? A twenty-eight-year-old writing an autobiography? But..." She'd agreed to the project in the hope that writing about everything would help her understand the emotional roller coaster she'd been riding for about a year, and would help her find the closure she knew she needed.

"Let's take a look at the second floor," Joe said, heading for the stairs. He took them two at a time, while Molly followed at a more sedate pace.

That was one of the things she had noticed immediately, his vitality. He couldn't sit still, he kept jumping up and moving when he talked as if he had more energy than his lean, lanky body could contain.

And, of course, he was great-looking. Being tall herself, she liked tall men. And there wasn't an ounce of fat on him, he was all muscle. Even in January, his face and arms were tanned, evidence that he spent a lot of time outdoors. That was appealing.

The feature most women would notice first, she supposed, was his eyes. Joe had deep blue eyes that sparkled mischievously. Molly had read about sparkling eyes, but she'd met only three people in her life whose eyes actually did sparkle. Joe Townsend was one of them.

She followed a nice fanny up the basement stairs, across the living room, then up another flight of stairs to the second floor. Here, a sitting room and hallway were open to the living room below.

Joe checked everything out, making notes, then looked inside the bedroom. "This is where you'll be sleeping until we're finished?"

"Yes." When he stepped back to the hallway, Molly closed the bedroom door, wondering what he made of the fact that the bedroom floor was covered with boxes she hadn't yet unpacked.

He started down the staircase, giving her a curious look over his shoulder. "When we're finished, this is going to be a big house for just one person. Do you have a husband who'll join you later? Any children?"

"No." She gazed at the back of his head when he stepped into the living room. She didn't know why her grandparents had put in so few windows, and small ones, at that. "How about you? Do you have a wife and a family?" she asked in a light tone.

"Nope. Not yet." Walking to one of the small living room windows, he gazed outside. "This is a beautiful tract of land. Will you be using the barn and pastures? Do you have horses?"

"When I was a kid, my grandparents had a couple of horses that I rode when I visited." She shrugged. "Maybe if I stay here. I don't know."

He looked at her for a long moment, then walked back to the kitchen and poured fresh coffee for both of them before he sat down at the card table and placed his notepad in front of him. "There are a few more things.... Do you object to dogs on the site?"

"Dogs? I guess I don't object." She watched him place a checkmark beside one of the items on his list. "You have a tattoo on your arm." She hadn't noticed it before. "Is that a tree?"

"A redwood," he confirmed, grinning. "I had the tattoo done the day I set up my own construction company." He rubbed a hand along his forearm. "This is to remind me where lumber comes from. It's a reminder to plan ahead and not waste wood."

"You like your job, don't you?" she asked softly. "That makes you a very fortunate person." She had been fortunate, too. She had loved being the Apple Girl, loved the million-dollar contract and the attention and the fame. A year ago, she had been sitting on top of the world and loving the view. She had believed it would last forever.

But that was then. And this was now.

When she realized she was smoothing a fingertip back and forth across the scar above her lip, she made herself drop her hand. "Is there anything else we need to discuss?"

"I think that covers it," Joe said, rising to his feet.

Molly followed him out to his pickup. The air was cold enough that silver puffs appeared before her lips when she spoke, but the mountain sunshine felt warm on her back.

"You and I have met before," she said impulsively. "A long time ago."

Joe smiled at her out of the pickup window as he switched on the ignition. "Mrs. Paulson's English class. You sat in front of me, one space to the right. You wore your hair in a ponytail then. We had history and Spanish together too."

Molly stared at him.

"*Adiós, chica,*" he said laughing. "See you in the morning."

Starting to shiver, she stood in the snowy yard and watched the old green pickup zoom down the driveway and swerve onto the no-name road.

Joe Townsend was an interesting man.

It would be diverting to have him around for the next four months, and that was something she badly needed. A diversion to take her mind off of herself. She'd spent far too much time during the past six months thinking about herself and her problems. She needed something else to think about for a while. Then maybe she would see her problems in a fresh perspective when she returned to them.

When she heard the phone, she shook Joe out of her thoughts and sprinted back to the house, snatching up the receiver on the fourth ring. "Hello?"

"Hi. It's Darcy Connors-slash-Arden. How are things out in the sticks?"

Molly laughed, happy to hear the voice of her oldest and best friend. "Don't tell me that you're going to have one of those hyphenated last names?"

"Hey, I'm a nineties woman. And I hope you're not in any hurry, because I want to tell you all about the wedding. If you ever want to elope, Las Vegas is the place to go!"

"Did an Elvis impersonator perform the service?" Molly asked, grinning and stretching to reach the coffeepot. After twenty minutes of delicious details about the wedding and about Darcy's wonderful new husband, Bruce, Darcy demanded to hear all about Molly's move and the house. "Do you remember Joe Townsend from middle and high school?" she asked, turning her gaze to look out the fly-specked window.

"How could I forget a guy that good-looking? What made you think of him?"

"He's my contractor on the remodel job. And he's even better-looking than you remember." She talked about Joe, liking the sound of his name on her tongue, and her plans for the house. "Oh, jeez, look how long we've been on the phone. And it's your dime."

"Molly? Remember how we sent out for Chinese the day the movers packed up your stuff? Remember what the fortune in your cookie said?"

"I had my mind on other things that day." And she

didn't have much faith in things like horoscopes and fortune cookies, anyway.

"Your fortune told you to follow your heart," Darcy reminded her. "One of my fortune-cookie predictions came true. I wonder if yours will. Maybe you and Joe—"

"Bite your tongue! I've got enough problems right now. The last thing I need right now is a man in my life."

Darcy laughed. "Honey, that's when the right man always comes along."

"HONEY, rise and shine. The coffee is almost ready."

Molly sat bolt upright in bed and stared at her bedroom door, toward the voice floating up the staircase. "What time is it?"

Squinting, she peered at the clock. Ten minutes to seven. She'd overslept. Jumping out of bed, she pushed her bare feet into her slippers and jerked on her robe. The minute she stepped out of her bedroom, she realized there was no way to reach the bathroom without being seen from below. She looked over the balcony railing and saw Joe standing in the living room.

"Nice robe," he said, grinning up at her. "But the hair needs some work."

Flustered, she tossed her braid over her shoulder and frowned down at him. "Give me a couple of minutes to brush my teeth and get dressed." She'd skip a shower this morning. Take one this evening.

"The pooches will be here in thirty minutes. That's Aspen."

An enormous German shepherd bounded up the staircase and raced toward her. He licked her hand, his tail wagging, his big brown eyes as happy to see her as if the two of them were lifelong buddies.

"Ah, good morning, Aspen." Living in apartments and traveling a lot hadn't been a life that lent itself to pets. Molly hadn't been around dogs much since she left home at age eighteen. Eyeing Aspen warily, she glanced down at the dog spit smeared across the hem of her robe, then hurried into the bathroom and closed the door when Aspen would have joined her.

Already she suspected the remodeling project would be more chaotic than she'd originally guessed. But she could stand anything for four months. Couldn't she?

When she rushed downstairs fifteen minutes later, Joe was seated at the card table as if he lived here, drinking coffee and reading the morning paper he'd brought with him.

"Coffee's on the stove," he said, looking up with a cheerful smile.

He'd made the coffee in a beat-up, ancient-looking coffeepot that he must have brought from home. He'd also brought a sack of jelly doughnuts. Molly peeked inside the sack and made a face. "Lard balls," she commented. "If you can stand to eat in the morning, it should be eggs or pancakes or something like that."

"Not a morning person, right?" He watched her avoiding the sunlight streaming through the kitchen window and laughed.

"Never have been." Sitting down across from him, she tasted the coffee and sighed. It really was better than hers. "Sunrise ought to be outlawed."

"Morning is the best time of the day, honey."

"Don't call me honey."

"Today we're going to pull up the old carpet and see what shape the flooring's in. We'll start knocking down the interior walls. It's going to be dusty and noisy."

"I'll be in the basement, remember? I probably won't hear most of it."

She could not have been more mistaken. The first thing the pooches did when they arrived was set up a boom box. Hard rock seemed to shake the ceiling above her head. Molly leaned back from her desk and stared up at the basement rafters. That was when the pounding started. Followed by a series of deafening crashes.

Dust floated down from the rafters and settled in a gray film over her shoulders, and her computer and printer.

After twenty minutes, she gave up staring at the blank screen on her computer and reached for her calculator, grimly working some simple figures. Four months equaled a hundred and nineteen days. The book she had agreed to write was due to the editor in one hundred and fifty days. If she waited until the construction was finished before she started the book, that meant she would only have a month. She suspected even a seasoned author couldn't write a book in thirty-one days.

"Honey?" Joe appeared at the foot of the stairs. She hadn't heard him come down the staircase. "Bad news. We've just discovered that we're in a pocket out here where our cell phones don't work." He indicated the phone on her desk. "Next week we'll be tearing out the wiring upstairs. From then on, your desk phone is going to be the only working phone on the premises."

"I see," Molly said slowly. "So every time you need to call out, and every time you receive a call, it's going to be on my phone."

"Right," he said cheerfully. "Thought I'd let you know." Frowning, he cocked an ear toward the ceiling. "I'll ask the pooches to turn down the music."

"Could they maybe turn it off?" she asked hopefully, glancing at her computer screen. A film of dust coated the surface.

"Honey, this is a construction site. Music makes the pooches happy, and happy pooches do good work."

Suddenly Molly had a suspicion that she would be hearing that explanation often.

"Uh-huh." She would have to live with the music. "I don't suppose you have any pooches who like classical music?"

Joe grinned at her. "It's going to be rock on even-numbered days—that's Al's preference—and country-western on odd-numbered days. That's Coke's preference."

"Coke?" she asked weakly.

"We call him that because he drinks a couple of six-packs of Coke a day. Come on. I'll introduce you to the people who are going to wreck your house and then rebuild it.''

''Okay,'' she said, making herself stand and follow him upstairs. Joe led her into the back bedroom on the ground floor. This was the room where Molly had slept when she visited her grandparents as a child. The room had shrunk over the years.

And even though she sort of knew to expect it, it shocked her to see that someone had knocked a hole in the wall that would come down.

Leaning over, Joe reduced the volume on the boom box. Four young men stopped pulling up layers of old carpet and looked up.

''This is Al, Coke, Trey and Z,'' Joe said. Sure enough, the one called Coke had a red can sitting on the floor near his work boots. ''This is Molly Stevens, the lady who signs the checks, so treat her nice.''

The pooches grinned at her. Then a mutt a little smaller than Aspen bounded out of the hallway, ran straight to Molly and pushed his nose into the crotch of her jeans. Face flaming, Molly backed away.

''Honey,'' Joe said to the young man he had introduced as Z, ''how about putting Bob outside for a while? That's Bob,'' he said to Molly, who was trying to keep the dog away from her.

Z caught the dog by the collar and smiled. ''I'm sorry, Miss Stevens. Bob always does that. But now that he's got your scent, he probably won't do it again.''

She couldn't think of anything to say. Then she realized that Joe had addressed Z as ''honey.'' She stared at him in disbelief. Good heavens, he really did call everyone honey. Even men.

''Ah, it was nice to meet all of you,'' she said faintly.

They smiled and returned to jerking up the layers of old carpet. The air was hazy with dust. A hard-rock group screamed out of the boom box. Joe took her elbow and led her down the hall and into the living room, where it was marginally quieter.

"Some clients give the pooches a six-pack of beer at the end of the day, but that isn't necessary or expected on a long job like this one," Joe said, looking into her dazed eyes.

"My God. I never thought of hors d'oeuvres."

He laughed and glanced at the window. "Gotta go. The Dumpster just arrived."

She stood where he'd left her, listening to the pounding beat of the music, hearing the clash of metal against metal coming from the yard, and the rumble of a bulldozer. Even in the living room, she could smell the musty scent of old dust.

After a full minute, she spun and fled back to the basement.

Half an hour later, she discovered that there was no bathroom in her basement haven, something she hadn't thought about or noticed until now.

But there was also good news. Her computer screen was no longer blank. She'd typed two words: *Chapter One.*

Chapter Two

On the way home from work, Joe stopped at the Goosed
Moose for a beer and a burger. Sandy, the bartender, placed
a frosty mug of Coors in front of him then asked the same
question he'd asked every evening this week. "How's it
going out at the old Stevens place?"

"Fine," Joe said, glancing at himself in the mirror over
the back bar. He had to find time to get a haircut. Maybe
tomorrow. "Does anyone know if Clive is still keeping the
barbershop open until eight on Friday nights?" he asked,
looking down the bar.

But no one was interested in the barbershop. They were
interested in Molly Stevens.

"I read that piece in the *Vrain Sentinel* about her," Bernie Schadler said, leaning forward over his beer. "But it
didn't say how bad she was scarred."

Joe had read the article, too, a piece stitched together
from other sources. Clearly, Moe Dietz, the *Sentinel*'s sole
reporter, had not actually interviewed Molly.

"Yeah," Bonnie said, sliding onto the stool next to him.
"How bad are the scars? Is she grotesque?" A light shudder shivered over the red satin blouse that was part of her
waitress's uniform.

"She's beautiful," Joe said, studying the foam on top of
his beer. "If you weren't looking for the scars, you
wouldn't even notice them."

"Then why hasn't she shown herself in town?" Bonnie asked, her expression a mixture of relief and disappointment. "Is she too good for us? Is that it?"

"She's been to town. I saw her." Everyone but Joe leaned forward to stare down the bar at Wiley Oats. "She came in and bought two hundred and eighty-three dollars' worth of groceries. Bought a lot of fresh stuff like carrots and celery and apples. And those low-cal, low-fat TV dinners."

"What was she wearing?" Bonnie demanded. "Was she wearing a mink coat? God, I'd love to own a mink coat!"

"No, she wore a blue parka. And big sunglasses, like you'd expect."

Joe picked up his burger when Sandy set the basket in front of him, and he carried it to a booth back near the fireplace. Eventually, the feverish speculation about Molly Stevens would die down, but Molly would always be an object of interest. The report of her arrival in Vrain had been the most exciting news to hit town since the first miner looked up from the banks of the St. Vrain River a century and a half ago and shouted, "Gold!" As far as Joe knew, Molly was the first real celebrity to live in Vrain, and she might well be the last. Vrain was a nice little mountain town, but it was too far from Denver for commuters, and not close enough to the nearest ski area to attract tourists.

"Hi. I've been looking for you." Jim Enders slid into the booth and set his burger basket on the table. He took a long swallow from his beer, then smiled. "Okay, I've tried to respect our friendship and not ask you anything about Molly Stevens, but there's something I've gotta know."

Joe sighed and rolled his eyes. "She's beautiful. She only has two scars and you can hardly see them."

"Not that. I want to know about her hair. You know that commercial for waterproof cosmetics? Where she's standing at the edge of the surf wearing that black bathing suit? Well, her hair is blowing back from her face." He unwrapped his burger. "Was that a wig, or does she have long hair?"

Joe thought about the wheat-colored braid that hung down to the small of Molly's back. All week he'd been wondering how she'd look if he opened that braid. He kept thinking about white-gold hair spread across a pillow like strands of silk. "She's got long hair," he said, staring a warning across the table. "And if you ask me one more question about her, I'm going to find another plumber."

Jim laughed, then bit into a bacon cheeseburger. Every man in town loved Sandy's burgers, because if you squeezed them, grease dripped between your fingers. Sandy didn't buy into that low-fat garbage. He still made burgers the way burgers were intended to be made.

"What are we looking at out there? How many bathrooms will there be?" Jim swallowed a swig of beer. "I thought I'd drop off some catalogs next week. Get her started thinking."

Joe put down his burger, his mind racing. For the first time, he realized there was no bathroom in the basement, and the prints didn't call for one to be installed. Swearing softly, he wiped the grease from his hands. "We're going to have to install a bathroom in the basement. Damn it." That would mean coring out the concrete to accommodate the plumbing. It was going to be expensive. One week into the job, and he was going over budget. "We're putting two bedrooms in the basement. The architect should have provided for a bathroom down there."

"I heard she used Hal Morris to draw up the prints. Hell, he hasn't been sober since Jimmy Carter was in office. What are you worrying about, anyway? She's got money. Everybody in America knows Apple Cosmetics signed her to a million-dollar contract."

"That's not the point," Joe said, frowning. "I don't want it to look like I bid the job wrong."

"Pride goeth before the falleth," Jim said, laughing. "You don't want to look bad in front of our celebrity."

Joe didn't care about Molly's celebrity, but he did care about her, and had for a long time. He'd developed a tongue-twisting crush on Molly Stevens in Mrs. Paulson's eighth-grade English class. At that time, she'd been an inch taller than he was, so he hadn't asked her to the end-of-the-year eighth-grade mixer, figuring she wouldn't accept a date with a shorter guy. In high school she'd been a cheerleader and popular, whereas he'd played drums in the band instead of playing sports, and while he had a lot of friends, he hadn't been one of Lakewood High's choices for homecoming king, or anything like that. He'd thought about asking her to their senior prom, but that had been the year he shot up nine inches in height and felt about as graceful as a skinny rag doll and it seemed that he always had a pimple on his chin, and he hadn't thought she knew he was alive, anyway. After graduation, she went back east to college, and he went to Colorado State University.

Former classmates in Denver had fed him tidbits about Molly Stevens over the years. He'd seen her smiling from the covers of women's magazines near the checkout stand when he paid for his groceries. A couple of years ago, there had been a big media splash when Apple Cosmetics chose her from thousands of hopefuls to be the Apple Girl. Joe had watched her on "Good Morning America" while he drank his morning coffee. He'd seen her on other TV shows, in magazine ads. He'd even seen her gorgeous face on a billboard when he drove to Las Vegas for a mini-vacation last fall.

Molly Stevens had always been part of his life and his fantasies, but he would have sworn that he was a total nonentity in her life. Hell, he'd seen her photo in the tabloids, hanging on the arm of film stars or handsome Europeans with fancy titles. He was so far out of her league, they might have lived on different planets.

A whisper could have knocked him over when she mentioned that she remembered him from long ago. He'd been that astonished, and flattered and pleased.

"We're not going to let it go to our heads," he told Aspen when he slid into his pickup. He unwrapped the plain hamburgers that Sandy had cooked up especially for man's best friend, and crumbled them into the dog dish he kept on the floormat. Aspen licked Joe's hand, then gobbled his supper while Joe pulled out of the parking lot and drove to his cabin.

That Molly remembered him from way back when didn't mean anything except that she had a good memory for names. And she hadn't chosen him to rebuild her grandparent's place because she was hot for his bod. She'd liked the quality of work on the homes he'd proudly shown her, and she'd liked the bottom line on his bid.

When he got home, he snapped on the lights, filled Aspen's water bowl, then went into his office and turned on his computer, pulling up the file that contained his bid for the Stevens job. Two hours later, he had worked up an estimate on the bathroom and found ways to shave costs without hurting quality.

Before he turned in, he stepped outside on his deck, Aspen beside him, and inhaled deeply, pulling icy air into his lungs. On a cold, clear night like this, with the stars thick and sparkling like diamonds, he was glad that he lived far from a big city's bright lights. Bending, he looked through his telescope, focusing on the rings circling Saturn.

Molly wouldn't stay in Vrain. He'd have bet his construction company and his bank account on that. She wasn't a small-town girl. She'd grown up in a suburb of Denver, she'd worked in New York City, she'd traveled and played in Europe. Once she finished her book and pulled herself together, she'd take a look at Vrain's short Main Street, count four thousand residents, shudder, and run for the big city lights as fast as she could.

As much as Joe liked to think that he was building a house for Molly Stevens, he wasn't. He was building it for the people who would buy the Stevens place when Molly returned to the glamorous jet-set life her beauty and fame had won for her.

"We need to remember that she'll be leaving," he said to Aspen, still peering through his telescope. Tonight, Saturn was heartachingly lovely, as distant and out of reach as Molly had seemed the first time he saw her smile on a magazine cover.

"EN GARDE," Molly muttered, then swung the flyswatter at the window and executed a series of rapid-fire strikes. Smiling in grim triumph, she watched three dead flies drop to the dusty, debris-strewn floor. Stepping over a pile of junk that used to be a wall, she moved to the next window and slapped down five more.

"It's you or me. This place isn't big enough for both of us," she warned, slapping the flyswatter against the window.

"Honey, where are you?"

"Moving toward the kitchen. Relieving some tension before I go to work." The book was not going well. Four pages in four days wasn't cutting it. The problem was, she'd had a happy, uneventful childhood. There was nothing to say about her childhood that anyone could possibly be interested in reading.

"Honey, I want you to meet Daddy Romaine. Daddy and his boys will do the excavation for the garage and the study."

Turning from the window, she studied Joe, deciding he must own a bottomless wardrobe of flannel shirts. She also decided that he was a man who looked terrific in flannel shirts and a leather tool belt. Then she looked at the man standing next to him. If Colonel Sanders had been taller, skinnier, and a little younger, he and Daddy Romaine would have been dead ringers.

"What the hell are you doing, girl, wrecking up a perfectly fine house?"

Her mouth dropped open, and she glanced quickly at Joe, who shrugged and grinned back at her. While she was trying to think of an answer, she noticed a girl dressed in skintight jeans and wearing a black leather motorcycle jacket walking around the living room. She had five earrings in each ear, none of which matched.

"That's my, ah, secretary," Daddy Romaine said, clearing his throat. "Dumpling likes to see the job sites where me an' my boys are doing bidness."

Dumpling undulated into the kitchen, popped a wad of gum, and looked Molly up and down. "You got a lot of flies in here," she said.

Molly drew a deep breath and flicked a look a Joe. "If I have to tear this place down to the foundation, I'm going to find that queen fly and kill her." She smiled sweetly at Daddy Romaine. "That's why I'm wrecking the house. I'm looking for the queen fly."

She heard Joe chuckle, and his eyes sparkled like sapphires. But Daddy Romaine and Dumpling stood looking at her as if she belonged in a lunatic asylum. Without a word, they both turned and walked out of the house.

"Who *are* those people?" Molly asked, stepping to the window and watching them climb into a pickup that sat up high on oversize tires. She wished she hadn't made the dumb remark about a queen fly.

Joe laughed, poured two cups of coffee from the pot he kept bubbling on the stove all day and handed her one. His fingers brushed hers, and Molly looked up quickly, then glanced away with a frown. She didn't recall the last time she'd been aware of a casual touch. The realization made her feel a little strange inside—or maybe she was still reverberating from his warmth.

Joe's eyes still twinkled and sparkled with amusement. "Daddy and the Romaine boys work a bulldozer like a scalpel. Best excavators in the state." He glanced over his shoulder toward the sound of a crash as another wall came down. "The man coming through the door is your plumber. Jim Enders is a friend of mine."

As always when Molly met someone new, she had to resist the impulse to cover the scar above her lip. Then she realized that Jim Enders wouldn't notice the scars. He looked at her with a dazzled expression that told her loud and clear that he'd never met a celebrity before.

Joe winked at her and rolled his eyes before he elbowed

Jim in the ribs. "You're in a trance, honey. Wake up and talk toilets."

Jim gave her a sheepish smile. "I need to know what color you want for the shower base."

"All right. Leave me a color chart, will you?" It hadn't occurred to her that she'd have to choose a color for the shower floor.

"Well, actually, I need to know today, because the pigments have to be special-ordered."

Not wanting to look foolish in front of Joe, Molly sat down at the card table and picked up a pencil to give her hands something to do. "I don't know what colors are available."

"Well, you can't go wrong with biscuit," Jim offered. "It's a hot color this year."

"Good. Buscuit sounds fine." Molly swallowed. Just when she'd thought she was making a little progress, a decision as simple as selecting a color was throwing her into a state of near panic. Plus, from the old bathroom the pounding of sledgehammers against the cracking tile was giving her a headache.

Her heart sank when Jim handed her a four-inch-high stack of catalogs. "You'll need these to pick out the rest of the fixtures."

She stared at the pile and gave Joe a look that clearly pleaded for help, hoping he could read her mind. Joe raised an eyebrow, his eyes narrowed on her for a moment. Then he led the plumber into the next room.

While they conferred, Molly looked on with an anxious expression. This whole thing had been a mistake. She wasn't up to this. Writing a book was enough of a challenge, she should never had taken on a major remodeling project at the same time.

She drew a deep breath. On the other hand, she hadn't had time to feel sorry for herself since Joe Townsend and his pooches came whirling into her life like a minihurricane. Besides, it was too late to stop now.

Joe touched her shoulder, and she roused herself with a

startled expression, lifting a hand to the spot he had touched.

"Are you all right?" Joe asked. Gently he smoothed back the braid that lay on her shoulder, his touch soothing and oddly intimate.

"I'm just…having trouble making decisions recently." What she wanted to do right now was step into his arms, place her head on his shoulder, and beg him to make all the decisions for her. Or maybe she just wanted someone to hold her. Someone…or Joe?

"Jim won't like it, but you can take your time deciding on the fixtures," he said quietly. He sat down at the card table and studied her. "Molly, are you sure you're all right?"

Pride stiffened her spine. She didn't want him to think she was a basket case, and she wasn't. Merely a little unsteady right now. "Your friend just threw me a curve, that's all." She returned his gaze, borrowing some of the strength and calmness in his face. Not only was he a ruggedly handsome man, but there was a steady solidity about Joe that invited her to lean. She'd have to be careful not to take advantage of that. "Now what the hell color do you suppose biscuit is going to turn out to be?"

Joe smiled. "It's an off-white. You might consider checking out a few plumbing-supply places in Denver. Get some ideas."

"I don't think I've ever been in a plumbing-supply place in my life."

He pushed up from the card table. "Gotta get back to work, honey."

"There's something I've been meaning to ask you…. It's about the TV. I've never had a satellite dish before…. Is it usual for different televisions in the house to get different channels?"

"What?"

"The TV in the bedroom gets even-numbered channels, and the TV downstairs by my desk gets odd-numbered channels. Is that the way a satellite dish usually works?"

"None that I've heard of. Call Mr. Melvin at Melvin Smith's Satellite Systems."

Mr. Melvin, Daddy Romaine, and Dumpling. Her head was reeling. "Okay, thanks."

Molly almost fled to her desk in the basement, seeking solitude and quiet. Solitude was possible, but not quiet. Directly above her head, the boom box was blasting out a song about a cowboy and a lady and a hoss named Blue. Sure enough, it was the seventeenth, an odd-numbered day. Tomorrow, it would be Al's turn again, and hard rock would rain down on her.

Sighing, she wiped dust off of her computer screen and placed her fingertips on the keyboard. Okay, where was she? Trying not to think about Joe, trying to think of something remotely interesting to say about her childhood. Maybe she should mention coming to this house for summer vacations and holidays. Talk about how it had always felt safe here.

Tilting her head back she gazed up at the rafters and watched dust dribbling down on her. A nail fell between the studs and bounced off her desk. A piece of broken tile dropped down into her lap. She picked it up and turned it between her fingers. Salmon-colored. Salmon must have been the hot color sixty years ago. The biscuit of its day.

BY THE TIME Joe appeared at the end of the day, she'd written two pages about the house as she remembered it from those long-ago vacations. Okay, she wasn't blazing along, but two pages was one more page than she'd been doing per day so far.

"My God, honey. Why didn't you say something?"

Following Joe's gaze, she inspected the dust filming her desk, her printer, herself. "I'm trying to convince myself there's nutritional value in old dust. Every time I breathe, I'm sucking in vitamins and minerals."

"I'll be back in a minute." When he returned, he had two sheets of heavy black plastic. "Move over there for a sec." Flipping a hammer out of his tool belt and filling his mouth with nails, he hung the black plastic over her desk area like a canopy, then stepped back and studied it. "That ought to catch most of the dirt and debris," he said.

It was such a simple solution. Molly wished she'd mentioned the problem earlier. She returned to her desk chair, and Joe sat across from her. "My hero," she said lightly. "It seems that all I've done today is thank you for one thing or another. I'd offer you a beer, now that you're off duty, but I don't have the energy to run up those stairs one more time."

"I'll get it. You want one?"

She hesitated. Ordinarily, she wasn't a beer drinker. "Sure. Why not?" When he returned, she noticed that he drank out of the can but he'd brought a glass for her. "I've never seen anyone with as much energy as you have." He seemed as fresh as he had been this morning, when he shouted her out of bed with the promise of hot coffee, a ritual that was becoming a habit. But Joe wasn't a man who stood by supervising while his crew did all the work. She'd seen him prying off sheets of old drywall, and swinging a sledgehammer against the tiles. He set the pace for his pooches, not by word, but by example. She didn't know why he wasn't dragging at the end of the day. "Where's Aspen today?" Usually, Aspen followed at his heels.

"She's at the vet's for her annual checkup."

At first Molly thought he was making a joke, but his eyes were serious. She placed her elbow on the desk and propped her chin in her hand. "You can't imagine how different my former life was from…all this."

"Do you miss that life?" he asked, his eyes curious.

She thought about her condo in the east fifties, the limos and the restaurants and the clubs and parties. The travel, and the photo shoots at exotic locations. People rushing to ask whether she needed this or wanted that. The fabulous clothes. Frowning, she looked down at herself. She didn't recall wearing anything but jeans since she'd arrived in Vrain.

"Yes."

Right now, she wished she was whirling out the door of her clean, quiet town house, wearing something wonderful, on her way to someplace like Madame Wu's, with plans to see the latest Broadway production after dinner.

"Does Vrain have any Chinese restaurants?" she inquired wistfully. "Suddenly I'm in the mood for mu shu pork and steamed rice and green tea." And a fortune in her cookie that said something like "You will live through your remodel project."

That thought reminded her of her conversation with Darcy Connors-slash-Arden, and the last fortune she'd received. She could almost hear Darcy whispering in her ear, telling her to follow her heart, and Darcy would mean Joe. Like it or not, she really was attracted to him.

Before he came downstairs, she'd been feeling tired and discouraged. Now she felt as if a current of electricity ran between her and Joe, flashing back and forth, carrying an exchange of heat. She wondered what her hair and makeup looked like this late in the day.

"I think Ma and Pa's Café has chop suey on the menu," he said, making a face.

She laughed at his expression. "I take it you're a meat-and-potatoes type of man?"

"There's no better meal than a bacon cheeseburger and a big side of home fries." Eyes twinkling like blue lights, he stood, looked at her for a long moment, then glanced at his watch. "Well, I've got to run—the vet will be waiting. See you on Monday, honey."

"What happens next week?" Disappointment tightened her chest. She didn't want to see him go.

He crumpled the beer can in his hand and tossed it toward the trash can. "The Romaine boys will start digging the foundations on the ends of the house. The new windows should be delivered. We'll start tearing out the old chimney chase on the second floor. And we're going to get you a bathroom down here. At least we'll get started on it."

"Sounds interesting." She stood up, and there was an awkward moment when it almost felt as if she should kiss him goodbye. Pink flooded her cheeks. "Well...have a good weekend," she murmured, glancing at his mouth and then dropping her eyes.

The house seemed very quiet when he'd gone. That was another difference. It was never quiet in New York City. There were always sirens and traffic and the sounds of the people living on either side. Quitting for the day, Molly shut off her computer, admired her new black plastic canopy for a minute, then went upstairs to the kitchen, listening to the quiet. After years of living in Manhattan, and after a day of pounding and hammering and crashes and bangs and music played at head-splitting decibels, the quiet of a country house seemed awfully loud.

Remembering that she hadn't called Mr. Melvin, Molly flipped on the little TV mounted beneath a kitchen cabinet, seeking the illusion of company, wondering whether she'd get an even-or odd-numbered channel. She got nothing; it didn't work. Sighing, she turned on the oven, then opened the freezer above the fridge and chose a TV dinner, wishing she'd asked Joe to stay a while.

When the phone rang, she walked to the telephone on the kitchen wall, but it was dead. How could it ring if it wasn't working? Then she remembered Joe telling her that the wiring had come out this week. Almost running, she rushed back downstairs and snatched up the telephone on her desk. "Hello?" she said breathlessly.

"Honey, I've been thinking about plumbing fixtures."

"Joe?" It surprised her how glad she was to hear his deep voice.

"You really should drive down to Denver and look at what's available, but you won't do that, will you?"

"Not in a million years," she agreed, noticing three flies crawling on the window above the basement door. She was living in the Amityville Horror. Every day she killed at least thirty flies, but they kept coming. "Listen, would you happen to know the life span of a fly?"

"I don't know. A day, maybe? What's the answer?"

"I don't know, either."

"Look, honey, I was thinking…I've got to go to Denver tomorrow to pick up your new front door. Would you like to ride along? We could stop by a couple of plumbing-supply places, then afterward we'll find a Chinese restaurant for dinner. If you don't want to go, that's fine. It isn't like you have to or anything. I mean, I'm sure you can find everything you need in Jim's catalogs, it's just that I thought you might like to see what's available before you make a decision. But if—"

She interrupted him, smiling. "Joe? I'd love to go to Denver and look at plumbing fixtures with you." Suddenly she needed to get out of here. She needed to hear traffic and sirens and see people, and eat something that didn't come in a carton. She needed a day away from the damned flies.

"You would?" He sounded surprised.

"What does a person wear to a plumbing-supply place?" she asked, unable to resist teasing him a little.

"Throw a little more dust on what you were wearing today and you'll fit right in," he said. She could hear the grin in his voice. "I'll pick you up at seven in the a.m."

Suppressing a groan, she laughed and agreed, hung up the phone, then leaned back in her chair. She liked Joe Townsend.

She liked him a lot.

Chapter Three

"Is there any graceful way to jump up into the seat of a pickup?" Molly asked in dismay, studying the height of the truck compared to the short length of her skirt.

Grinning, Joe showed her how to grasp the handle above the window, step up and swing herself inside. She got the hang of it on the first try, folded her hands in her lap and beamed at him. He was glad he'd cleaned the dog hair off the seats and left Aspen home, because her tan skirt, while casual, looked suspiciously like cashmere. So did the blue sweater that matched her eyes and parka. Both would have acted like a magnet for dog hair. Today she wore her long hair wrapped in a coil on her neck and she'd chosen small tan-and-blue earrings. She was so beautiful that she simply took his breath away.

By the time he'd walked around the truck and climbed behind the wheel, she had slipped on a pair of dark glasses that covered the upper part of her face, and he was glad. Maybe he'd have a slim chance of concentrating on his driving, instead of on her.

"One of those coffees is for you," he said, nodding toward the cup holder as he shifted into gear and pointed the pickup down her driveway toward the no-name road.

"Thanks." She tasted hers and sighed with pleasure. "I like coffee in the mornings, but if I drank coffee all day like you do, I'd never be able to sleep at night."

"Coffee is as much a part of the construction business as a hammer and a nail gun."

She shifted on the seat so that she was almost facing him. "How did you get into this business? Is construction something you always wanted to do?"

"I came by it naturally. My father owned a construction business in Denver before he retired and moved to Vrain. When my Dad died a couple of years ago, my mother sold the house and moved to Florida, where her sister lives." Pausing, he wondered if she was really interested in any of this. He couldn't imagine why she would be. "Anyway, I used to work on Dad's crew in the summers. I liked the physical part of it, and being outdoors. I couldn't see myself sitting at a desk in some airless office building." He shrugged, and turned the pickup onto the highway.

"It must be nice to drive around the county and see houses that you've built, houses that wouldn't exist it if hadn't been for you."

He glanced at her, surprised that she'd guessed how he felt. "Yeah, it does feel good."

"I envy your ability to create something that will last. Something solid and real that touches people's lives." She gazed out the windshield as they drove toward town.

The highway followed the St. Vrain River, swept into a broad curve, then straightened out. Joe slowed as the highway became Vrain's Main Street for a short stretch. He waved at Wiley Oats, who stood on the sidewalk washing the grocery store's windows, and nodded at Mrs. Stetson, who was unlocking the door of her small hardware store.

Molly twisted on the seat to watch as they drove by, then she laughed. "Small-town America. I didn't know this kind of town existed anymore. I thought it went out with Norman Rockwell."

"Nope. And small-town America is just where I want to be." He honked the horn at Marsha Fiddler, who looked up from fitting her key into the door of the bank and waved, pointed out Mr. Melvin's satellite shop to Molly, and then they were past the business district, such as it was, and

driving past Ma and Pa's Café and the lumberyard on the
way out of town. "So, I've told you my history, now it's
your turn. How did you get into modeling?"

She took a sip of coffee and adjusted her dark glasses.
"There's some skill involved, I guess, but nothing like the
talents you have." A light shrug raised the front of her
parka. "It just happened that I have a face the camera
loves." She fell silent for a moment, and her fingertips
wandered to the tiny scar above her lip. "I was buying
clothes one day when I was about fourteen, and the store
manager asked if I'd like to model some items from their
teen line at a show that weekend. It was fun and I made a
hundred dollars, so when my mother suggested I take modeling classes that summer, I agreed. By the time I left for
college, I'd earned enough money to pay for most of it."
She was quiet again until Joe turned at the junction road
and headed toward Denver.

"Mostly out of curiosity, I made an appointment with
one of the big modeling agencies in Manhattan when I was
a sophomore in college. To my astonishment, they signed
me on the spot. I'm one of the lucky ones, a Cinderella
story, I guess. I started getting plum assignments right
away." She turned to look out the side window. "So, I
dropped out of college and worked it full-time. It was a
great job while it lasted."

"You make it sound like you'll never model again."

"I won't."

"I don't want to say anything that will upset you or make
you uncomfortable..."

"But?" she said, giving him a long, steady look.

"As far as I can see, you only have two scars, and I
probably wouldn't have noticed them if I hadn't been looking." He frowned and gripped the steering wheel. "I was
only looking because the tabloids made such a big deal
about it after your accident."

"It was a big deal," she said sharply. "I don't know
how fast I was traveling when I went out of control on the
ski slope, but it felt as if I hit that tree at three hundred

miles an hour. Facefirst." A long pause opened. "I broke my nose, a cheekbone, my collarbone and an ankle. When I came to, I was spitting teeth and trying to see through all the blood. My face was all cut up. I knew right then that my career was over."

"Seriously, the doctors did a great job. Looking at you now, you'd never know all that happened to you." He wasn't paying an idle compliment. He meant it. She was the most exquisitely beautiful woman he'd ever seen.

Her short laugh sounded bitter. "The camera knows." Her hand crept to her upper lip. "The camera sees all, exaggerates all. The scars you say you can hardly see look like deep valleys on a black-and-white glossy. They're less noticeable in a color shot, but you *do* see them."

"So what's wrong with that?" He was genuinely puzzled. "Most people get a few dings and dents along the way. That's how life is. What's wrong with looking like a real person?"

"The thing is, Joe, modeling is all about fantasy and illusion. Models aren't supposed to look like real people. It's about Ms. Average looking at a photo in a magazine and thinking, Wow, I could look like that if I buy this cosmetic or that dress. She wants to imagine herself as perfect as the vision she's looking at. She doesn't want to imagine herself with scars on her face."

He glanced away from the road to give her an incredulous look. "That's the craziest thing I've ever heard. Are you trying to say that a woman like…like Dumpling, for instance, looks at a picture of you in a magazine and imagines that buying the dress you're wearing will take off twenty pounds, reduce the size of her nose, add six inches to her height and tame a head of frizzy hair?"

She smiled. "That's the theory."

"Well, it's nuts, that's all I've got to say."

"I wish Apple Cosmetics shared your opinion." She faced forward, watching Denver's skyline grow taller as the highway curved around Boulder, then straightened. "So, what are we doing first today?"

He understood that she wanted to change the subject, but he wished she hadn't. He had a suspicion that she needed to talk about the accident and losing the Apple contract. Instead, he talked about the chores for the day, casting occasional glances at the acres of long legs that extended from her hem. At least she'd worn low-heeled brown shoes. "Did you have a chance to look through any of the catalogs that Jim left with you?"

"Are you kidding? I spent most of last evening trying to work out the wardrobe logistics for today."

He liked the sound of her laugh. He'd discovered that she had an appealing sense of humor. Years ago, he'd realized that when he could joke about something, it meant he'd come to terms with it. Maybe she was the same way. He hoped that someday she'd find something to laugh about when she remembered losing the Apple Girl contract. On the other hand, he couldn't think of anything amusing about losing a million dollars a year.

Joe studied her profile from the corner of his eye, awed that her face and body were worth a million dollars a year. He'd never in his life earn a million dollars in one year, certainly not in Vrain, no matter how large his company grew. He doubted he could earn that kind of money even in Denver.

He didn't need the frustration of a big metropolis. He liked living in a town where everyone knew his name, where he was the man to call if you were planning a large or complicated project. For a minute he thought about telling her that he'd begun to get a few jobs in Longmont, Boulder and Estes Park, that he'd probably have to double the number of pooches next year. Then he realized he was feeling defensive about a subject that she hadn't even mentioned.

"Why are you smiling?" she asked curiously.

"No particular reason. It's a beautiful day and I'm feeling good." He winked at her. "I have a great pickup and a pretty girl at my side. The guys at the loading dock are going to turn surly with envy when we drive in to pick up your door.''

He wasn't wrong. The warehouse manager kept looking over Joe's shoulder, stealing peeks at Molly when he should have been examining Joe's paperwork. ''That is one gorgeous woman. Your sister?'' he asked hopefully.

''Nope.'' Joe grinned. Molly had removed her dark glasses and was sending him such exaggerated looks of adoration that it seemed impossible that the warehouse manager didn't realize she was mugging.

''A cousin, maybe?'' Molly blew Joe a kiss, and the warehouse manager sighed. ''I guess not, you lucky dog. Jeez. Where'd you find a woman like that? And what does she see in your skinny butt?''

Joe laughed and watched two men lift Molly's front door into the bed of his truck. He liked her for making him look like a stud in front of the warehouse guys. He liked her, period. Liked her enough that he wished she hadn't been teasing. He wished the adoring looks and the thrown kisses had been real.

While he wrapped up the paperwork, he tried to remember the last time he'd been this fascinated by a woman. It had been a while. Occasionally he dated Ellen O'Ryan, a teacher at the high school, and he saw an aerobics instructor in Longmont every now and then. Last year he'd dated Jim Enders's sister, who owned a souvenir shop in Estes Park. He had enjoyed her company, but it was a long drive to Estes, especially in winter, and eventually he and Janice had agreed their relationship wasn't strong enough to justify either of them making the drive. He hadn't seen much of the aerobics instructor this winter, for the same reason.

It occurred to him that he wouldn't think twice about icy, snow-packed roads if Molly Stevens was waiting for him at the end of the drive.

The odd thing was—and he doubted any of his male friends would believe this—it wasn't her looks that attracted him the most. She was beautiful, yes. Amazing, really. She was tall and gracefully slender, larger-breasted than most models. Her eyes were china blue and thickly fringed by long lashes. Her mouth was lushly full and shaped like a kiss. And when she stood in the sunlight, her hair glowed like spun gold. No man could look at her without wanting her.

All that was undeniably true. But what fascinated him most was the vulnerability in those lovely blue eyes. The shy hesitation when she met people for the first time. He liked it that she noticed the absurdities in life and could laugh about things like her address, the color biscuit and the flyswatter that she carried as if it were as much a part of her outfit as her shoes or belt.

A low sigh reminded him that he needed to be very careful with her. She was a shooting star streaking across his horizon. Something bright and beautiful that a man could wish on but never own. Molly had ranged within his orbit for a while, but he couldn't imagine that she would stay. Sooner or later, gravity would pull her back to New York City, where, he conceded, she probably belonged. Beauty like hers was wasted on the small audience Vrain could provide. She deserved a much larger stage.

She beamed at him when he climbed back behind the steering wheel. "Well? Did the warehouse guys go surly with envy?"

"They all think you should dump me and take up with them," he said, pulling away from the loading docks. "In fact, you might consider the warehouse manager. His tattoo was a lot more interesting than mine. His read Born To Party."

"I'm afraid the warehouse manager and I wouldn't hit it off. After years of early wake-up calls, I start yawning about ten o'clock. Not much of a party girl."

"What?" He pretended indignation, fought imagining her in bed. "You've been faking it about not being a morning person?"

"Not on your life," she said, smiling. "Now that I'm unemployed, I'd like nothing better than to revert to my stay-up-late and sleep-in-late inclinations. Unfortunately, you and your pooches won't let me.''

Joe headed deeper into the heart of the industrial district. Visions of Molly lying in bed spun in front of his eyes. He wondered whether she wore her braid to bed or loosened her hair at night. ''Seriously, you don't have to get up early on our account. Sleep in if you want to.''

''Like I could with the boom box shaking what walls I have left. Besides, sleeping in doesn't get books written.''

''How's that project coming along?'' he asked, cruising slowly, looking for the entrance to Hardbaugh's Plumbing. He was so focused on her that he could easily miss a place he had been to a hundred times before.

''So-so. It's a struggle.'' She peered at the buildings they passed. ''What are we looking for?''

''There it is.'' After parking, he walked around the pickup bed, but she'd already dropped to the ground and was tugging down the hem of her skirt.

''Thanks, but I can open my own doors.''

''It's a habit,'' he said truthfully, smiling at her as he opened the door to Hardbaugh's and waited for her to pass by him. Whatever perfume she wore was faint enough that he hadn't noticed it until now, when she stepped close to walk through the door. Her scent was light and made him think of the lilacs that had grown in the backyard of the house in Lakewood where he lived as a kid.

''Good Lord,'' she said softly, halting just inside. ''This place is huge!''

''Come on,'' he said, touching her elbow, trying not to imagine the softness of her skin beneath her jacket. ''Fixtures are in the back.'' He couldn't help noticing that everyone in the store looked at her, some with puzzled expressions, as if they were trying to place where they might have seen her before. He walked a little straighter, proud to have her on his arm. ''This is one of my favorite places. They carry new and used.''

She looked at him over her shoulder, and her eyes widened. ''I don't think I want a used toilet, thank you.''

"Not even an antique?" he asked, grinning at her. "They have a special showroom on the other side of the salvage yard where you can buy restored chain-pull toilets and claw-foot tubs."

"I haven't seen a claw-foot tub in years," she said, stopping in the aisle.

"Keep going." But she was staring at a wall of faucet sets.

"That's a pretty set."

"Gorgeous," he agreed. "But do you know what gold-plated fixtures would do to your plumbing budget?"

"I have a plumbing budget?" she asked, moving down the aisle toward the showroom.

The minute he heard that question, his heart sank. And his mood followed, sinking toward his boots as the day wore on.

When they finally left Hardbaugh's Plumbing, Molly had purchased fixtures for all the bathrooms, even though he had all but begged her not to make impulsive, and expensive, purchases. The total cost came to a little over eleven thousand dollars, even with his discount. Which put her over budget by five thousand dollars, and she still needed kitchen fixtures.

As they walked toward his pickup, she gave him a playful poke in the ribs. "Now stop sulking. I love everything I bought, especially the Jacuzzi bathtub. In biscuit, I might add," she said, smiling. Gazing down the street, she lifted a hand and pointed. "There's another plumbing place. Let's see what they have." She grinned at him before she swung gracefully into the truck.

He thrust his hands into his pockets and looked through the open door at her legs, hoping to cheer himself a little. "It's closing time, and we have reservations at Fung Shui's."

Tight-lipped and silent, he drove across town to the restaurant, frantically trying to figure out how he could shave five thousand dollars off something else.

For the first time, it occurred to him that Molly Stevens

was going to be a difficult client. Not only did she distract him with her beauty, not only did he spend too many hours thinking about kissing her until they were both dizzy, but she was also going to go way over budget.

THIS MORNING Molly would have said touring plumbing-supply places was not exactly her idea of a great day. But she had to admit she'd had fun, and she was delighted with her purchases.

"I've been so worried about the book, and getting unpacked—so distracted and self-absorbed if you want to know the truth—that I haven't really thought about all the things I'm going to have to buy for the house," she said, reaching for an egg roll. "If I thought about it at all, I dreaded all the decisions. But I'm beginning to see that this can be fun." She bit into the egg roll, then snapped her fingers. "I should buy a bunch of decorating magazines, shouldn't I? Get some ideas. I wouldn't have had so much trouble making up my mind about the toilets if I'd realized beforehand how many different designs there are." She gave him a sheepish look. "I guess talking about plumbing fixtures isn't the greatest dinner conversation. Sorry."

Joe waved her apology aside. "It's shoptalk to me," he said absently, looking down at the egg roll he turned between his fingers. "Honey, you spent four hundred and fifty dollars on each toilet."

Molly tilted her head and frowned. "Okay, I went over budget. What's the big deal?"

"The big deal is that I bid this job as close to the bone as I could. I really don't know if I can shave five or six thousand dollars somewhere else. And, honey, we're just getting started. That worries me a lot."

This was turning into one of the strangest dinner conversations Molly had ever had. She would have laughed except that Joe looked so uncharacteristically glum. Impulsively she reached across the table and took his hand.

"Joe? Look, I know honoring your bid is important to you. But today showed me just how important the house is to me. It suddenly hit me that this is my home. I've never owned a home before, and I want it to be wonderful. Can you understand that?''

"Of course I can.''

He didn't take his hand away, so she kept her own on top of his. His skin was warm, and she felt the strength in his fingers. "Joe? Can I ask you something?" His hand was hard, tanned by winter and summer sun. "What are we doing today?''

He turned his hand beneath hers, and she felt the calluses on his palm, was fascinated by the contrast of his tanned fingers lacing through her pale fingers. "I'm not sure I understand the question," he said, looking at her across the table.

Pink colored her cheeks. "I mean…is today work or play?" She almost laughed at the absurdity of having to ask if she was at a business meeting or on a date.

A smile lit his eyes. "A little of both." Suddenly he laughed. "Okay, no more shoptalk. This part of the day is reserved for two old friends to get reacquainted.''

It was a cautious answer, a safe answer. Molly wasn't sure it was the answer she'd hoped for. Surprised by her reaction, she gently removed her hand from his and reached for her chopsticks. She needed to employ a little caution too. "How's your stir-fry?''

"What?" Blinking, Joe gazed down at his plate, as if noticing it for the first time. "Fine, I guess. It isn't a steak, but it's okay," he said with a smile. "How's your mu shu pork?''

"As delicious as I'd hoped it would be.''

"Do you eat this kind of stuff a lot?''

Molly laughed. "New Yorkers live on Chinese food, especially takeout. I have a friend back home who recently got married. Darcy and I met for lunch once a month, and it was always for Chinese food." She fell quiet for a moment remembering those long lunches, remembering them laughing or moaning about their lives. Hoping the fortunes in their fortune cookies would be wonderful and come true.

"You just referred to New York City as home," Joe said lightly. "But a minute ago you were talking about your grandparent's house as being home."

Her head came up. "I did, didn't I?" She frowned then shrugged. "It'll take some time to get used to, I guess."

"Did you keep your place in New York?"

"Yes," she said, looking down at her plate. But she didn't want to talk about a life she had left behind. Smiling, she gazed at him across the table, noticing that he'd gotten a haircut since yesterday. And this was the first time she'd seen him when he wasn't wearing a flannel work shirt. "You look nice today."

"Thanks," he said, grinning. "But isn't that supposed to be my line?"

"You already told me that I look nice today. About three times," she said, teasing him.

"So did every plumbing salesman we ran into," he said. One of his eyebrows lifted. "Does it upset you when people tell you that you look like the Apple Girl?"

There was no way to escape the Apple Girl thing, she thought. She had one of the most recognizable faces in America. Even when people couldn't place where they knew her from, they still felt as if they did know her.

She looked at Joe. "Do you mean, does it upset me that people look at the scars and think I couldn't really be the flawless, unscarred Apple Girl? Or did you mean, does it upset me to be reminded that because of the scars I'm no longer the Apple Girl? Or were you asking if it's upsetting when people act as if they somehow know me?"

Instantly he looked embarrassed. "Honey, I just… Look, I'm sorry I said anything."

"Don't be. I'm just trying to figure out what you wanted to know."

"Since you mentioned it, my guess is that none of the people we ran into today even noticed your scars. I think people mention that you look like the Apple Girl only because they can't imagine the real Apple Girl would show up in a plumbing store. That's all. It has nothing to do with your scars.''

She didn't believe him for a minute. When she looked into a mirror, the only thing she saw was the scars. ''Of course it upsets me to be reminded that I'm no longer the Apple Girl.'' She met his eyes. ''I loved being the Apple Girl. I was damned proud that they chose me over a thousand other models. It was a very lucrative contract, and a good job.''

He nodded but didn't comment. ''I was mostly curious about how it feels to be famous.''

''That's tougher to answer.'' Sighing, she dropped back in the booth. ''In the beginning, that's what I thought I wanted. Fame. And it was thrilling the first time a stranger said, 'I saw your picture on the cover of *Cosmo*.' Even more amazing was the first time someone asked for my autograph.'' She shook her head. ''I couldn't believe it.''

''I'd fall over laughing if anyone asked me for my autograph.''

''I think I laughed, too.'' She thought for a minute. ''But then, as that sort of thing starts happening more frequently, you start thinking that everyone recognizes you and they're watching you.'' She shrugged, frowning. ''You start behaving as if they are. I wouldn't dream of going out of the house without makeup, for instance. And this is a small example, but…I always return my grocery cart to the stacking area, no matter how exhausted I am, because I don't want anyone recognizing me and then saying that I was too good or too spoiled to do what everyone else is expected to do.''

''You have to be perfect? Is that what you're saying?''

Nodding, she stared at him. ''That's how it feels, yes. It feels as if privacy is only an illusion. Someone is always watching. Believe me, I don't want to lose my cool and then pick up one of the tabloids and read that Molly Stevens was involved in a brawl in public. And that's what happens. Some bystander sees a way to make a quick buck through exaggeration or embellishment. The tabloids pay for junk like that.''

''You're sure that you aren't imagining...''

As if to prove her point, a woman approached their table, her eyes fixed on Molly, a paper napkin and pen in her hand. Knowing what was about to happen, Molly straightened, pressed her lips together, then curved them into a smile.

''Excuse me,'' the woman said, stopping beside their table and staring. ''I don't mean to intrude, but could I have your autograph?'' She glanced at Joe, then back at Molly. ''I just love Apple Cosmetics, I won't use anything else. And I love that commercial where you paint a face on an apple with your eyeliner.'' Without waiting for Molly's assent, she placed the napkin and pen beside Molly's plate.

''I'd be glad to give you an autograph,'' Molly said, picking up the pen.

''Make it to Irene, will you? Say something like 'I love your makeup.'''

Molly paused, then dutifully wrote what the woman had requested.

While Molly was writing, the woman examined Joe with a long, speculative stare. ''Are you somebody too?''

Startled, Joe stiffened, and a dark flush rose from his collar. ''No, honey, I'm no one.''

''Oh. Well, you're cute enough that you could be somebody,'' she said, batting her eyelashes.

Glancing up at his expression, Molly stifled a laugh. After the woman collected her napkin and finally left their table, Molly grinned. ''You'll always be somebody to me,'' she said.

''Let's get out of here,'' Joe said, sliding toward the edge of the booth, ''before someone else spots you.''

''Wait. You didn't open your fortune cookie. That's the best part.''

He slid back into the booth and took the crescent-shaped cookie she handed him. Molly opened hers and withdrew the thin slip of paper. '''Follow your heart,''' she read aloud, disappointed. "I got the same one the last time I opened a fortune cookie. What does yours say?"

Joe rolled out the tiny slip. "'Remember the bottom line.' I think I got the one that you were supposed to have," he commented with a humorless grin. Then he stood up beside the table. "Are you ready to leave? I just spotted someone else headed this way carrying a napkin and a pen."

"Yep," she said cheerfully, collecting her purse and parka. "Once one person asks for an autograph, it's like opening a floodgate."

She signed three more napkins while Joe paid their bill. Then she took his arm and they left the restaurant. "It's getting cold." Tilting back her head, she gazed up at the dark sky. The city lights made it impossible to tell whether there were stars tonight. "Do you think we'll get snow before morning?"

He unlocked the door of the pickup and opened it for her. "You were a lot more gracious to that first woman than I think I would have been. She said she didn't want to intrude, but that's exactly what she did."

She waited to answer until he had slid behind the steering wheel and backed out of the restaurant's parking lot. "I really don't think people realize that they're being rude or intrusive. There's no sense getting annoyed by it. I try to remember when I dreamed about someone asking for my autograph. It's very flattering, really."

And at the back of her mind was the sobering reality that it would end. Soon Apple Cosmetics would announce the name of the new Apple Girl. Some lucky model would step into Molly's place and become the center of an intense media blitz as Apple Cosmetics launched a new advertising and promotion campaign. If they were as successful with the new Apple Girl as they had been with Molly, the new Apple Girl would pop up on "Good Morning America" and the "Today" show. Soon her face would be on billboards and commercials, in magazines and newspapers.

Molly would be forgotten. A has-been.

Her chest constricted painfully, and she gripped her hands tightly together in her lap. What was she going to do with the rest of her life? She'd been a model since she was fourteen. And twenty-eight was too young to retire, to devote the rest of her days to sitting on the porch in a rocking chair.

This was the point where her mind froze and panic set in. This was the moment when her confidence eroded and she suddenly questioned every decision she had ever made.

It had been too late in the spring to ski that day. At least three of the resort people had warned her and her party to stay on the main trails. But Molly had decided to ski anyway, wanting to ski fast, feel the wind in her face and experience the exhilaration of a bright spring day on the mountaintop. Why not? She had the world by the tail; she was riding a crest of fame and fortune. The rules didn't apply to her. She was charmed. Bulletproof.

But she was as vulnerable to the consequences of foolish decisions as anyone else. Slamming into a tree at full speed was the inevitable result of foolish, arrogant decisions that she had regretted ever since.

Gripping her hands so tightly that her nails dug into her palms, she suddenly wished she hadn't bought the painted sink. Maybe she wouldn't like it after all. Maybe it would look stupid or pretentious in her guest bathroom. Or maybe she should have bought the one with the butterflies in the basin instead of the one with the wildflowers. Why hadn't she remembered that making sound decisions was not her forte? She'd been dumb to surrender to impulse.

There was another thing. Was it a good decision to spend this much time with Joe Townsend? She flashed him a quick, anxious look. She enjoyed his company, and she liked him, but she didn't know why she liked him.

Was she drawn to Joe because she'd run away from all the people she knew and she was lonely? Was it because he seemed so solid and grounded and right now she wasn't?

Or was it because Joe was so different from most of the other people she knew? Perhaps she liked him simply because he reminded her of her roots and her beginnings.

It was also possible that she was making things unnecessarily complicated. That was what usually happened when her mind started questioning everything. Maybe she liked Joe because he was a great-looking, likable guy.

Lowering her head, she closed her eyes and touched trembling fingertips to her forehead. Damn it, she hated being so fragile that a few negative thoughts could explode in size and gobble her judgment and her confidence. She'd always thought she was so strong. Then her world had changed overnight, and suddenly she was floundering and questioning everything. And she usually did it after the fact.

"You're awfully quiet, honey. Everything A-okay?"

"It's been a long day. I'm just tired," she said, hedging.

"Lean your head on my shoulder and take a nap if you like. I'll wake you when we get to Vrain."

She hesitated, then decided the offer was too appealing to resist. Sliding across the seat, she nestled her head on his shoulder and let her eyelids drift shut. After a minute, she felt his arm close protectively around her.

Maybe she liked Joe because he was a man she could lean on.

"HONEY?" Joe said softly. "Wake up. We're home."

It was warm and cozy inside the cab of the pickup; large, puffy snowflakes floated out of the night sky and silently slid down the windshield. If it had been up to him, he would have stayed here forever, watching the snow, with Molly's head on his chest and the light fragrance of her scent in every breath. Fifteen years ago, he had fantasized about a moment like this. He'd dreamed of taking Molly Stevens to a movie, then parking somewhere private. He had dreamed of her snuggling her head on his shoulder, of putting his arms around her. Funny how life worked out.

Stirring, she lifted her head at the same moment he

looked down at her. His chest tightened when he found himself looking directly into her eyes, his mouth less than an inch from hers. For Joe, time spun backward and he was that unsure boy again, wanting to kiss the most beautiful girl in high school, but unable to believe that such an exquisite creature would want to kiss him. Back then they'd called it first-date jitters.

Clenching his jaw and staring at her lips, he reminded himself that they were no longer teenagers. In this situation, a man kissed a woman.

She lifted a hand and lightly touched his cheek. "Joe? Thank you for a lovely day and evening. I enjoyed it."

Damn, he'd missed the moment. He who hesitates is lost, he thought ruefully as Molly moved out of his arms and sat up straight, pushing at the long tendrils of hair that had worked their way out of the heavy coil on her neck. "It's snowing," she said, covering a yawn.

"Stay put," he said in a gruff voice. "Like it or not, I'm going to open the door for you." When he stepped outside, he took his time walking around the pickup, letting the cold, frosty air cool his face.

If he had any sense, he'd be grateful that the moment had passed. Molly was the boss lady; he was her employee. She was a naturally warm woman—he might have misinterpreted a lot today. Finally, she was at a very vulnerable time in her life right now, and a real man didn't take advantage.

He could think of a lot of reasons why it was the right thing not to do what his brain and body shouted at him to do. Drawing a deep gulp of cold air, he pasted a smile on his face and opened her door, then helped her out of the truck. She held on to his arm as they picked their way through construction debris that was quickly being covered by the falling snow.

And then came that awkward moment in front of her door, when they turned to face each other. This moment hadn't been easy as a teenager, and it wasn't easy for a man. Joe knew what he wanted to do. He wanted to lean her up against the side of the house, then let his body melt into hers. He wanted to open her jacket and slide his hands from her slender waist to those magnificent breasts. And he wanted to kiss her until they were both breathless and fiery with needing each other.

But he didn't know what she wanted. Or what she expected. When he realized they had been standing together looking at each other for several minutes, he laughed, and some of the tension went out of his body. What were they doing? Waiting for each other to make the first move? If so, he had a suspicion they would still be standing here, waiting, when the sun came up.

Someone had to do something. Stepping close to her, he framed her face in his hands, suddenly conscious of the hard calluses on his palms brushing her soft smooth skin, and, exercising more control than he'd known he possessed, he dropped a light kiss on her forehead, then stepped away from her.

Every muscle in his body was tight as he made himself walk down the porch steps and into the snow. "See you Monday," he called over his shoulder, hoping his voice didn't sound as hoarse to her as it did to him.

Without looking back, he drove out of her yard and toward the highway. But he stopped on the side of the road as soon as he was out of her sight, and he gripped the steering wheel and clenched his teeth.

Molly Stevens was a client. He'd bet everything he owned that she was a short-timer in this part of the world. Only a fool would pursue a woman like this. If he let himself fall for her, he was going to get hurt. Badly. Frowning, he told himself that he should start a checklist of all the reasons he ought to keep Molly at arm's length.

Unfortunately, he wanted her a lot closer than that. A lot closer. He had never wanted a woman like he wanted Molly. Being close to her revved his heart like an engine, turned his bones to liquid.

He stared at himself in the rearview mirror and sighed. "You're a fool, Joe Townsend. She's dated film stars and celebrities. You can't compete with that kind of competition. Forget it."

Chapter Four

On Sunday, Molly slept late, had her coffee and read the newspaper in bed, then put on her oldest pair of sweats and wrapped her hair in a bandanna. Cleaning up her living areas would give her something to do, and maybe take her mind off Joe Townsend. In New York, she'd had a cleaning lady. She hadn't polished furniture, vacuumed or scrubbed a kitchen in years.

And it was futile to clean now, she knew that. Tomorrow Joe and the pooches would create more dust and debris. But she lived here, and she had to make an effort to keep the house clean. She realized what she was up against when her wet rag turned the dust on the kitchen countertop to mud. Staring down, she tried to think whether she had ever seen that happen before. No, she had never lived where that much dust had accumulated, and she never would again. Grimly she attacked the muddy countertop, and then, when the old kitchen sparkled, she carried her cleaning supplies to the basement and cleaned the area around her desk.

And while she was scrubbing and polishing, she kept thinking about yesterday, trying to figure it out. If yesterday had been about business, she'd messed up by going over her plumbing budget. If it had been a date, then she had messed up by falling asleep. She poured furniture polish on her desktop and sighed. If yesterday had been business, then she'd ended the day badly by wanting Joe to kiss her.

If it had been a date, then she'd ended it badly because she didn't kiss him. The whole thing was crazy.

When she'd finished cleaning her living areas, an all-day project, she jumped in the shower, then put on her plaid bathrobe and fuzzy slippers and went down to the kitchen, where she poured a glass of wine. Outside, snow had started to fall again, and frosty patterns laced the corners of the window.

She toasted her reflection. "It feels great to have accomplished something, doesn't it?" Piles of debris lay mounded on bare floors where carpet used to be. A haze of perpetual dust hung in the air. But her areas were clean. She felt tired but good. She would have felt better if she could have gotten a handle on her confusing feelings for Joe.

After she ate a sandwich and a bowl of soup, she planned to spend the evening phoning friends and tracking down her parents, who were exploring the U.S.A. in an RV. But she didn't think she'd call Darcy, because Darcy would ask about Joe, and Molly didn't know how to answer.

Standing in her kitchen, watching the snow tumble past her window, she wondered what he was doing tonight. Did he have a date? Was he seeing someone?

After thinking about it again, she concluded that yesterday had not been a date. They had picked up the front door and they had purchased the fixtures for the house. She decided the day had been business as usual for Joe. It embarrassed her that she'd been wondering if it was anything else.

In retrospect, she realized that of course Joe had to be present when she bought things like fixtures. Otherwise, she wouldn't receive the benefit of his contractor's discount. Feeling foolish that she'd been so naive, she finally realized that he must take all his clients on similar outings.

Molly sipped her wine and watched the snow, listening to the silence. With a long night's sleep and a satisfying day behind her, the panic and negative thoughts of yesterday seemed silly and embarrassing. She was going to love her home spa and the painted sink, and she was glad she had bought them.

In about two minutes, her thoughts returned to Joe.

He was a nice man, great to look at, easy to be with, and she enjoyed his company. She hated to think what it would have been like if that wasn't true, considering that she would be seeing him every day for the next three and a half months. Shoot, her last romantic involvement hadn't even lasted three and a half months.

With Peter, the short time they were together had seemed like an eternity of misunderstandings, arguments, and hurt feelings. By the time they decided to call it quits, they'd both been emotionally exhausted and wondering what they had ever seen in each other. She had accused Peter of being shallow and drifting through life spending his father's money. He had criticized her for single-mindedly thinking only of her work. It hadn't been a pleasant parting.

That had been last year, shortly after the skiing accident. Peter had been decent enough to send flowers to the hospital, and he'd called in June to wish her a happy birthday, but she hadn't heard from him since. She didn't want to.

During most of last year, she'd been so involved with doctors and plastic surgery and recovery, then the next surgery and the next recovery, that she didn't think much about her dwindling social life. Then Dr. Holyrood had told her the surgery was finished. He'd been exceptionally pleased that she would have only two small scars. Considering how severely her face had been devastated, anyone else would have been hysterically grateful to emerge at the end with "only" two small scars.

But Apple Cosmetics had spent a week doing test shots and analyzing the results. The corporate powers who made such decisions had not been pleased. After an intense flurry of Apple's lawyers talking to Molly's lawyers over the course of several weeks, Apple had bought out her contract, and suddenly she'd been unemployed and basically unemployable.

A month later, she had fled to Vrain and a house where she had felt safe as a child.

It must have been a good decision, she concluded, drawing a heart on the steamed-up window, because for the first time in nearly a year she was worrying about something other than herself. She was thinking about her book, and the house, and she was speculating about a man again. She was even beginning to make decisions again, though it was only because she was forced to and her confidence wobbled every time she made some kind of choice. But she was doing it.

"So where are you tonight, Joe Townsend?" she murmured, staring at the heart she had drawn with her fingertip. "Having dinner with someone who isn't a client?" A woman?

He was ruggedly handsome, and his blue eyes twinkled and sparkled as if lit from within. He was always cheerful, usually smiling. A man gifted with curiosity and a quick laugh. A man who opened doors, a man who made a woman feel safe and protected.

Of course he was seeing someone.

JOE CROSSED HIS ANKLES on the ottoman and dropped a hand to scratch behind Aspen's ears, gazing at the flames crackling in the fireplace grate. He liked his cabin, liked spending a cold, snowy night here, but tonight the silence bugged him. Setting aside the book he'd been trying to read, he rubbed the bridge of his nose and wondered what Molly was doing tonight.

After a while, he stood, stretched, then picked a pizza box off the floor and carried it to the trash can in his kitchen. Glancing out the window, he noticed that it had started to snow again. Maybe he'd go skiing next weekend. In his opinion, February was the best month for downhill. More likely, he realized with a sour smile, he'd be sitting in front of his computer studying the Stevens bid, trying to find places where he could cut expenses.

It was odd to think of someone Molly's age never having

owned a home before. But it explained his conviction that there were a lot of things about the project that she hadn't thought through. That being the case, she was having to make decisions on the spur of the moment that most people had thought out by the time Joe ran into them. Fortunately for her, she had enough money that if she made a mistake, she could afford to correct it.

The money was another big difference between them that he needed to keep in mind. She didn't date men who drove old pickups. Chauffeurs and limos were more her style. She was so far out of his league that he didn't know why he kept torturing himself by thinking about her. She could pick and choose, date the cream of the crop. Suave film-star types who made millions. Guys who didn't wear baseball caps or crawl around dusty houses.

When the phone rang, it was a relief. Even if the caller was Jim Enders, wanting to talk about his breakup with Avis—yet again—it would be better than thinking about Molly.

"Joe Townsend here," he said into the telephone, leaning a shoulder against the kitchen wall.

"Hi, it's Ellen."

Guilt tightened his chest. He hadn't called Ellen in over a month. Not since he took her to Don White's New Year's Eve party, in fact. Glancing at the calendar, he realized it was longer than a month, more like six weeks. "I was going to call you," he said, knowing how that overworked phrase would sound to her. Damn.

"Have you heard my news?"

"What news?" Cradling the phone between his ear and shoulder, he opened the fridge and took out a beer. Molly drank beer, he knew that, but she probably preferred wine. She probably knew what was a good year and what wasn't. He popped the tab and took a long swallow. He was always going to be a beer man. It made him smile to imagine ending a day on a construction site by opening a chichi bottle of Chablis. It would never happen.

"Don White and I are engaged."

He straightened. "No, I hadn't heard. Congratulations to both of you."

Her voice turned shy. "You aren't upset or...or hurt, are you?" She rushed on. "I mean, we had some good times, Joe, but the thing is, I never felt it was serious with you. I always felt like you were sort of marking time. You know, while you waited for someone who'd been gone a long time to come back. Does that make any sense? Probably not, but that's how I felt. Then, after Don's New Year's Eve party, he and I got together for lunch, and...well, we just..."

"I'm happy for both of you. Really." To ease a twinge of guilty relief, he told himself that Ellen and Don were perfect for each other. "When's the wedding?"

"We haven't set a date yet. But listen, I didn't call to talk about Don and me. I called to ask you about Molly Stevens."

He sighed. "You can hardly see the scars." Was there anyone in town who hadn't asked him about Molly?

"I heard. What I want to know is...the Vrain Ladies Society would like to have a potluck to welcome Ms. Stevens to town. Do you think she'd come? And if so, well, is there a man living with her? Does the invitation go to her, or to her and also someone else?"

"I don't know if she'd go to a potluck dinner." Unless he missed his guess, Molly had never been to a small-town potluck in her life. And since he really couldn't imagine that she'd stay in Vrain very long, he doubted she'd want to bother with meeting the residents. "Invite her, if that's what you want to do, and see what happens." His voice didn't offer much encouragement.

"Well, it would be pretty dumb to have a party in her honor if she isn't interested in showing up."

"Look, why are you asking me about this?"

"You see her and talk to her every day. You know her better than anyone else does."

"Ellen, would the VLS have a welcome dinner for Molly if she weren't a celebrity?"

"Sure," she said, sounding surprised. "Don't you remember the party for Ed and Marie Costa? You and I won the door prize."

He'd forgotten. "She isn't living with anyone," he said after a minute. "But why don't you phone her instead of sending an invitation? Then you'll know if she's interested before you and the VLS go to a lot of work planning something."

"What's your opinion? Will she think a potluck is just for small-town hicks? She probably will, won't she? And we'll have paper plates, like we always do. And square dancing afterward. It won't be anything like what she's used to."

Suddenly he felt angry. "Ellen, Molly is real people. She's not royalty. She's not a snob. She knows Vrain isn't a magnet for the jet-set. And I'm sure she's eaten off of paper plates before."

After he got off the phone, he walked out on the deck with Aspen, lifting his face to the falling snow.

The frosty air cleared his head, but he still felt annoyed. Everyone in Vrain had an insatiable curiosity about Molly, and everyone had an opinion about her. They'd all made assumptions. She was stuck-up. She was too sophisticated for small-town people and small-town events. Most people seemed to assume that she was bitchy to work with and the most demanding client he'd ever had.

Frowning, he peered through the snow and waited for Aspen to return from a stand of snowy pines. What assumptions had he made?

WHEN JOE ARRIVED, it was like a hurricane of energy entered the house, Molly thought, listening to the sound of hammering and pounding. Shaking her head, she stared at the computer screen and tried to recapture her thoughts. Sighing, she pushed back from her desk. The good news was that after a dozen false starts, she thought she had composed a fairly interesting first ten pages for the book. The problem was trying to concentrate when the ceiling was shaking above her, bits of debris were falling into her plastic canopy, and she was intensely curious about what was going on upstairs. Adding to the chaos, the phone had rung several times this morning, confirming her suspicion that interruptions were deadly for would-be writers.

"Hello?"

"Can I speak to Joe Townsend, please?"

Well, she was looking for a reason to find out what was happening upstairs. And to see Joe. "Hang on," she said into the phone. "This might take a while."

Actually, her mind was on the last call she'd received. A smile curved Molly's lips. She'd never square-danced in her life, or supposed that she ever would. Therefore, she didn't own anything remotely resembling a square-dance dress that she could wear to the welcome dinner and dance next Saturday night. She wasn't sure she even knew what a square-dance dress looked like. It occurred to her that perhaps she should have declined the invitation. She wasn't going to be dressed properly, and she didn't have an escort. Thinking about it, she wondered if she should call Ellen O'Ryan back.... On the other hand, her social calendar wasn't exactly overflowing with engagements.

Putting the problem out of her mind for the moment, she wondered why it felt so cold today. Frowning, she glanced at the staircase. A frigid breeze flowed down the steps. She'd already added a sweater over a shirt and turtleneck, but her hands were so cold that, even if she had fewer interruptions, she probably couldn't have typed comfortably.

Rubbing her hands to restore some circulation, she ran up the stairs, calling Joe's name.

Noise and dust and pounding country rock hit her at the top of the staircase. A crash vibrated the floor and made her jump as the last interior wall came down, sending a cloud of dust rolling toward Molly and the front of the house. There was no way to avoid inhaling the choking haze. When the dust settled somewhat, she noticed that the only wall left on the ground floor was the bearing wall that supported the second story.

But what shocked her was the huge hole cut in the outside wall. Mouth falling open, she stared at the snowflakes blowing into the foyer. As usual, Joe and the two pooches working in the foyer area made no concession to the icy temperature. None of them wore coats.

"No wonder it's freezing in here," she muttered, wrapping her arms around herself. How did they stand it? None of the men looked as if they had even noticed that warm puffs appeared in front of their lips when they spoke.

"Hi, honey. Guess I should have warned you. The contractor rules say we can't cut a hole in an outside wall unless it's snowing outside and the temperature is below freezing." Laughing, Joe instructed Al and Trey to fetch the new front door. "Have you met the Johns?"

"I beg your pardon?"

"The electricians." Taking her by the arm, he led her into the dust-hazed living room where three men were kneeling on the floor removing the heating units. "Hey, honey," he said to the closest. "Meet the boss lady."

They all got to their feet and smiled at her. One with a long, dark, beautiful ponytail stuck out his hand. "Hi. I'm John Mason."

It turned out that all three of the electricians were named John, which would make it confusing. Molly smiled, then turned to Joe. "I almost forgot why I came up here. You have a phone call." The smile faded from her lips, and she cast a quick look at the snow blowing through the gaping hole in the side of the house. "Oh, boy." It was freezing.

"Thanks," Joe said, looking at her. They held each other's gaze for a minute, and then he started toward the basement staircase. "Mr. Melvin just arrived to fix your television."

Molly turned as the tallest, thinnest man she had ever seen walked through the hole in the side of the house as if holes in houses weren't unusual enough to notice. He wore jeans that hung on pencil-thin hips and, astonishingly, a woman's pink ruffled blouse and a pair of dangling pearl earrings. Molly was five feet ten inches tall, but she had to look up when he stopped in front of her.

"I am Mr. Melvin, owner of Melvin Smith's Satellite Systems. I have arrived to restore your entertainment," he announced grandly. "The even-odd-channel thing is a fascinating problem." He laughed at Molly's expression. "I know. You're thinking I'm so skinny that if I closed one eye, I'd look like a needle."

Actually, she was thinking about his pink blouse and pearl earrings.

By the time she returned downstairs, Joe was off the phone. He adjusted his tool belt and gave her a reassuring smile. "Don't let the blouse fool you, honey. Mr. Melvin is brilliant. Best satellite man in the state."

Molly nodded, then picked up a pencil from her desktop and inspected it closely. "I wonder where a person would buy a square-dance dress...." At least, as the guest of honor, she didn't have to bring a dish for the potluck, thank God. The woman who called had seemed shocked by the question.

"I'm the wrong guy to ask about women's fashion," Joe said in a distracted voice, glancing at his watch. "Damn. The new windows should have been delivered an hour ago. See you later, honey."

Molly watched him bound up the stairs. Then, shivering, she reached for her parka and pulled it on. Frowning, she sat down at her desk and idly tapped the pencil against the surface. Joe was all business today. Rushing here, racing there. Avoiding her? Trying to remind her that theirs was strictly a business arrangement, nothing more? Certainly, he hadn't picked up on her comment about the square-dancing dress. Maybe he didn't know about the dinner and dance yet.

Well, nuts. She had almost a week to worry about dresses and escorts. Right now, she needed to get a few pages done on her book. She'd typed a couple of paragraphs before she became aware of someone standing behind her. Thinking it might be Joe, she whirled around with a smile on her face. But it was one of the pooches—Z, if she remembered correctly. He stood at the bottom of the staircase, looking very young and holding one hand up in the air. Bright red blood dripped down his fingers.

"What happened?" Molly gasped.

"I cut my finger," he said solemnly, staring at her with an expectant expression.

At once she realized he was only about eighteen or nineteen. Big brown eyes examined her face.

"Let me see it," she said, when she realized he was hoping she would do something. "How deep is the cut?" It wasn't too bad, she decided, peering down. Probably it didn't need any stitches. "Okay. Let's go to the bathroom and wash it out." She led the way upstairs, and they crowded into the bathroom. Molly turned on the cold water, then took his hand and held it under the flow.

Mr. Melvin leaned in the doorway to see what they were doing. "Oh, blood! Yucka-yucka." Making a face, he disappeared.

"I think I've got some disinfectant." Molly opened the medicine cabinet and rummaged through bottles and tubes. "Yeah, here it is."

Z stiffened his shoulders and stared stoically into the mirror, not watching as she applied the disinfectant and then a Band-Aid. "Do you think I should go home?"

"No, honey," Joe said from the doorway. "Not for a little cut like that. If you slice off your hand, then you get the rest of the day off. Now go back down there and help Coke with the front door." He dropped a hand on Z's shoulder, and Molly noticed a gentle squeeze. "Thank Mother before you go."

Z flashed her a grateful smile. "Thanks, Miss Stevens. You saved my life."

"Please. Make it Molly." When he'd gone back downstairs, Molly looked at Joe and raised an eyebrow. "Mother?"

He laughed, flashing white teeth and sparkling eyes at her. "You're spoiling my pooches."

Before she tore off some paper towels and wiped out the sink, Molly looked in the mirror. "Your pooches are just babies. Suddenly I feel a hundred years old."

"Believe me," he said, in a voice that made her look up at him, "you look just fine."

In ordinary circumstances, a man and a woman didn't occupy the same bathroom unless they were intimate. Joe was probably accustomed to talking to clients in bathrooms, but Molly wasn't. She found herself acutely aware of standing close to him, tried not to remember waking up with her head on his shoulder and her mouth inches from his.

"Joe?" she asked, meeting his eyes in the mirror over the sink. God, he had beautiful eyes. "I guess you probably know how to square-dance...."

He shrugged and grinned at her in the mirror, holding her gaze. "I can do-si-do if I have to."

"Hey, Joe! Where do you want us to put these windows?"

"Joe? The Romaine boys are here, dropping off a dozer."

"Gotta run, honey." Watching him in the mirror, she saw his gaze flick to her mouth. Then he touched her shoulder lightly and strode away.

Sighing, Molly touched her shoulder, then put the tin of bandaids back in the medicine cabinet. She'd done everything but come right out and ask him to be her escort. Damn. She wasn't good at asking a man for a date.

The following day, she tried again. Taking a break from her frustrating attempts to write, she came upstairs and watched Joe for a minute. He was striding around shouting directions, and the pooches seemed to know which honey he was addressing, although Molly didn't see how they could. The activity and noise seemed chaotic and disorganized to her untrained eye. It wouldn't have surprised her if the Red Queen suddenly appeared, shouting, "Off with their heads!"

When Joe stopped long enough to inspect what the electricians were doing, Molly walked up to him. When he saw her, he gave her one of those electric smiles that made her toes curl.

"I've figured out that the house is not going to get warmer," she said, watching the heaters come out with a sinking heart. "So where can I buy an electric blanket?"

"Probably at the new Wal-Mart," he said. "Want a cup of hot coffee?"

"Thanks." She curved her cold hands around the lid of his thermos, then took a sip, wondering if he'd been using the lid as a cup before he offered it to her.

Just ask him, she told herself irritably. *Just say, "Would you be my escort to the dinner and dance on Saturday night?" Just say the words, damn it.*

"Actually, this would be a good day to shop for extra blankets," he said, flicking a look toward the open second floor and the door of her bedroom. "Today we're going to knock out the basement wall next to your desk and install some windows for you down there. Get you some light. And we'll start coring out the cement floor to put in a bathroom drain. Ever tried to work with a jackhammer right behind you?" he asked with a laugh.

"Joe?" *Just come out and ask him.* "All we talk about is the job."

He looked at her, and his eyebrows soared. "Honey, for what you're paying me, we'd better be talking about the job."

But there was a look in his eyes that she couldn't read.

"Right," she murmured, ducking her head. Was he reminding her that theirs was only a client relationship? Or was he assuring her that he wasn't wasting her money on idle chitchat?

After an awkward minute, she sighed, then went in search of her car keys and drove into town to buy an electric blanket. For some reason, she felt mad at the world today.

On Wednesday, she asked him if he liked potluck suppers. He said he loved them, then went running off to investigate a loud crash. On Thursday, she asked if he knew where the high school auditorium was, where the dinner and dance would be held. He said of course he did, then used the telephone on her desk to call a supplier.

On Friday morning, Molly sat at her desk, ready to throw her hands up in the air in frustration. When the phone rang, she snatched it up and answered with a snarl.

Darcy Connors-slash-Arden laughed in her ear. "In a bad mood, are we? The construction driving you crazy?"

Molly pushed a hand through her hair and glared at her wonderful new windows. Finally, her cave was opened up and flooded with winter sunlight. "The contractor is driving me crazy," she said with a sigh.

After she explained her problem, Darcy laughed again. "I don't believe it. The beautiful and famous Molly Stevens can't get a date. Listen, dummy. Remember what your fortune said? Follow your heart. You ask him."

"I've been trying to," Molly said in exasperation. "I don't know how to do it. I've never had this problem before." She glared at the open rafters above her head and the haze of dust filtering through the cracks. "As for a silly fortune in a fortune cookie, you're putting entirely too much credence in something that doesn't mean anything."

"You couldn't prove it by me," Darcy insisted. "My fortune came true."

Joe came bounding down the stairs, bringing his usual energy and vitality. Molly could have sworn the room suddenly got hotter and started to sizzle with Joe's unique electricity. "Darcy? I have to run."

"Don't hang up on my account," Joe said.

"No, no, it's all right." She had to ask him about tomorrow night. Time was running out. If she didn't make herself say something today, she'd be going to the dinner and dance alone. Visions of being a wallflower made her shudder.

"Are you doing anything important right now?" he asked, his blue eyes sparkling. She looked up at him and suppressed another sigh. She'd always been a sucker for sparkly eyes. "I want to show you something."

"Nothing important," she said. Just trying to write a book that she wished she had never agreed to attempt, and not getting very far with it. "What's up?"

"Come upstairs."

She followed him, amazed that he had the energy to run up the staircase two steps at a time. This was her fourth trip upstairs, and her feet were dragging. When she stepped into the living room, a blast of frigid air turned the tips of her ears red. Today they were cutting more huge holes in the outside walls.

"Outside," Joe said, grinning with the pleasure of a surprise.

For all she knew, he was seeing someone else. He could have a serious lady friend. Maybe he was engaged. Asking him to the dance would be hideously embarrassing for both of them if he was involved with someone. He was a nice man, and he would make it as easy as possible on her. He wouldn't say, "I'm sorry, this is strictly a business relationship. How could you possibly have imagined it was anything else?" More likely he'd say, "My fiancée and I would be happy to have you hitch a ride with us."

And then she would drop through the floor with mortification. And she would feel like a fool about all the hours she had spent thinking about Joe and daydreaming about him. She would regret and feel foolish about all the long looks and speculation.

Frowning, Molly pulled her parka around her and followed him outside, then stopped dead and stared. Already the Romaine boys had dug a trench around the base of what would be the new garage. A huge mound of muddy dirt had been pushed to one side, and she saw a pile of large rocks that they had pulled out of the excavation site.

"Look at that," Joe said, pointing.

The bucket of the bulldozer was banging and pushing and clawing at a boulder that must weigh six or seven tons. It was huge.

"It has to come out," Joe said. "So. Women are good

at arranging things.'' He laughed, sunlight dancing in his eyes. ''Where do you want us to put that boulder?''

She leaned against someone's muddy truck and watched the bulldozer rock up on one side. Molly gasped and held her breath, certain the dozer was going to crash over on its side, but it didn't. The man at the controls was a younger version of Daddy Romaine. He wore a black cowboy hat and rode the bulldozer as if it were a bucking bronco. Fully concentrated on the boulder, he didn't seem aware that the bulldozer teetered precariously on the lip of the excavation.

Molly gazed at the pile of rocks, then returned her stare to the boulder that Toots Romaine was trying to coax out of the ground's grip. ''I can see why they call them the Rocky Mountains,'' she murmured. ''This land must be on a glacial moraine.''

Daddy Romaine stepped up beside her, his eyes narrowed on the dozer bucket. ''You want me and my boys to haul that rock out of here?''

''Or you could have them put it at the end of the driveway,'' Joe suggested. ''Might look nice down there.''

''Do you have to have an answer right this minute?'' What she hated most about all this was the need for instant decisions.

''Toots is gonna pop that rock out any second,'' Daddy said. ''Gotta know what to do with the damned thing. 'Scuse me for swearing.''

Now Molly noticed Dumpling leaning against Daddy's big-wheeled pickup, chewing gum and filing her fingernails. Today Dumpling was wearing skintight jeans, a pearl-buttoned shirt and a fringed leather jacket. Long feather earrings swung down past her shoulders. When she saw Molly watching her, she called across the yard, ''Looks like you found that queen fly. The flies are gone. I checked.'' She went back to filing her nails.

Daddy Romaine cut a sideways glance at Molly. ''That was a joke, about the queen fly. We figured it out. Ain't no such thing as a queen fly.''

''Dumpling doesn't talk much, does she?'' Molly asked.

A dozen men stood around the excavation site, watching Toots maneuver the bulldozer. Only Dumpling appeared indifferent to the battle with the boulder. She stood apart, absorbed by her fingernails.

"Well, just look at her." Daddy Romaine rocked back on the heels of his cowboy boots and sucked in his cheeks. "A woman that gorgeous don't have to talk. Spoils things when a gorgeous woman talks too much."

"Can't argue with that," Joe agreed, his eyes flashing and sparkling as if he were holding in a laugh. When he gave Molly a teasing glance, she noticed his chest moving beneath his flannel shirt. "Well, where do you want to put that rock, honey?"

"I don't have a clue," Molly said, throwing up her hands. When Daddy Romaine curled his upper lip, she added hastily. "Okay. Place it at the end of the driveway, like Joe suggested."

"End of the driveway, huh? Well, now, that there is gonna be an interesting challenge," Daddy Romaine said, narrowing his eyes on the boulder, gauging its size. "If we bring the big dozer in, we can do it. But you got those electrical wires crossing overhead. Gonna have to study on this." He wandered down the driveway.

"All right, all right, who did it?" Mr. Melvin glided around the end of the house and walked up to the edge of the trench to shout at Toots Romaine. "Gosh darn it, Toots! You dug up the TV cable." He threw out a long, skinny hand and pointed to the broken ends of cable protruding from the ground near the giant boulder.

"Nice blouse, Mr. Melvin," Dumpling called, glancing up. "Lace looks good on you."

"Thank you, darling. I'm crazy about your earrings. They're so you."

"You'll have to wait until we get this rock out of here, Mr. Melvin!" Toots shouted back. "It would be better if you'd wait until tomorrow!"

"Then Miss Molly won't have *any* entertainment tonight. That won't do."

Her eyes fixed on the bulldozer, Molly decided to swallow her pride and give it one more try. She had to be a glutton for punishment. Turning to Joe, she said, "I wonder if Dumpling and Daddy Romaine will be at the welcome dinner...."

"Those two wouldn't miss a chance to dance," Joe said absently. He scanned the line of men watching Toots wrestle the boulder. When Toots bucked the massive rock up out of the foundation hole, a cheer went up. Even Molly gave a shout and grinned.

"That's it, pooches," Joe shouted, smiling broadly. "On that triumph, we'll call it a day."

Almost instantly, beers appeared out of pickups, music blared from truck radios. Everyone hung around to watch Daddy Romaine direct the bulldozer down the driveway and beneath the electrical wires, and finally, to the accompaniment of honking horns, Toots placed the huge boulder at the side of the driveway entrance.

Joe cupped his hands around his mouth and shouted. "The Goosed Moose. First round's on me!"

Molly stood beside him, hands thrust deep in the pockets of her parka, and she watched the pickups rev their motors, then race down the driveway and spin plumes of cold dust as they wheeled onto the no-name road. The cavalcade roared off toward town.

Joe opened the door of his truck, then grinned at her. "What time shall I pick you up?"

Molly stared at him, incredulous. "What did you say?"

"Honey, I hope like hell that I'm not making a mistake, but it occurs to me that you've been doing a lot of hinting lately about the dinner and dance tomorrow night. And I've been doing a lot of thinking about it too. So..." His grin widened.

She looked at him, then laughed in relief. Thank God. "Does seven o'clock sound about right?"

"I'll be here whenever you want me," he said in a gruff voice, holding her gaze.

"Seven's fine," she said, in a voice that was suddenly

dry. Lord, she felt like a teenager again, tongue-tied at the prospect of a date.

And this time there was no question. They had agreed to a date.

She stood in the yard watching him drive away, wistfully wishing that he'd invited her to join him and the pooches at the Goosed Moose to celebrate the removal of the boulder.

Well, good grief. One date wasn't enough, she thought, smiling. And eight hours a day wasn't enough. She wanted to be with him all the time. When was the last time *that* had happened?

Shaking her head, she walked back to the silent house. That was when she discovered that there was no electricity on the ground floor. For a moment, the realization was so dismaying that she felt like crying. The cold was making her miserable. The constant noise during the day gave her headaches. The dust and debris were driving her crazy. And the decisions made her stomach cramp.

If it hadn't been for Joe...his sparkling sexy eyes, his constant cheerfulness, his good natured calm in the midst of bedlam...she thought she would have lost her mind by now.

She would have bet every cent in her stock portfolio that every female client fell madly in love with him.

"YOU LOOK BEAUTIFUL," Joe said admiringly as Molly spun across the old kitchen linoleum in a flare of blue ruffles. She caught herself against the countertop and laughed. "Where did you find a square-dance dress on such short notice?"

"At the Wal-Mart, when I went into town to buy an electric blanket." She gazed down at the off-the-shoulder ruffled blouse and full skirt. "You're sure I'm not going to be the only woman dressed like this? I like it, but it feels like a costume."

"You'll fit right in, but believe me, none of the other women will look as fabulous as you do."

"Thank you, kind sir. You look pretty darned fabulous yourself. With that pearl-buttoned shirt, crisp new jeans and shiny boots...all you need is a Stetson to look like a real cowboy."

"Or to look like Toots Romaine," Joe said, grinning. "The day you bought the dress is the day we put the windows in downstairs. Do you like having more light down there?"

"Oh, Joe." Eyes shining with gratitude, she gazed at him with an expression that made his stomach tighten and his mouth go dry. "I haven't raved nearly enough. When I came home that day and saw the windows...I could have kissed you!"

"Wish I'd been here when you got home," he said softly, smiling. A light flush of color tinted her cheeks. It must be her makeup, he decided.

"I'd offer you a drink," she said, smoothing down her skirts, "but it's freezing in here." Pursing her lips, she demonstrated by blowing a plume of silver vapor.

Showing him how cold it was had formed her lips into a kiss. Joe stared at her, then bit down on his back teeth and walked to the hall closet. He slipped a mink jacket off a hanger, holding it out for her.

"I'd rather wear the camel's hair coat," she said lightly.

"You're going to disappoint the ladies." After hanging the mink back in the closet, he helped her on with the cloth coat.

"My folks gave me the mink jacket for Christmas last year, so I can't give it away. But I don't wear fur." She preceded him out the door, talking over her shoulder. "My mother knows how I feel about fur, but she refuses to believe it."

Joe followed her to the passenger side of the pickup and opened the door, even though she offered a mild protest. "I guess I sort of picture you in fur, too," he said. "I didn't figure you for a furballer."

"You're thinking, she won't wear fur but she's wearing leather shoes," Molly said as he started the pickup. "I know. It doesn't make sense to do it halfway. And I can't explain why it seems okay to wear leather but not to wear fur."

"Maybe because leather is a by-product, but fur *is* the product."

The light from the dashboard illuminated her smile. "Good explanation. You aren't a hunter, are you?" she asked, obviously trying to hide a touch of anxiety.

"Nope. I used to do some duck hunting, but not anymore. I realize the deer and elk herds need thinning or many of the animals will starve over the winter. I don't object to hunting or hunters per se, it just isn't right for me." He turned his head to look at her, thinking that he'd done her an injustice. He'd assumed she would look uncomfortable and a little silly in something as unsophisticated as a square-dance dress. But she didn't. She was lovely. "I do fish, though. Have you ever been fishing?"

After the cold in her house and outside, the pickup seemed overly warm. Or maybe sitting this close to her was heating his system. He couldn't seem to come within two feet of her without thinking about taking her into his arms.

"Me? Fishing?" She laughed. "Not since I was a kid."

"You ought to give it another try. You're outside, close to nature. It's quiet, and you can think about things. Relax. And, if you're lucky, you take home supper."

"What else do you do on your days off?" she asked, twisting on the seat to look at him.

He shrugged, inhaling the seductive sweetness of her perfume, aware of her eyes on his face. "The usual things. I play golf. Fish. I try to work in a couple of pack trips with Jim Enders every summer. I like to ski." He paused, kicking himself for mentioning skiing, but she said nothing. "I've been wanting to do a little snowshoeing before the snow melts, but recently I've spent my weekends working up bids or catching up on the paperwork."

"You don't have a secretary?"

"My business is at the point where there's too much

paperwork for me to keep up with, but not really enough to justify hiring a secretary." He cast her a rueful smile. "If you're ever interested in a part-time job…"

"Be careful what you say," she said lightly. "I don't think this author thing is going to work out."

"It's not going well?"

"You're kidding, right? I defy anyone to concentrate with everything that's going on in my house! The noise, the constant interruptions…"

"Sorry, honey, you're looking to the wrong guy for sympathy. I begged you to take an apartment for the duration."

"'I told you so?'" She gave him a mock glare. "You're a hard man, Joe Townsend."

Her comment made him laugh. "Don't I wish. I'm the first guy the Girl Scouts hit when it's cookie-selling time. When they need volunteers for some town project, they call me first. I sponsor a little league team every year, and every year I get drafted to help build the sets for the drama club at the high school. The truth is, I'm a pussycat who can't say no."

She studied him so long that her steady gaze made him uncomfortable. "You like living in Vrain, don't you? You're thriving in small-town America."

"I grew up in a Denver suburb, just as you did," he said after thinking about the question. "My folks lived on the same block for eighteen years, but they didn't know the names of the people who lived in the house at the end of the block. I never felt any sense of community or connection when I lived in a big town."

He spoke slowly, thinking about his feelings. "You're known all over America, Molly, so maybe you won't understand how good it feels to walk into any store and know the person behind the counter. Plus, in Vrain I feel that I'm really participating in democracy. In our last election, the mayor won by four votes. Here you know your vote counts. It matters."

"Is it true that everyone knows everyone else's business in a small town?" she asked.

He laughed. "I'm afraid so. And no one is shy about expressing an opinion about your business, either." His expression sobered, and he turned to look at her. "There's a nice side to that, too. People care. They look out for each other. There's room for individuality, and an attitude of live-and-let-live. But people are going to talk."

"I'll say there's individuality," she said, smiling at him. "Just look at Mr. Melvin."

Joe turned off the highway toward the high school, a three-story building fashioned out of the stone quarried above the town. "Mr. Melvin created something of a sensation when he first moved here. But by and large, the people in Vrain accept people for who they are."

"Does that apply to me, Joe?" she asked softly.

"It will if you stay," he said after a minute. "Right now, you're new in town, and you're a celebrity. Everyone is fascinated by you. But I won't lie to you. Most of them have formed an opinion without having met you." Switching off the ignition, he turned on the seat to look at her. "But these people are fair, honey. As they get to know you, their opinions will shift more toward reality."

Sliding out of the pickup, he walked around the truck bed to open the door for her, and this time she didn't protest. Arm in arm, they followed a freshly shoveled sidewalk toward the lights blazing out of the gymnasium windows.

"Joe? What did you mean when you said, 'if I stay'? I've come here to live. This will be my home."

"Choosing a home is one of the biggest decisions people make," he said, not looking at her. For an instant, he considered changing the subject, but then he decided to say what was on his mind. "You've said yourself that making decisions is difficult right now. You've come home to a place that was safe and happy when you were a child, but I'm not sure if you've realized yet everything that's attached to that choice."

Near the door, she withdrew her hand from his arm and stopped, frowning up at him. "Like what?"

"Like shopping at Wal-Mart instead of designer boutiques. Like driving fifteen miles to Longmont to see a movie because there's no theater in Vrain. Like watching the senior class perform *Arsenic and Old Lace*—yet again—instead of seeing the latest hit on Broadway. Like having dinner at Ma and Pa's Café instead of dining at the latest trendy spot in Manhattan. Honey, the nearest airport is in Denver, eighty miles away. The closest shopping mall is in Boulder, twenty miles away. The nearest dentist is in Longmont. If you have a recipe that calls for, oh, say shiitake mushrooms, you'll have to notify Wiley Oats a few days in advance so he can special-order them for you. One of the things that big cities offer is choice and convenience. Small towns are short on both items.''

Molly thrust her hands into her coat pockets and studied his expression. "You don't think I can adjust?"

"I didn't say that, honey. I'm just pointing out that Vrain isn't what you're accustomed to. You haven't been here long enough to know yet how much aggravation you're going to feel the first time you're longing for a cup of mocha latte and discover you'll have to drive to Longmont or Boulder to find it. Small towns aren't right for everyone.''

"Do you think I'm that superficial?'' she asked softly, staring up at him.

He gazed into her lovely eyes and remembered Ellen O'Ryan's concern that Molly would dismiss a potluck dinner and square dancing as an event for small-town hicks. Suddenly he realized that he'd harbored the same thought.

"No, I don't think you're superficial,'' he answered. "I just don't think you're destined to be a longtime resident.'' To soften his opinion, he lifted a hand and let his fingertips rest lightly on her silky cheek. She had the softest skin he could ever have imagined. "Let me ask you something. Would you have moved home to your grandparents' place if you hadn't hit that tree facefirst?''

"Probably not,'' she said after a long moment. She stared into his eyes. "But I did hit that tree facefirst. And the minute I did, Joe, everything—and I mean everything—changed.''

"Right now I think you're hurt that your world rejected you," he said gently. "So you're rejecting it, too, by running away." He stroked her cheek, unable to take his hand away. "But you're getting stronger every day, honey. And I think the time will come when you're ready to go home, and I don't mean the old Stevens place. I mean home to Bloomingdale's and Saks and a deli on every corner. Home where celebrities are a dime a dozen and people don't gawk at you. Home where you can eat French cuisine tonight and Korean tomorrow night. Art galleries and museums and high fashion, that's your world. Theater openings and nightclubs and stretch limos.''

She stepped back from his hand. "Looks like you've formed an opinion, just like you said everyone else in Vrain has," she said coolly.

The look in her eyes told him that he'd bungled this badly. But he was in it now, and he might as well see the subject through. "You tell me…am I wrong?" When she didn't answer, he shrugged, suddenly depressed. "If you do plan to eventually return back east, then why are you bothering to go to this party and meet everyone? What's the point? The folks inside have gone to a lot of trouble to arrange a welcome party for you. If you go in there, they'll expect you came tonight because you want to be part of this town. Are you sure that's what you want?''

Molly simply stared up at him with a frown.

Chapter Five

"Hi, Miss Stevens. Can I take your coat?"

Joe recognized Avis Morrison's daughter, Cheryl. Cheryl had made the cheerleading squad this year. She colored prettily as she took Molly's coat, tagged it and handed him the end torn off the tag. Like she would forget which coat belonged to the Apple Girl. Smiling stiffly, Joe handed her his topcoat and scarf and dutifully tucked his tag and Molly's into the pocket of his jeans. Molly lifted her chin in a challenging expression, then turned away from him to look around.

The Vrain Ladies' Society had set up long food tables on the stage at the end of the gym. Tables crowded the floor, the collapsible kind that could be easily removed for the dancing after supper. Crepe-paper streamers and balloons decorated the walls, and helium balloons bobbed above each table, stenciled with the word *Welcome*.

Everyone present must have been watching for her, because Molly hadn't taken three steps forward before it seemed that a hundred people turned to stare at her. A beat of silence opened, and then the buzz of conversation resumed. Joe moved up beside her seconds before Ellen O'Ryan, Avis Morrison and the Van Tine twins bore down on them.

Ellen smiled at him and then introduced herself and the others to Molly. Molly smiled, too, and shook hands and

complimented the decorations and the savory scents waft-
ing from the tables set up on the stage. The ladies complimented her dress and her hair and then, when everyone had
run out of things to compliment, they proudly escorted
Molly—and, almost as an afterthought, Joe—to the stage
and the array of potluck dishes.

"Be sure to try Avis's famous baked beans," Joe advised, picking up a plate. Like most men, he enjoyed potluck dinners, where all the women vied to outdo each other.

"Isn't he a sweet-talker?" Avis said, blushing. To Joe,
she added in a pleased stage whisper, "My dish is the
Corningware with the blue flowers around the rim."

"Do you like to cook?" one of the Van Tine twins shyly
asked Molly.

"I haven't done much cooking in recent years," Molly
answered, giving Joe a quick, defiant glance, "but I used
to enjoy it. I'm afraid I'll never be any competition for you
ladies, though. Everything looks and smells wonderful."

Ellen and the others gave each other pleased smiles, and
Joe realized Molly had answered the question exactly right.
She had turned a question into a charming word of praise.
It occurred to him that she could probably charm people in
her sleep. She was used to this kind of thing.

Each of the tables was set for eight. After filling their
plates they were led to a table with a reserved sign in the
center, where Steve Castle, the mayor, sat with his wife,
along with the chief of the volunteer fire department and
his wife. The men stood as Molly approached, and Ellen
made introductions, then Don White joined her and everyone sat down.

Joe didn't say much throughout dinner. The conversation
began with everyone asking Molly how the renovations
were progressing on her house. She responded with funny
stories about sharing one bathroom with pooches and workmen, and she mentioned the boulder in the garage foundation, making it a hilarious tale. Soon everyone was join-
ing in with remodeling stories of their own, offering Molly

encouragement, then relating disastrous experiences that had everyone at the table holding their sides with laughter.

After dessert, Avis Morrison went to the microphone on stage and made a few announcements, then cleared her throat and launched into a prepared welcome speech. "Actually, the lady we're welcoming tonight needs no introduction. We've seen her lovely face on magazine covers, on billboards, and in the newspapers." She went on to detail Molly's career, ending with Molly's selection as the Apple Girl, America's sweetheart. Tactfully, Avis didn't mention the skiing accident or the fact that Molly was no longer the Apple Girl.

Next the mayor made a few announcements, then presented the official welcome to "our very own celebrity." He talked a few minutes about the proposed new community center, then said he hoped Molly would enjoy living in Vrain as much as he and Edna did.

Next, to Joe's surprise, Molly stepped forward and took the microphone. He hadn't noticed when she slipped from the chair beside him. Immediately all the little rustling sounds stopped and everyone stared at her.

He couldn't guess what the rest of the town saw, but he saw a blindingly beautiful woman whose smile stopped his heart and made him ache inside just to look at her. The overhead stage lights shone down on her hair and made it shine like a halo. Her bare shoulders gleamed as if they had been polished. If Joe had been seated closer to the stage, he knew, he would have noticed that the china blue of her square-dance dress matched her eyes. When he realized he was comparing her mouth to a rosy valentine, he sighed and cursed himself for a fool.

"As many of you know, my grandparents, Ed and Eleanor Stevens, lived most of their life right outside of Vrain," Molly said. "They loved it here, and so did I when I visited them in the summers. What I remember most are the apple blossoms in spring and the scent of lilacs. I think it must be a town ordinance that every resident in Vrain is required to plant at least one lilac bush in his or her yard. It's wonderful.''

The crowd chuckled, and Joe felt them warming to her. He knew the residents well enough to understand that a few would remain aloof and almost rude, to prove to her and to themselves that celebrity didn't impress them. But he'd already seen enough to know that after tonight, Vrain would claim her as one of their own.

''I don't recall ever receiving such a generous or enthusiastic welcome,'' Molly said, smiling at the crowd. ''Your warmth and hospitality make me very glad that I've come home to a town my grandparents loved so much. Now I know why my family chose to live here, and I expect to follow in their footsteps in every way.'' She looked directly at Joe, and her chin rose a notch. ''I'm very happy to be here.''

Everyone rose to their feet and applauded her enthusiastically. Yeah, Joe thought, she had them in the palm of her hand. Oddly, he didn't know how he felt about that. He was happy for her success tonight, but he also felt protective toward the people in this room. He hated to see them invest a lot of themselves into making Molly feel welcome and accepted, when he truly believed she would be a short-timer. And he didn't care what she said, he truly believed she would return to New York City. Right now, she thought she knew what she wanted, but she was one phone call away from chucking Vrain and heading back east. If that call ever came…she'd forget that she'd ever heard of a guy named Joe Townsend.

Avis returned to the microphone and watched the mayor assist Molly down the steps leading off the stage. ''Okay, everyone. We need some volunteers up here to clear the food and tables so Shorty and his musicians can get set up. And will you men clear the tables and chairs off the floor, please?''

While Joe helped stack tables and folding chairs, he watched the women converge on Molly near the bleachers. She greeted all of them as if they were as fascinating to her as she undoubtedly was to them. And, hell, maybe they were. Maybe a president of the PTA was as foreign and as exotically interesting to her as a creature from Mars would be to him. Or maybe she was collecting stories to tell her New York friends after she returned home.

He could picture it. "The town had a quilting club? And they actually asked you to join?" her friends would inquire incredulously. "The mayor is also the town's undertaker? That's hysterical." Her friends would laugh and beg for more, and she would tell them about Mr. Melvin and Avis Morrison's famous baked beans, and about a party held in a crepe-paper-draped gym.

What would she tell her fancy, sophisticated friends about him? That he thought formal meant new jeans that still had a crease down the legs? That he was a mountain rube who couldn't bring a project in on budget?

Jim Enders stacked the last of the folding chairs, then straightened and studied Joe's face. "For a man who's the envy of all his friends tonight, you look pretty glum."

"I'm thinking about the budget on the Stevens job. Wondering if she's going to go over on the fireplaces."

"No rest for the wicked," Jim said, smiling. They both pushed their hands into their pockets and stood looking across the gym at Molly and the knot of people surrounding her. "Be careful, pal," Jim said after a minute. "You're wearing your heart on your sleeve. I'm not the only one who's noticed, either."

Frowning, Joe rocked back on his heels. "She's just a client, honey. That's all."

"Yeah, and a fully loaded Dooley with mag wheels is just a truck, right?" Jim smiled. Then he looked back at Molly. "She's a world-famous model, and the most gorgeous woman anyone in this town has seen outside of a movie theater. How long do you think she'll stay here before she's bored out of her mind?"

Joe had been asking himself the same question, but somehow he resented hearing Jim say the same thing.

"Look, Joe, you've been in the business long enough to

know that clients form a close and dependent relationship with their contractor. Until now, you haven't mixed business and social.'' He nodded toward Molly. ''Hell, I wouldn't say no if she wanted to play footsie with me either. What man would? But—''

''Watch it,'' Joe warned, his eyes narrowing. ''We've been friends a long time, but there are some lines that even friends don't cross.''

''All I'm saying is you're setting yourself up for a fall, that's all. To you, she's Christie Brinkley, Princess Di and Marilyn Monroe rolled into one fascinating package. But to her, you're just a small-town contractor who rides around in a dented pickup that's usually covered with dog hair.'' He looked into Joe's eyes, and he wasn't smiling. ''Just keep things in perspective, okay?''

''You're a fine one to give advice. Aren't you the guy who's been calling to ask *my* advice about you and Avis? Get your love life in order, then maybe you can advise me about mine.''

''I rest my case,'' Jim said with a humorless smile.

Scowling, Joe thrust his hands deeper in his pockets and watched Jim walk toward the stage to talk to Shorty, who was almost finished setting up his amplifiers.

It had been stupid to mention Molly and his love life practically in the same breath. What had he been thinking of?

He knew what he'd been thinking about. Molly. That was all he seemed to think about lately. Frowning across the gymnasium, he looked at her. As far as he was concerned, she was the only woman in the huge room.

He should stay away from her. He knew that. But he couldn't resist her. She was like a magnet drawing him closer and closer, a force he didn't know how long he could fight.

DUMPLING breezed past the group around Molly, looked her up and down, then said, ''I saw that dress at Wal-Mart. Almost bought it myself.''

Daddy Romaine tipped his hat in Molly's direction, then beamed down at Dumpling. "She has wonderful taste."

Molly smiled as they strolled by, watching Dumpling's sashaying hips. Dumpling wore a yellow-and-green square-dance dress that made her look like a plump Gypsy, and four or five earrings dangled from each of her ears, some of them swinging down to her bare shoulders.

Mr. Melvin was the next familiar face to push forward with a word of welcome. For the party he wore straw-thin doe colored jeans and a turquoise off-the-shoulder blouse with matching drop earrings. "Darling, I should have your entertainment restored by Tuesday," he promised happily. "Wednesday at the latest."

She met two of Toots Romaine's ex-wives, an elderly lady who had known her grandparents, a wide-eyed teenager who wanted to be a model, the town policeman, several teachers, a man who had the lopsided grin of a happy alcoholic, and then the names began to blur. When she heard Shorty's musicians tuning their fiddles, she scanned the gymnasium, looking for Joe.

He stood apart from a group of men, his hands pushed in his jean's pockets, looking across the room at her with an expression that was part scowl, part admiration, and entirely sexy. The brooding look was one she hadn't seen before, and it sent an electric shiver down her spine. For a moment, she puzzled over the fact that some men, occasionally some very handsome men, did nothing whatever for the libido, while other men could make her heart pound with a glance. Granted, she hadn't met very many men who could make her knees feel weak with a glance, but Joe Townsend was one of them. Maybe the only one, now that she thought about it.

After excusing herself from the group surrounding her, she walked across the floor and stopped in front of him.

"Penny for your thoughts," she said lightly. There were a lot of good-looking men at the party tonight, but none of them exuded Joe's energy and restless sexuality. Joe was a man who effortlessly drew others into his orbit, without seeming to be aware that he did. Men, Molly guessed, would be drawn to his lean, nail-hard masculinity. He wasn't wearing his tool belt tonight, of course, but there was something about him that suggested he'd cut his teeth on power tools and he probably spent his weekends rebuilding his truck's engine, watching football, or something equally macho. Women would be attracted by his sparkling electric eyes, his potent sexuality, and by an intuitive certainty that Joe was a man who liked and appreciated women. He also moved with a fluid grace that managed to suggest that he would be lithe and tigerish in bed, something she doubted many women missed noticing.

She touched the tip of her tongue to her upper lip and drew a breath. It was crazy to wonder about Joe in bed. He hadn't given her any indication that theirs was anything other than a friendly business relationship. She was the one who felt a tingling when she gazed at him. There was no sign that he reciprocated her speculation about how they might mesh on an intimate basis.

"My thoughts aren't worth a penny." Tilting his head back, he gazed up at the gym's high ceiling for a long moment, then looked back down at her. "Look, I apologize for getting this evening off on the wrong foot."

"It's all right," she said lightly.

"No, it isn't. We were both getting irritated."

"That's because you were dead wrong," she said with a smile. "But that's an issue we fight about some other time. For tonight, how about a truce?"

"I'm dead wrong?" He smiled, then gave her a thoughtful look. "Oh, hell. We're here. Let's try to have a good time."

"I am having a good time," she said. "These are nice people."

"Come on." Taking her hand, he led her onto the floor. "The sets are forming." Joe pulled her into a square that included Daddy Romaine and Dumpling, the mayor and his wife, and one of her electricians and his wife or girlfriend.

Molly stood waiting, acutely aware of Joe's hard hand wrapped around hers.

"Are we having a good time?" Shorty shouted into the microphone. A hundred voices returned a resounding affirmative. "Are we ready to dance the night away?"

The crowd shouted, "Yes!" and Molly laughed aloud, enjoying herself. This was an entirely different kind of evening from anything she was used to, in a lot of ways. Aside from the wine on the tables, alcohol was not a factor at this party. The intoxicated man who had come up to welcome her sat on the bleachers to watch the dancing, a goofy smile on his lips, but no one else had drunk too much. And they were about to square-dance.

She glanced up at Joe, who was watching her with that intense, almost brooding look that called to mind wild, heated actions that had nothing to do with dancing. Molly wet her lips and focused on the string tie he was wearing. "I hope I don't humiliate either of us," she said in a low voice. "I've never done this before."

"Just listen to the words," Joe said, dropping her hand to clap along with everyone else. "You'll get the hang of it in a hurry."

"Then let's do it!" Shorty shouted into the microphone. Behind him, a row of cowboy fiddlers swung into a lively tune that had Molly tapping her foot in spite of herself. "Face your partner, bow down low…" Shorty called in a singsong voice. Joe caught her hand and turned her to face him as the partners in all the squares bowed to each other. "Ladies to the right and do-si-do…"

When Daddy Romaine reached for her hand and pulled her past him, toward the mayor's outstretched hand, Molly caught on about do-si-doing. Laughing, she wound around the square until she reached Joe again, keeping her eyes on him as she moved closer.

"Swing your partner, swing her high…hug her tight and my, oh, my…"

All over the gym, brightly colored ruffled dresses swung out behind dancing legs, just as Molly's dress did when

Joe's strong arms caught her around the waist and he swung her in a circle that ended in a close embrace. She caught a quick breath and held it, feeling her heart pound.

Being pressed against the long length of him, melded to the muscled heat of his rock-hard body, took Molly's breath away. Eyes wide, she stared at him as he held her a beat too long and electricity leaped and sizzled between them. Gazing into his eyes, pressed hip to hip with him, she felt his instant arousal, and her own. It was as if she had been waiting for him to take her in his arms and pull her roughly against his body all her life. As if her body recognized the end of a long, long wait and didn't want to move away from him.

She didn't know how long the two of them might have stood there, wrapped in an embrace and staring into each other's eyes, if Daddy Romaine hadn't caught her hand again and spun her away from Joe and into a swing. Confused and stumbling, Molly tried to follow as Daddy's boots moved up and down in time with the fiddlers. And then she was do-si-doing around the square again, her eyes locked with Joe's across the square, working her way back to him.

His hand slipped around her waist like a brand, searing through the material of her blouse, and her lips parted breathlessly. Following the caller's instructions, Joe swung her in a tight circle, his arm muscled and hard across her back. Then she was bowing to Daddy Romaine, her cheeks flushed and hot, sashaying around him before turning back to Joe and the electric heat burning in his eyes.

There was something teasingly erotic about the parting and coming back together of square dancing. About passing from man to man around the square, then returning to Joe's powerful, possessive hands on her waist. He lifted her effortlessly and swung her in a circle, then brought her feet back to the floor by sliding her along the length of his muscled body. And she felt the hard heat and tension in his body, saw it in his eyes, and listened to the answering tension in her pounding heart. Her face flushed with the exertion of the dance and from being so near him. Once his fingertips brushed her cheek, then dropped to her bare shoulder, another time his hand settled on her hip. Under the guise of the dance, she gave in to an irresistible impulse to flatten her palm against his wide chest, and she let her fingers splay over the muscles rising on his forearms.

When the dance ended, Molly stood facing him, panting slightly, her hands and lips trembling. She wanted to race home right now and fall into bed with him. She'd never wanted to be with a man so badly in her entire life.

Before either of them could speak, Mr. Melvin claimed her for the next set, and then the fire chief led her though a Virginia reel. Next came Toots Romaine and Wiley Oats. Molly thought she held her own, but it was Daddy Romaine and Dumpling who were the Fred and Ginger of the square-dance set. Smooth as glass, Daddy anticipated Shorty's calls. Dumpling twitched her skirts, tapped her boots, tossed her dark hair and moved around Daddy and the square as if the dance existed merely to showcase her flashing feet and whirling skirts. When Dumpling snapped her gum and blew a bubble without missing a step, Molly laughed out loud and joined her square in a burst of applause. No one seemed to care about the large difference in age between Daddy and Dumpling, and Molly found herself forgetting about it, too.

Occasionally she heard Joe's distinctive rumbling laugh. He danced with Ellen O'Ryan, Avis Morrison and other women, but he didn't dance with Molly again and it was hard to hide her disappointment. No matter who she was dancing with, her gaze constantly swept the floor, looking for him. And when she found him, he was gazing at her over his partner's head. Each time their eyes met, Molly's heart skipped a beat and she drew in a sharp breath. Wanting him, willing him to come to her.

Finally Shorty wiped his forehead with a red-and-white bandanna, murmured to his fiddlers, then smiled and signaled for the lights to dim. "The last dance is a round dance, folks. Find your sweetheart, hold her close, and warm yourself up for the drive home." He waited while couples drifted toward each other, then the fiddlers drew out the long, sweet opening of "Good Night Sweetheart." Shorty leaned to the microphone, picking up the song and crooning, "...till we meet tomorrow... Good night, sweetheart, parting is such sorrow..."

And suddenly Joe appeared out of the darkness, standing in front of her, gazing down at her flushed face and searching eyes. Without a word, Molly stepped up to him, walking into his arms. His hand claimed her waist, and she leaned into him, resting her forehead against his cheek, inhaling faint traces of his clean, lime-scented cologne.

For a long moment, they didn't move. They stood locked together as other couples moved past them, their hearts beating against each other, almost clinging, as if they had endured a long separation. When Joe moved, Molly discovered that he was a strong lead and she had no difficulty following him. It was as if they had danced a thousand times before. She could have sworn this was not the first time that her arm had rested on his shoulder, that she knew in advance how thick and silky his hair would be when she let her fingers move at the nape of his neck. She knew the rough, callused feel of his hand holding hers, the solid power of his hips moving, guiding hers.

Holding each other close, their bodies moving in slow, sensual harmony, they circled the darkened gymnasium, and Molly felt his arms around her, inhaled the scent of his skin. Her head moved and her lips were against his cheek and she felt his lips on her forehead. If either of them moved just a little... Her heart thundered in her chest and her fingers trembled and she wished the music would never end.

But of course it did. The last note died away, and the lights came up. Avis Morrison took the microphone and thanked everyone for coming, advised everyone to drive home safely. A flurry ensued as dishes were claimed, and coats. Then people spilled out of the gymnasium, calling good-nights across the frosty tops of cars and trucks.

Self-consciously silent, Molly waited while Joe collected their coats, then followed him to the parking lot. Inside the pickup, electrically aware of Joe sitting close to her, she searched for something to say. "This was a wonderful evening. I really had fun." Resting her head on the back of the seat, she thought about every part of the evening except Joe. "Did you know that Wiley Oats wants to buy Mrs. Stetson's hardware place so he can expand the grocery store? And, gasp—one of the Van Tine twins is having a winter fling with Dale Winston, who owns the gas station?" When Joe didn't say anything, she continued. "Avis is the postmistress, I guess you know that. But did you know that her daughter Cheryl has been accepted by Harvard University? And Ellen O'Ryan got engaged to Don White last week?"

"I heard," Joe said, his eyes on the road. "Sounds like you received a thorough introduction to Vrain. Right down to the latest gossip."

"Yes," she said, smiling. It was strange to know things about people she didn't really know. At the same time, knowing those things made her feel that she did know them. "I had a great time. How about you? Did you have a good time?"

"Honey, wherever I am, whatever I'm doing, I'm having a good time."

She wished he'd said that he'd have had a better time if he danced more often with her. But he seemed as self conscious as she was. "Joe? Can I ask you something?" She rolled her head on the seat back to look at his profile. "Why didn't you ask me out when we were in middle school and high school?"

"I thought about it once or twice." He shrugged. "We didn't have the same friends, didn't move in the same circles. You were part of the in group—I was part of the rest of the student body." Turning his head, he looked at her curiously. "Would you have gone out with me way back then?"

"I don't know," she said truthfully. In middle school

she'd been intensely aware of Joe, she remembered that. By the time they entered Lakewood High, she'd decided he wasn't interested in her and pushed him to the back of her mind. Even then, she hadn't dealt well with rejection. She doubted that many people did. "You seemed kind of stuck-up back then," she said with a smile. "Now I'm wondering how I ever thought that. Did you think I was stuck-up, too?"

"No, I just thought you were beautiful." He cleared his throat and drove down her driveway, braking in front of her porch. "Well, honey...Monday's going to be a busy day. The Romaines should finish the excavation on both ends of the house, and we'll start framing inside. It's going to be noisy. Alan will be here to finish the concrete coring behind your desk. Monday would be a good day for you to run errands or something."

"Can't do it," she said drowsily. It was warm and intimate in the cab of the pickup. She didn't want to move, didn't want to go into her icy house. "I already lost Friday. Didn't get anything done on the book. I'll work on it a little tomorrow after I finish cleaning my living areas, but I need to make some real headway on Monday."

A nice fantasy rose in her mind. Waking up with Joe beside her. Spending a lazy Sunday in bed, drinking coffee, reading the newspapers...making love.

A small sigh lifted her breast. Nothing like that would happen. Already Joe was backing away, moving the conversation to work, placing a distance between them. But she hadn't imagined the sizzling sexual tension. She'd felt his arousal when he held her, and he must have noticed her quickened breath and pounding heart.

Headlights swept around a curve in the county road, then drove past the turnoff to the no-name road. Joe cleared his throat. "I'd better get you inside and get me out of here. If people see my pickup parked here too long, they'll get the wrong idea."

The wrong idea? Or the right idea. Before Molly could murmur a husky question, Joe had stepped out of the pickup and was opening the passenger door on her side, extending his hand to help her outside, into the frosty air. He walked her up the porch steps, then hung back as she opened the front door.

All evening Molly had wondered if he would kiss her good-night. After their last dance together, she'd expected him to kiss her, if not on the dance floor, then certainly later. Like right now. Gazing at him, she knew without the tiniest doubt that his kiss would be hot and wild and passionate. She hadn't realized how much she wanted Joe to take her in his arms until it became devastatingly obvious that he wasn't going to.

Looking at his starlit silhouette on the steps, she asked softly, "Joe? What happened between the time we left the party and now? Something changed." She'd felt him pulling back from the moment the music faded and she reluctantly moved out of his arms.

"Did it?" His feigned surprise didn't sound convincing. "I'm sorry it seems that way. Everything feels the same to me." He moved down a step. "Well, I'll see you Monday. Unless you want me to check inside and make sure there's no bogeyman?"

"No, but thanks."

She stood at the door and watched him walk back to his pickup, then swing inside. He tapped the horn once, and then his taillights moved down the drive.

Molly gathered her coat around her and watched until he turned onto the county road, then curved out of sight. A deep sigh of disappointment fogged the cold air in front of her lips.

They had had a definite date, there was no doubt about it this time. And they had set each other on fire. Maybe Joe could ignore what was happening between them, but Molly couldn't.

She had never wanted a man to kiss her more than she had wanted Joe to kiss her tonight. She had never felt as aroused or as ready for a man as she felt for Joe. He must have known it. Yet he had walked away.

Tilting her head back and gazing up at the cold stars, she tried to figure it out. Her first thought, of course, was that Joe was repulsed by her scars. But she was making progress—she had moved beyond blaming everything on her scars. She didn't think that was the reason he'd left her standing on the porch tonight.

Maybe he had a rule about not romancing his clients? If so, that was a sensible rule, she decided. As long as it didn't apply to her.

Was it possible that she intimidated him a little? She knew there were men who backed away from beautiful women who commanded large salaries. But Joe Townsend didn't impress her as a man who was intimidated by anything or anyone.

So what was the problem here?

MOLLY wasn't in a particularly good mood on Monday, and the constant ringing of the telephone didn't improve things. Every time the phone rang, she had to interrupt her work on the book and run all over trying to track down the person wanted on the phone. This time, Dumpling wanted to speak to Daddy Romaine.

At least he was easy to find. All she had to do was follow the roar of the bulldozer. As usual, a group of men were standing around watching Toots Romaine do battle with the huge rocks he fought to coax out of the foundation excavation for the garage. Pickup trucks crowded the driveway. Barking dogs chased each other through mud and slush and melting snow.

Wondering if she was paying the men who were standing around watching, Molly headed toward Joe and Daddy Romaine, not realizing they were arguing until she was standing beside them. Loud voices broke off as she approached, and they both scowled at her.

When she told Daddy that he was wanted on the phone, he spun on the heels of his boots and strode to the house. Molly turned to Joe, who had taken off his baseball cap to rake a hand through his hair. "What's that all about?"

"The Romaines should have started on the foundation for your study this morning, but they're still working on the garage. Damn it! There's no way they'll finish the job today. Do you know what this means?"

Molly pulled the collar of her parka up around her throat. "I don't have a clue."

"It means they are going to go way over what they estimated in their bid, that's what it damn well means!"

"They keep hitting those huge rocks."

"Come on. If you dig a hole in the Rocky Mountains, you're going to hit a damned rock. This isn't the first time the Romaines have done an excavation, for God's sake."

Molly studied his handsome face and raised an eyebrow. "You know something? I think this is the first time I've seen you in a bad mood."

"I'm not in a bad mood," he said, staring at her. "I am never in a bad mood."

Somehow it pleased her that he was in no better frame of mind than she was. "Is that so?" she said, smiling at him and trying to coax a smile in return.

Daddy Romaine reappeared and spoke directly to her, ignoring Joe. "What do you plan to do with all these rocks we're digging up, girl?"

Molly shaded her eyes and scanned the piles of dirt and rocks. "It hadn't occurred to me that I had to *do* anything with them."

"I'll give you a good price to haul 'em out of here. You think about it."

Joe rocked back on his heels and watched Daddy saunter away, heading toward the excavation. "I wouldn't be in any hurry to accept that offer, if I were you. I've never known the Romaines to cut anyone a break."

"You're being a real tough guy today," Molly said lightly.

He looked at her, his eyes on her lips. Then he made a point of glancing at his watch. "Gotta get to work, honey. Time is your money."

Frowning, Molly watched him stride away. Nope, her mood was not improving.

THE CROWD at the Goosed Moose had the usual questions about how it was going out at the Stevens place. But this time no one asked about Molly's scars or what she was really like.

"You can't even see the scars," Bernie Schadler said indignantly.

Bonnie served Joe a beer and his usual burger in the basket. "That's right. I looked, too. If you ask me, she was robbed. Those Apple people shouldn't have fired her!"

"Damned shame," Wiley Oats agreed. "Nice woman like her getting shafted by a big corporation."

Joe walked away from the conversation and carried his burger to the booth back by the fireplace. Taking a bite, he gazed out the window. It was snowing again, great puffy flakes that floated out of a black sky.

Would the world have skidded to a halt if he had kissed Molly after the party? Maybe. Maybe not. Damn.

What did she do at night, after he and the pooches left the site? Huddle near her space heater and work on her book? Crawl under her electric blanket and read? He'd forgotten to ask if Mr. Melvin had fixed her TV yet. He hated to think about her out there all alone.

Dipping a french fry in ketchup, he ate it absently, frowning out the window at the falling snow. It was time to face the question he'd been avoiding.

Was he willing to crawl way out on a shaky limb and pursue some kind of personal relationship with Molly Stevens?

A personal relationship wouldn't end well, he knew that going in. Getting hurt was such a given that he didn't even have to think about it. She was chateaubriand; he was burger in a basket. She'd earned a million dollars last year; he'd be dancing in the streets if his business netted a hundred grand this year. She was big-city; he was Podunk, U.S.A.

For a brief while, they had one point in common—her house. But shortly after the remodel project ended, whatever relationship they experimented with would also end. Right now, Molly's days were busy and interesting. It was a rare day when there were fewer than ten men working at the house. Their presence was an inconvenience for someone who was writing a book, but the men were also company, and she was clearly captivated by the work the pooches and the subcontractors were doing. Once the job was finished and everyone departed, that big old house would seem very quiet and isolated. Joe was willing to bet that she'd last about a month, maybe, before she hightailed it back to Manhattan.

And then, what happened to him? He dipped another french fry in ketchup and imagined the whole scenario. She'd feel bad about going, about appearing to have led him on. If the relationship turned serious, she'd ask him to go with her. He'd explain that his home, his business, his life, was in Vrain. He'd ask her to stay, and he'd feel guilty about that, because he'd always known she would eventually go. She would say that she had moved to Vrain with every intention of staying here, but she'd made a mistake. Her life was in New York City. They would argue, they'd both feel guilty and miserable, and in the end he'd drive her to Denver and put her on a plane for New York and that would be that.

Then his friend Jim Enders would say, "I told you so, pal."

And the whole town would shake their collective heads and say they hadn't realized that Joe Townsend was such a fool. He should have known better than to set his cap for a woman like Molly. Pride would force him to walk around the county with an aching grin on his lips, slapping backs and pretending that his few weeks with Molly had been nothing more than a fling, pretending that it hadn't hurt like hell when she left him.

But it would hurt like hell. He knew that going in. For as long as he could remember, he'd carried Molly's memory, like a low-grade fever that wouldn't go away. In the past week or so, he'd realized that every woman he ever met he had compared to Molly. Without him being fully aware of it, she had influenced his social life for years. Now she was here for a brief time. And his low-grade fever had flamed into full-blown delirium. He thought about her day and night. Felt his heart skip a beat when she appeared unexpectedly. When he held her in his arms at the dance, he hadn't been able to breathe properly, had thought she would surely notice the trembling in his fingers or hear his pulse pounding in his chest.

Oh, yeah. It was going to kill him when she left.

But on the positive side—and his nature tilted toward the positive—he would have had a few weeks with Molly. He would sample the joy of a long-held dream coming true. He would know the scent of her hair and the taste of her skin. He'd know what it was like to wake up in the morning and see her lovely face on the pillow next to his. That is, of course, if she wanted to be with him, too. And he had to start with the assumption that she did. He didn't think he'd imagined the way she responded the night of the dance.

So the question became: Was grabbing part of a long-held fantasy worth the pain and misery that was certain to follow?

"Do you like cold burgers, or are you on a diet?" Jim Enders asked, sliding into the booth. "Are you going to eat that thing, or just sit there staring at it?"

"What's up?" Joe put the burger back in the basket. There was nothing better than a hot cheeseburger just dripping good grease, and nothing worse than looking at a dead burger with cold, shriveled cheese and congealed fat.

"Do you know if Molly has picked out the rest of the faucets yet? I need to get them ordered."

"I don't know. You'll have to ask her."

"I heard you tore down the old kitchen and moved part of it downstairs so she has something to cook on. I figured me and my pooch would start running pipe next week."

"Sounds good." Usually he thrived on shoptalk, but his mind wasn't on work tonight.

He and Jim watched fresh snow accumulating on the windowsill. After a while, Joe called to Bonnie and ordered a pitcher of beer. "I'm sick of snow," Jim said glumly. "I've got a drift in my yard that must be ten feet tall. On nights like this, it feels like spring will never come."

"February and March are the snowiest months," Joe agreed.

But, for the first time in years, he was in no hurry for spring and summer to arrive.

HAVING PIECES of a kitchen scattered around the basement wasn't working out well, Molly decided at the end of the day. She could operate the oven or she could operate one burner. She couldn't use both at the same time, and she couldn't use two burners at the same time without blowing the circuit breakers for the whole basement.

Joe bounded down the steps and helped himself to a beer from the refrigerator shelf Molly had given to Joe and the pooches for their lunch items, soft drinks and beer. He popped the tab, then crinkled his eyes at her. "What's going on with you, honey? You've been in a funky mood all week."

That did it. She exploded. Rounding on him, she planted both fists on her hips and shouted, "You want to know what's going on with me? I've got pooches peeing in the yard—I saw them! You knocked out the entire end of the house and now there's only one thin layer of plywood between me and a blizzard. There isn't a guy on this project who can drive a nail without grabbing his crotch and spitting first. FedEx can't find me because I don't have a real address. Daddy Romaine now wants to haul the big rocks out of here at no charge, and that makes me suspicious as hell. Your pal Jim Enders is bugging me daily about picking out faucets. I'm cold, tired, and hungry. I can't operate the damned stove without blowing the breakers down here, and I only wrote four pages today. *That's* what's going on with me!''

The amusement sparkling and flashing in his eyes made her cheeks grow hot with anger.

Then he set down his beer, clasped her by the shoulders and pulled her against his body. He gazed into her eyes, and then he kissed her so hard and deep and long that Molly's knees collapsed and she sagged helplessly against him.

When his mouth finally released hers, all she could do was stare, wide-eyed and shaken. Never in her life had she been kissed like that!

"Grab your hat and some gloves, honey. Let's go get something to eat." He gave her a pat on the fanny and headed for the stairs.

Chapter Six

Aspen rode on the seat between them, and they didn't speak much during the drive into town. Occasionally Molly slid a glance over Aspen's head toward Joe. Something had changed. Whatever it was that had made him decide to kiss her, she was glad; she'd been yearning for him to kiss her for what seemed like a very long time. And what a kiss it had been. Her fingertips wandered to her lips, which still tingled.

Judging from previous experience, Molly had concluded that most men believed they needed a technique for kissing, and therefore had worked out a routine designed to demonstrate skill, sensitivity, gentleness or seduction, whatever they thought would lead to arousal, she guessed. And there were those who bought into the glamour of the modeling profession and felt they had to impress her with their prowess, assuming she was sophisticated and experienced.

She didn't recall a man ever kissing her for the first time impulsively, or with as much emotion as Joe had done. His technique, if he had one, was an exuberant expression of what he felt at the moment. And it had blown her socks off. His ardent kiss had told her that he'd wanted to kiss her for a long time too, and that he desired her and cared for her. His kiss had kindled an answering passion in the pit of her stomach, had left her trembling and feeling dumbstruck at the depth of her own response.

She was still thinking about the electric effect of that single kiss when he parked in front of the Goosed Moose. Letting the engine idle, he rested his forearm on the steering wheel and examined her over Aspen's head.

"Honey, before we go inside, I need to tell you that if we walk into the Goosed Moose together, it's the same as tacking up a notice in the post office saying that we're now an item." He smiled and shrugged. "Sounds old-fashioned, doesn't it? But I don't know how else to say it. By this time tomorrow, everyone in town will know we're seeing each other socially. Are you sure that's what you want to do?"

"Why is tonight different from you escorting me to the welcome dinner?"

"First, everyone recognized that you didn't know a lot of people. I was a natural choice as your escort for that reason, and it could be explained as a professional courtesy between client and contractor. Before the welcome dinner you were a newcomer, a stranger. Now you aren't. You've met the town, they've met you." His shoulders lifted. "There isn't a man in Vrain who would have presumed to phone you for a date without having met you first. Now a lot of choices open up."

She smiled. "You think my phone is going to be ringing off my desk with Vrain's bachelors calling to ask me out?"

"Not if you walk into the Goosed Moose with me. Every single guy in the county wants to ask you out—trust me on this. But they won't if they know you and I are seeing each other off the job. This is a small community, honey, we all have to get along together. Unless it's an unusual situation, most of us don't poach in another man's territory."

Molly rested her hand on Aspen's head, scratching behind his ears. "Joe, are you asking if there's someone else I'd like to date?"

"Something like that." He drew a deep breath. "I'd like to see you socially, but—"

"I'd like that, too."

"I don't want to put you in a situation where you've entered into an exclusive arrangement without knowing it. And that's what will happen if you and I walk into the Goosed Moose together. That's just how it is here. It's not like a big city, where people date several others at once and no one thinks anything of it. Here, if you want to date others, you date someone in Vrain, maybe someone else from Longmont, Boulder, or Estes Park."

"So if we go inside together, I've just declared that you're my Vrain steady, right?" she asked, teasing him.

He didn't return her smile. "You've got it, honey. No one else will call and ask you out. As dumb as it sounds, we'll have made some kind of commitment in Vrain's view. That's not our point of view," he hastened to add. "We aren't making any commitment whatsoever, except to have dinner together. We're both free to date anyone, see anyone we want to. I just want you to know that if you do go out with someone else after tonight, it will cause gossip. People will say that Joe Townsend's girl is cheating on him."

Joe Townsend's girl. It had a nice, old-fashioned ring to it. "Is that what they said when Ellen O'Ryan started dating Don White?" she asked, lifting a curious eyebrow.

"You know about that?" A sigh collapsed his chest. "You really did pick up a lot of gossip at the welcome dinner." He reached to pat Aspen's head, too, and their fingers brushed, sending a fresh tingle up Molly's arm. "Sure. That was the gossip, even though Ellen and I never had an exclusive arrangement between us, and our involvement was more friendship than romantic. But right now there's a lot of dumb talk about Don stealing my girl."

Leaning forward, Molly made a decision by turning the key in the ignition, shutting off the engine. She could almost have sworn that Joe was blushing, not liking the idea that it might appear he'd been dumped in favor of Don White.

"Oh, dear," she said, lifting her hand to briefly touch his lips. "I'm getting you on the rebound. You're using me to soothe your broken heart." Chuckling, she opened the door and jumped to the ground. "I'll take my chances, I guess."

Joe met her in front of the pickup, took her arm, and led her toward the heavy carved doors. "You do know that's not true, don't you? This sure as hell is not a rebound thing."

"So you say," she said, sliding him a sparkling look. "We'll see."

"Ellen and I were just friends. That's all it ever was." He opened the door for her, then winced at her smug expression. "You're enjoying putting me on the spot, aren't you?"

"I'm loving it," she admitted, laughing. "It's nice to see you on the defensive for a change, you're always so sure of yourself."

They walked into the cheerful warmth of the Goosed Moose, and Molly recognized at once that here was where the locals hung out. She had an idea that Bernie Schadler sat on that same stool every evening after work, and Wiley Oats sat at the other end of the bar every evening. The Goosed Moose was Vrain's version of Cheers.

Then she heard what the crowd at the bar was discussing, and she laughed out loud.

They were engaged in a heated discussion about whether or not rocks could move under their own power. "I'm telling you," the bartender insisted stubbornly. Joe whispered that his name was Sandy. "I saw it on a television documentary. Daddy Romaine is full of crap. It's against the law for a TV documentary to lie!"

"No, sir," Bernie Schadler protested. "Daddy is right. Those TV documentaries lie all the time. There's no such law like you just said. Ask Matt."

Everyone at the bar peered down at Matt Anderson, the town policeman.

"Well, I don't know about TV law, but I think documentaries are entitled to present a point of view, and if the producer believes some foolishness about rocks moving on their own, I guess he can make a documentary saying that.''

"Well, I know for a fact that rocks can move on their own, and I can prove it," Wiley stated. "You ever see rocks laying on a highway? 'Course you have. Do you think someone came along and put 'em there? Now why would some durned fool do that? No one would. The rocks got there on their own, that's how they got on the highway. They're trying to get to the other side of the road. It's just logical, just stands to reason. The part that isn't too logical is why does the rock want to go to the other side of the road in the first place?''

Bernie Schadler threw up his hands. "There are prettier rocks on the other side?" He glowered. "Wiley, that's the stupidest thing I ever did hear you say!''

Joe led Molly to an upholstered booth at the end of the building, and gave her the side where she could see a cheerful fire crackling in a big stone fireplace.

"The way you're pinching your lips together and sort of gasping makes me think you know something about that rock discussion," he said, grinning at her across the table.

"Daddy Romaine hangs out here, doesn't he?" She couldn't help it—she gave into a gust of laughter, then wiped her eyes.

"He and Dumpling and the boys usually come in around eight o'clock." The frown cleared from between his eyes. "Aha. You've been pulling Daddy's leg. *You* started the walking-rocks discussion?''

Molly placed a hand over her heart and gave him her most innocent expression. "I swear. I saw something on television about moving rocks. I didn't make it up." She batted her eyelashes. "I may have mentioned something to Daddy Romaine about big rocks moving around my yard." After Joe stopped laughing and shaking his head, she touched his hand. "No one even noticed when we walked in together. Looks like we're not engaged after all.''

"Don't kid yourself, honey. We're both committed. The news will be all over town tomorrow.''

"Hi, I'm Bonnie. We met at your welcome dinner."

"I remember," Molly said, withdrawing her hand from Joe's and smiling at the pretty dark-haired waitress. "Nice to see you again."

"Likewise. You guys want menus?"

"No," Joe said. "Just bring us the usual."

"I'm talking to Molly, you goof. She doesn't have a 'usual.'" Bonnie rolled her eyes, then winked at Molly.

"She does now. Her usual is the same as my usual." Joe grinned and said to Molly, "Trust me on this, you're going to like your new usual."

"So what is my new usual?" Molly asked after Bonnie headed back toward the bar.

"The best cheeseburger and fries you ever ate. This thick, and the fries are homemade."

"Oh, my God." She stared, then gave him a weak smile. "I don't think I've had a cheeseburger in years." For an instant, she rebelled. Then she remembered that she wasn't working anymore. She didn't have to maintain a low, camera-friendly weight anymore. She could eat anything she wanted to, and it didn't matter what the scales read tomorrow morning. It was a realization that was both liberating and depressing.

Joe folded his hands in front of him and cleared his throat. "We need to discuss the rules."

"What rules?"

"The rules for our relationship."

She blinked. "Our relationship, as you call it, is about an hour old. And we already need rules?"

"Honey, this is an unusual situation. I work for you. You're my boss for another two and a half to three months. I think we need to agree that we keep professional and private absolutely separate. Say I screw up badly and you have to fire me. I don't want you to keep me on the job because we're seeing each other, but you might be tempted to do that. See what I mean?"

"Joe, if you screw up so badly that I have to fire you,

there's no way that wouldn't affect a personal relationship. So—'' she smiled at him ''—don't screw up.''

A frown puckered his brow. ''I've already screwed up. As it sits now, the job is going to come in about fifteen thousand over budget. And, we've got a couple of months to go. I'm already staying up nights worrying about the estimates for the kitchen and the light fixtures.''

''Oh, God. I've got to decide on more stuff?''

He nodded and grinned. ''I hate to be the one to point this out to you, but have you noticed that you hardly have any furniture?''

Molly poured a glass of beer from the pitcher that Bonnie had brought automatically when she came to take their orders. ''I have a condo in New York filled with furniture. But you're right. The house is a lot larger. I'll have to buy more. Rats.'' She thought about styles, colors, coordinating everything.... At the moment, it seemed daunting.

''You haven't listed the condominium for sale?'' he asked, in a tone that impressed her as a little too offhand.

''I haven't decided about selling. I have a lot of friends in New York. It would be convenient to have a place to stay when I go there to visit.'' Or return to work? Was she still holding out some secret hope that her modeling career wasn't as dead as it appeared to be?

Joe leaned back as Bonnie placed a basket in front of him. ''I understand they have some wonderful places in New York especially for out-of-town visitors. I believe they're called hotels.''

''My God.'' Molly stared down at the basket Bonnie set in front of her. The cheeseburger and fries were cradled in a stiff paper liner that was shiny with grease. ''It smells wonderful,'' she finally admitted, ''but there must be a million grams of fat in this basket.''

''Yeah,'' Joe said happily, spreading ketchup on everything. ''Isn't it wonderful? It's hard to find burgers like this anymore.''

Gingerly Molly picked up the burger and blinked at thick waves of cheese oozing out of the bun. If Addie, who ran the top modeling agency in Manhattan, had seen Molly biting into this burger, she would have fainted in shock and horror.

The greasy cheeseburger tasted so fabulous that Molly almost swooned. Reading her expression exactly, Joe grinned at her across the table. "If I were the kind of guy to say 'I told you so…'"

"This is so good," Molly said, groaning with pleasure. "I'd forgotten how fabulous a really great cheeseburger is."

"Well, well," a voice said beside her. Lowering the burger, she looked up to see Jim Enders standing beside the table, smiling at them. "So it's official. You two are an item."

Something in Jim's expression made Molly suspect that he didn't approve of her being here with Joe. Or maybe he didn't approve of her, period. Was he that angry that she hadn't yet picked out the remaining faucets?

"We're just having dinner," Joe said, rolling his eyes. "Believe it or not, a man and a woman can share a meal without it binding them to a lifetime commitment."

"Not in Vrain they can't," Jim said, laughing. He sat on the seat facing Molly, forcing Joe to move over, which he did, grumbling.

"If I have to stay up all night to do it, I'm going to pick out faucets tonight," Molly promised. "Would you like some of these french fries? There's no way I can eat all of these."

"Don't mind if I do. Thanks." Reaching, Jim took several fries and dunked one in Joe's ketchup. "Did Joe tell you that any relationship with him means that you have to take Aspen and me, too?" He poked Joe in the ribs with his elbow. "Me and Aspen go with the deal."

"I hadn't gotten to that part yet," Joe said with a humorless smile. "She knows about Aspen, but I forgot to mention a certain buttinsky friend."

"So, Molly," Jim said, studying her across the table.

"Does this new development mean that you're going skiing with me and Joe this weekend?"

It was a tactless and deliberately provocative thing to say to her, and she recognized it as such. Slowly she lowered her burger to the basket.

"What the hell are you doing?" Joe demanded, a warning in his eyes.

Jim raised his hands, all innocence. "We talked about going skiing this weekend. I'm just asking if we're going to bring dates."

When Molly spotted the flush of angry red rising from Joe's throat, she leaned into the conversation. "I can't go through life expecting people never to mention skiing in front of me," she said quietly before she turned a thoughtful look on Jim. What was going on here? Was he afraid of losing Joe's friendship? Did he resent Joe having a lady friend who might cut into the time Joe spent with his male buddies?

"Joe asked me to join him for dinner," she said to Jim, speaking pleasantly. "We haven't made any plans beyond eating and sharing that pitcher of beer. But if Joe did ask me to go skiing on the weekend, I'd probably say no thanks. I enjoyed skiing once, and I hope to again, but I don't think I'm ready yet." She turned to look at Joe. "Honestly, it doesn't bother me to talk about skiing. It's a great sport. I hope the two of you have a wonderful weekend, and I hope you'll tell me all about it when you return."

"That's a far more gracious answer than you deserve," Joe said sharply to Jim. "Now if you'll excuse us, we're trying to have a meal here."

"That's fine with me. I guess I know when I'm being a third wheel," Jim said, sliding out of the booth. "Just wanted to say hi, that's all." He lifted a hand. "See you both tomorrow on the site."

Joe waited until Jim had reached the bar. Then he looked at Molly. "I apologize. I don't know what's gotten into him lately."

Molly sidestepped any comment. "Is Jim dating any-one?" she asked, picking up her burger.

"He was dating Avis Morrison, but the age difference bothered her," Joe said, pushing away his basket. "Avis is seven years older than Jim. She's got a seventeen-year-old daughter. You met her. Cheryl?"

"I remember. Harvard acceptance. She took our coats."

He nodded. "Anyway, Avis was convinced that every-one in town was laughing at her or calling her a fool for going out with a man younger than she is."

"Were they?" Molly asked, wiping grease off her chin. The small-town stories fascinated her, even though it felt a little strange to know intimate details about strangers. Even more so in this case, since she had met Avis and could picture her in her mind.

"Yeah," Joe said finally, "a few people did feel that way. A lot more people didn't care one way or the other, but Avis thought they did."

Molly finished the burger with a huge sigh of content-ment. A person could get addicted to greasy cheeseburgers if the person wasn't careful. "Why did Avis care what any-one thought?"

"Honey, I'm not sure you're getting the picture here. No one is anonymous in a town the size of Vrain. Particularly not Avis Morrison. She's the postmistress. Like most peo-ple, she wants other people to think well of her. She wants to be respected in the community where she lives. It can't feel very good to believe that friends and neighbors are whispering behind your back, saying you're a foolish woman."

"How did Jim feel about all this?"

"Jim? He didn't care about Avis's age. If someone made a joke about older women, he just laughed. He figured that eventually folks would get used to the idea of him and Avis. And that's what would have happened, if Avis hadn't broken it off."

"How about you, Joe? Do you care what people say or think about you?"

"Sure I do," he said promptly. "This is my home. I make my living in this community. Of course I want people to think well of me. Don't you care what people think about you?"

She hesitated, picking up her paper napkin and pulling it through her fingers. "Yes and no. Yes, it feels good when you believe people like you and respect you professionally. But I can't control what other people think. Maybe an act that is acceptable to me is offensive to someone else. I don't think I would have made the choice that Avis Morrison did, because I'm not willing to live my life to please other people. I guess that sounds selfish, and maybe it is. But I don't think it's anyone's business but mine who I date or what I do. I'm responsible for my own happiness—there's no rule that says I have to please everyone else or live the way they think I should."

They studied each other across the table.

"You and I have a lot of differences, honey," Joe said finally.

"We have a lot of similarities too," she mentioned softly.

"Maybe I need to be reminded of some of those similarities."

"We grew up in the same neighborhood, in families with the same economic background and basic value system. We went to the same schools. Had some of the same friends." She smiled at him, finding solid ground again.

"I'm a morning person, you're a night person."

"Neither of us finished college, but we're both ambitious. I was successful in my profession, you're successful in yours."

"I like greasy cheeseburgers, I suspect you prefer rabbit food. It'll probably be a month before you allow yourself another usual."

"We share a similar sense of humor. I suspect we're both a little obsessive."

"Well, hell," he said with a grin. "You convinced me. Let's get married."

Molly laughed, and the last of the tension between them evaporated. "Are you ever serious for longer than five minutes?"

"Only when I'm working." Pushing back a sleeve, he glanced at his watch. "Come on, honey, let's get out of here. Tomorrow's a workday. And Aspen's out there waiting for his supper."

On their way out, Bonnie handed Joe a couple of plain burgers for Aspen, and Molly laughed again. "Come here often?" she asked, raising an eyebrow.

"Just about every night," he said, opening the door for her. "I'm not much of a cook. Hardly seems worth turning on the stove for one person."

"One of these nights I'll cook you a meal," she promised once they were in the truck and Aspen was happily gobbling his supper.

"Would it be one of those low-fat, low-calorie things?" Joe asked with an exaggerated shudder. "Skinny-model food?"

"I'll try to come up with something you'll like. But I'm warning you—it won't be swimming in grease. How in the world can you eat those burgers every night without putting on a ton of weight?" If Molly ate like that every night and ate jelly doughnuts for breakfast every morning, she'd zoom up to a hundred and thirty pounds in less than a week.

As if he'd read her mind, Joe looked at her and smiled. "High metabolism, I guess. It wouldn't hurt you to gain a few pounds, honey. You look great, but you're a tad on the skinny side."

"The camera adds ten pounds, so I can't..."

Her voice trailed off, and she looked down at her lap. The camera's added pounds didn't matter anymore. When was she going to get that through her head? Watching what she ate for professional reasons was no longer necessary. And she could stay up until one in the morning if she chose to, without fearing she'd appear for an early-morning shoot with circles beneath her eyes. Her face would never again smile from magazine covers. Addie would never again phone, her voice filled with excitement, to tell Molly about a fabulous new opportunity or offer.

Joe was right. There was no reason to keep the condo in Manhattan.

"Honey?"

When she lifted her head, they were in her driveway, driving down a tunnel formed by tall snowbanks pushed aside by the county plow. She'd forgotten to leave a light on inside, and the house looked deserted, like an unoccupied construction site.

"Come out of your trance. You're home," Joe said, braking in front of the porch steps.

She would have liked to turn to him and burrow into his arms. Would have liked it if he held her for a few minutes. But Aspen was on the seat between them, his head in Joe's lap, most of his hindquarters in Molly's lap. She opened the door, eased away from the dog, then dropped to the frozen mud. Instantly the sharp cold air chilled her cheeks. Unfortunately, it wasn't going to be much warmer in the house.

For an instant, she considered asking Joe to stay over. But neither of them had planned for that. And there was Aspen to consider. And it was too soon. Sighing, trailing a silvery plume behind her, she walked toward her new front door, then turned as Joe caught up to her.

Sliding his hands up beneath her parka, he circled her waist and gently drew her against his body. Their first kiss had been impulsive, hard and ardent, but gazing into his shadowed eyes, Molly knew this kiss would be different, and it was.

This kiss was slow and deliberate on both their parts, a kiss that explored and experimented. There was an odd gentleness, a sweetness, to their porch kisses that Molly didn't recall ever experiencing before. It was Joe who finally pulled back. She could have stood there all night, kissing and holding him. Or at least until her toes froze.

"I was really dumb," she murmured against his lips. "I thought you weren't interested in me this way."

He kissed her lips lightly, then her nose. "I thought you weren't interested in me this way, either." He kissed her eyelids and her temple. "You know? I just realized something. It's very hard to neck when both people are wearing parkas. The puffy material won't let you get close." He grinned down at her. "If you've still got breasts in there, I can't feel them."

She laughed, releasing the tension that had begun to build when he started kissing her. "I think I still have breasts, but I'm too cold to know for sure. We'll have to check it out tomorrow."

"I'll add that to my to-do list," he said, laughing. He kissed her again, his mouth hot against her cold cheek. "See you in the morning, honey. Sleep well."

"I'll be asleep in ten minutes."

She would have been, too, if she hadn't suddenly remembered Jim Enders and his damned faucets. Muttering curses, she climbed out of bed, found her slippers and robe, then ran downstairs through the cold wind blowing past the gaps in the plywood. She snatched the faucet catalogs off her desk and ran back upstairs to dive under her electric blanket.

By two in the morning, she'd looked at so many faucet sets that they all seemed the same. Disgusted that she couldn't decide, she threw a handful of catalogs over the side of the bed. In the morning she'd look and see what page they had fallen open on. And that would be her choice.

Turning on her side, she nestled into the pillow and closed her eyes, a smile on her lips.

Joe had kissed her. They were an item.

"RISE AND SHINE, honey!" Joe shouted up the stairs. "The coffee's made! It's a beautiful day!"

"I'm up," Molly called back, stepping out of the bathroom. She moved to the balcony railing, tying her robe around her waist. "I've decided that contractors and pooches see more women in their bathrobes than hospital attendants do." She gazed down at him, noting how fresh and rested and ready to go he looked. And how handsome. What was it about jeans and a tool belt, anyway? She didn't know why the hip-slung tool belt seemed so sexy, but it did. "And it's not a beautiful day. It's snowing again."

"All in the eyes of the beholder," he said, laughing. Raising a hand, he waved a packet. "FedEx just delivered this for you. I'll put it on your desk."

By the time she pulled herself together and got downstairs, the pooches had arrived and Joe was outside supervising the unloading of foundation forms. Toots Romaine had already fired up the dozer. The Johns were stringing electrical wire on every floor of the house.

The phone rang as Molly was opening the FedEx package, and she held the receiver between her ear and shoulder, trying to wrestle the package into submission. "Molly, it's Addie. Did you get the proofs I sent you?"

"What a nice surprise to hear from you. I'm opening your FedEx package now. You said you sent some proofs?" Seeing her agent's name on the packet had surprised her. Addie was the last person she had expected to hear from, she thought, sliding the photos out of the FedEx package.

"The proofs are part of the test packet that Apple shot after the accident."

"The shots that decided them to fire me." Molly stared at her face, smiling up from the photos, then turned the proofs facedown on her desktop. She covered her eyes. "Addie, why did you send these to me?"

"I've been thinking…occasionally what first appears to be a handicap can be turned into a publicity asset. Maud has that gap between her teeth…. I'd like to send these around and get a few opinions other than Apple's."

Dropping her hand, Molly stared into space. "What's the point?"

"The point is, if you read the tabloids, then your impression of Molly Stevens is that she's badly scarred and she's finished in the business," Addie said bluntly. "I don't think so. I think experience and professionalism count for something. I think you're as beautiful and marketable today as you were a year ago. I'd like to find out if others think so, too.''

"The scars look like deep valleys in the black and whites."

"It's not that bad. Listen, years ago the so-called experts told Elizabeth Taylor to have the mole on her face removed. They said it looked like a dirt spot. Said it detracted from her beauty. It turned out that mole added to her distinctiveness and didn't hurt her career at all, now did it? So what do you think? Let's test the water. Let's send those photos out and find out if your career is as dead as you think it is."

It would be so easy to start fantasizing that she wasn't really a has-been. So easy to set herself up for more painful rejection. She shrugged, determined not to let herself get suckered by hope. "Do what you want, Addie. Whatever you decide is okay with me. But if you do send out the photos, I think you'll discover the accounts don't want a model who's scarred."

"Molly," Joe called, coming down the stairs. "I need to use the phone, and—" He stopped talking when he saw her and mouthed the words "I'll come back in a few minutes."

She shook her head and beckoned him forward. "Bye, Addie. Let me know what happens."

"Was that your friend in the computer business? The one who got married recently?"

"Nope. You're thinking of Darcy. What was all the commotion upstairs a few minutes ago?" Standing, she left her desk and went to the stove. After pouring two cups of coffee, she handed him one.

"About three dogs ran across the concrete they just poured into the foundation forms. Then Coke fell face flat in the mud. Toots Romaine gave the pooches a thrill when he damned near dumped the dozer in the foundation hole he's digging for your new office. It's been a morning."

Molly smiled as he gulped scalding-hot coffee. "How can you pour concrete when it's this cold?"

"It's a new process, only a couple of years old," he explained. Happy to indulge the opportunity for shoptalk, he told her all about the special cold-weather forms and concrete. Molly nodded and tried to look interested, but her attention kept wandering to his lips and eyes and the expressive way he moved his hands.

"Honey," he said, breaking off his monologue about foundation forms, "when you look at me like that, all I can think about is ravishing you."

Molly smiled. "Is that such a bad idea?" she asked softly.

"Right now, yes. I make it a rule never to ravish beautiful women while pooches are still on the site. It makes them crazy with jealousy." He glanced at his watch, then reached for the phone. "I wish we hadn't mentioned ravishing," he said gruffly, running a long glance over her body. "I've got something going every night this week, someplace I have to be that isn't here. Damn."

"And the weekend is out," she reminded him, trying not to look too devastated with disappointment. "You're going skiing with Jim this weekend."

"These things were scheduled before you and I became an item," he said, putting down the telephone and walking around her desk. Pulling her to her feet, he wrapped his arms around her waist and pressed her close against his body. "Remember our discussion about rules?"

"Hmm..." Molly murmured, kissing his chin and running her palms up his flannel shirt. "I think this is against the rules, actually. So what are you going to do? Have me arrested?"

He smiled, then kissed her, letting his lips linger at the corner of her mouth. "This is definitely against the rules. One thing we forgot to discuss. Eventually..."

She pulled his head down and lightly breathed in his ear, teasing him, feeling a shudder of pleasure ripple down his body. "Yes? Eventually...?"

"Eventually, I suspect this thing with you and me is going to go further than kissing." His hands slid up beneath her parka and stopped just beneath her breasts.

She drew a sharp breath, feeling the heat of his hands like a brand. "I hope so," she groaned. "You're torturing me." Teasingly, his thumbs stroked the underside of her breasts, and his hips moved against hers.

"I sure hope so," he said against her mouth. "What I'm trying to say is that I don't think I should ever stay over on a worknight."

"Don't want the pooches to catch you rolling out of the client's bed?" His touch was like fingers of lightning igniting her skin. Moaning softly, she pressed against him, nibbling along his jawline.

"Yeah." A low sound rumbled up from his chest. "Speaking of pooches, one of them could appear any minute. Honey, I've got to get back to work right now, or I'm going to do something that will embarrass us both." Stepping back from her, he picked up the FedEx folder and fanned his face, grinning. "You are one hot number. Set a guy on fire before he has to go back out in the cold."

It wasn't until everyone had gone for the day that Molly remembered that Joe had forgotten to make his phone call. She laughed out loud. Then, as she was eating a low-cal TV dinner at her desk, she realized she hadn't told him about Addie's call and her proposal to send out her test photos.

Well, it was too soon to mention anything, anyway, especially as she didn't expect anything to come of it. Addie was simply the type of person who didn't recognize defeat until she had exhausted every possibility.

After finishing her TV dinner, she tried to take advantage of the quiet and work on her book. But her thoughts kept drifting to Joe.

The implication was that sometime soon they would make love. Her heart rolled over in her chest at the thought of it. It would be wonderful. She knew that already. The chemistry between them was powerful and electric, and would only grow stronger in bed.

Between now and whenever that happened, she needed to find where she had put her filmy nightgowns. Most men didn't think a flannel sack was too sexy.

On the other hand, she thought, laughing again, Joe probably did think flannel was sexy.

Chapter Seven

It was so adolescent, Molly thought, making a face, but she couldn't resist taking breaks throughout the day to see where Joe was and what he was doing. This afternoon she'd found him standing in a haze of dust, supervising as the pooches cut holes in the side of her house.

"Looks to me like you're losing sight of the contractor rules," she said. "You're cutting holes in the walls for windows, but it isn't snowing."

He grinned and briefly touched her cheek. "Dinner tonight?"

She thought a minute. "I'll cook. If I can figure how to prepare a real meal without blowing all the basement breakers." She looked toward the sound of ringing hammers, just beyond the plywood that sort of closed off the garage end of the house. "Who's working out there? Did the pooches multiply?"

"Yeah," Joe said, smiling. "Honey, we're into the seventh week and it's going slower than I'd like. I hired on a couple of extra guys. Mike and Harry. It isn't going to cost extra," he hastened to add. "The electricians say they're going to come in under budget, so I'm taking the extra from there."

Molly looked around. The framing on this floor was almost finished, and she could see how the rooms were going to lay out. She especially liked the spaciousness of what would be the master bedroom. "I think I'm going to love this house when it's finished," she said softly.

"Great! That's what it's all about. See you later, honey."

Heading back downstairs, she tried to figure out how she was going to manage dinner. If she started right now and cooked one item at a time, then right before dinner she could warm everything in the oven. That would work.

Of course, it meant that she wouldn't get any pages written this afternoon.

"THAT was an excellent meal," Joe said, happily, leaning back in his chair. They had eaten at her desk, since she'd been thoughtful enough to leave the card table upstairs for the pooches to use during their breaks and lunch hours.

"Thanks for running to town and picking up some wine," she said, giving him a soft-eyed look that made his stomach tighten. She wore jeans, a red sweater and her parka, but she'd put on fresh lipstick before dinner and she was wearing her hair the way he liked, banded at the neck and flowing loose down her back. Raising her glass of wine, she saluted him. "I love the new windows. I can't believe how they opened the house. I don't know why my grandparents put in such small windows where there are such fabulous views."

"Maybe that was the style back when the house was first built. Insulation wasn't as good then. Lots of windows, and large ones, would have meant a cold house."

He loved to just look at her. Even though the one heater the electricians had left in the basement was operating full blast, the air was chilly enough to raise a lovely pink in her cheeks. Wisps of wheat-blond hair floated around her face when she turned her head.

He liked everything about her, beginning with the graceful way she moved, and the sound of her voice. It pleased him no end when he said something that made her laugh. He liked the way she wore jeans like anyone else, instead of foo-foo high-fashion stuff, as he'd half expected she would before he knew her better. He liked her quirky sense of humor and the way she made all the pooches forget that she was famous. He liked her lack of pretense and admired the way she was coping with living on-site, and doing it with a minimum of complaints.

"I know I'm obsessing on those rocks," she was saying when he tuned in again. "But Daddy Romaine keeps bugging me about hauling them off. And I keep remembering what you said about the Romaines never doing anything for nothing. So I called the local landscaper and asked him to come out here and tell me if those rocks are worth anything."

"Honey?" Right now, he didn't want to hear about the rocks, or anything else that didn't have to do with making love to her. "What are you doing this weekend? Any plans?"

"No," she said, drawing the word out. "What do you have in mind?"

Standing, he picked up their plates, stepped through the new wall studs and set the plates on top of the washing machine. "If you want to, I thought we could go to Denver and look at kitchen cabinets." Turning the taps on the utility sink, he filled the sink and added dish detergent.

"Joe, what are you doing?" she asked, watching him through the studs.

"I'm going to wash the dishes. Didn't I tell you my rule? The cook doesn't do clean up."

"I like that rule," she said smiling. She lifted a perfectly arched eyebrow. "I was sort of hoping for a different kind of weekend. Do we really have to buy the kitchen cabinets this weekend?"

"No, but soon, honey. So you need to get some ideas, and start thinking about what kind of cabinets you want." The hot sudsy water felt good, but there weren't many dishes. He washed and rinsed the plates and stacked them in a dish drainer. "It will take about six weeks for the cabinets to come in, so it isn't too soon to start thinking about them. I'd say we need to get them ordered sometime in the next three weeks. Not much later." They were back to shoptalk, but this time he was using it to lead into something else.

She leaned against the framework, watching him. "Did you and Jim have a good time skiing? You didn't say."

He dried his hands on a dish towel. "Sure you want to hear about it?"

"Until the accident, I loved to ski," she said slowly, her fingertips straying to the faint scar that went through her eyebrow. "I was a good skier too. At least I thought so, until I lost control that day."

"Even the pros lose control on occasion," he said, taking the wineglass she handed him through the studs. "It was great, actually. We went to Keystone. I bought a condo up there several years ago as an investment. The management company keeps it rented most of the year, but I reserve Christmas week and a week in the summer for myself. And they let me know when a weekend is vacant, like last weekend and next weekend." He watched her face to see if she had guessed where he was leading.

"When does the season end?"

"In a couple more weeks. Most of the areas close in early April. Why?" he asked gently, jumping on the opening he'd been looking for. "Were you thinking about going skiing?"

The pink in her cheeks deepened, and he wondered what she was thinking. "If I don't ski relatively soon, I'm afraid I never will again."

Leaning against the utility sink, he studied the fear darkening her eyes. "They say if you get thrown from a horse, the best thing to do is get right back on him. This may be the same kind of thing."

"I don't know, Joe," she said with a wobbly smile. "It's kind of scary to think about."

She'd never do it without someone at her side, pushing her a little. He understood that. "I was thinking…we could go skiing this weekend." The snow was still good, but it wouldn't be for long, not with the days getting longer and starting to warm up. The melt was coming.

"You said we should look at kitchens this weekend."

He shrugged, wanting to touch her, hold her, make love to her. His condo in Keystone would be the perfect place. He'd thought about it, and he didn't want their first time together to happen here, where it was cold and more a construction site than a home. He could have taken her to his place, and he hoped to in the future, but he didn't want to worry about Aspen nosing open the bedroom door and jumping on the bed at a crucial moment. Not the first time they were together. And finally, taking her to a motel would feel cheap and wrong.

"We could go down to Denver early Saturday morning, look at some kitchens, get some ideas, then drive up to Keystone. How does that sound? We'll have a nice dinner, a lazy evening, then ski on Sunday." He figured one day on the slopes would be enough for her.

Doubt clouded her face, and her fingertips dropped to the faint scar above her lip. "I just remembered. I didn't bring any equipment. My skis are still in New York."

"We'll rent some." He stepped through the framing and took her gently in his arms. "If we get there and you change your mind, that's okay. To tell the truth, the part I'm most interested in is the going-to-bed part. The part about staying with you in a cozy condo." He kissed her lingeringly, then gazed into her half-closed eyes. "It's your call, honey. Are we ready for a weekend together? Or do you need more time?"

She smiled at him, pressing her hips closer against his, driving him crazy with wanting her. "I think I've been ready for you for years," she said softly. "I think I've been waiting for a weekend with you since the eighth grade."

"Shame on you," he teased, nibbling her lower lip. "That's much too young to be thinking about sex."

"You weren't?" she asked in a throaty chuckle.

"Absolutely not." Lifting his head, he buried his face in the hair he pulled loose from the band at her neck. Her hair smelled like roses. And it flowed through his fingers like watered silk. He wanted to see it fanned out across a pillow, wanted to feel it against his bare chest. "I had my first thoughts about sex three months ago, when I came out here to present my bid and saw you standing on the porch stark naked."

She pulled back from him, laughing. "You're crazy, do you know that? The day I met you out here, I was wearing an Armani pants suit and a calf-length camel's hair coat."

"You're kidding. I could have sworn you were naked. I remember the moment so clearly." He kissed her hard on the lips. "Thanks for dinner, honey."

"Are you leaving?"

The disappointment in her voice made his chest swell and his thighs tighten. She couldn't possibly guess how much he would have preferred to stay. All day long he had fantasized about finishing dinner, then picking her up in his arms and carrying her upstairs to her bedroom.

But he didn't want to make love to her the first time when she might be thinking about freezing every time a bare part was exposed to the night air. And with both ends of the house open and only two heaters in the whole place, the inside air was cold. Plus, there was dust and sawdust everywhere, and there were nails loose on the floors, and power tools laying everywhere. It wasn't exactly a romantic getaway, particularly for a woman who was used to the best of everything.

Before he ran up the basement stairs, he looked back at her. She'd flipped on her computer and stood in front of it, frowning at the screen.

"Honey?" he called, his voice husky. "I'm going to be counting the minutes until Saturday night."

She turned toward him, and her expression grew sultry with promise. "So will I," she whispered.

He stared at her for a long moment, amazed that this fabulous woman was willing to spend the weekend with him. What had he ever done to deserve this? At this moment, he didn't care that she would eventually break his heart. He looked at her and thanked heaven for giving him even a little time with her.

It was an effort to make his boots march up the stairs and out into the chill night.

MOLLY HUNCHED over her computer, glaring at it and wishing she had never agreed to write about her life. She must have been crazy, she thought, glancing at the oven. She had the oven set at four hundred degrees and had opened its door. With her space heater on high and the oven radiating heat, her desk area was warm enough that she had unzipped her parka. But that didn't make concentrating any easier. Today, Jim Enders and his assistant were running plumbing pipe through the basement ceiling, working not three feet from her desk.

"Excuse me," Jim said, interrupting. "Do you mind if I set my handsaw on your desk?"

"Go ahead." The problem with writing a book about herself was that she didn't have anything very interesting to say. She'd had a happy childhood, a happy adolescence. There was nothing people would really want to read except the section addressing her experience as the Apple Girl. That, she figured, would take up maybe two chapters. She doubted her editor would agree to a two-chapter book. Well, damn. She was a model, not a writer. She should never have agreed to attempt to write a book.

Jim Enders positioned a ladder in front of her desk and studied the ceiling joists. "Heard you and Joe are going skiing this weekend," he commented.

Molly looked up from her computer screen and studied him for a minute. His tone signaled, loud and clear, that he didn't approve of her weekend plans. "Do you have a problem with Joe and me going skiing?" she asked, more sharply than she'd intended.

He didn't brush off the question. It was almost as if Jim had been waiting for just such an opening. He leaned against the ladder and folded his arms across his chest. "Joe's my friend, and I care about him. I don't want to see him get hurt."

"That's commendable," Molly said carefully, trying to

ease up a little. She had mixed feelings about Jim Enders, but one thing she was sure of, she didn't want to come between Joe and a longtime friend. Not if she could help it.

"Joe's been carrying a torch for you for years. Then you suddenly show up here in Vrain, and now…he's really falling for you."

"I care about Joe, too."

"Do you? Or is Joe just a way to pass the time for a while, until the house gets finished or until your career picks up again?"

Molly stood behind her desk and stared, feeling the heat rise in her cheeks. "I'm sorry to be rude, but my relationship with Joe is really none of your business."

"The minute Joe took you to the Goosed Moose, he made a commitment. I hope you understand that, Molly. He's in for the long haul. But a lot of people don't think you are. A lot of people think you'll be going back to New York, and you'll leave Joe high and dry, without a backward glance."

"Frankly, I don't care what people think. The way I hear it, you didn't care what they thought, either, so maybe you'll understand how I feel." To her surprise, he didn't get angry, didn't seem to think it unusual that she knew about his broken romance with Avis, or that she would comment on something that was none of her concern.

"The thing is," he said, studying her face, "I think it too. I don't think you're really interested in a small-town guy who isn't rich or famous. I think you're just passing the time, and Joe deserves better. So why don't you back off? You don't need another conquest."

"Is that what you think Joe and I are all about?" She was beginning to get really angry. "You think I'm just adding another notch to my romantic gunbelt, because I'm bored or something?"

"Come on. I've read the tabloids. The guys you usually date are millionaire playboys or film stars or sports figures.

Now you're suddenly interested in Joe? Sure you are.'' He looked disgusted. "Give me a break."

"Look," she said, coming around her desk and stopping in front of him. She poked him in the chest with her finger. "Don't tell me who or what I'm interested in, because you don't know. You don't know me at all. As for Joe, what happens between Joe and me is our business, not yours. And not anyone else's. I don't want to hurt Joe, and I don't want to get hurt, either, but every relationship carries the potential for a bad ending and pain. There aren't any guarantees, Jim. So *you* back off. Joe's a big boy, capable of making his own decisions. I don't think he needs you to run interference for him. And I sure as hell don't need it, either."

Angry and needing to cool off, she turned abruptly and walked upstairs. For a minute, she stood in the chill living room and watched chunks of the old kitchen ceiling falling into the house, sending bursts of cold dust rolling toward her. Joe was up on a tall ladder, beating at broken rafters, shouting instructions. He didn't see her.

Since she didn't want him to, she walked outside and turned toward the men building the walls of the garage. The sound of nail guns exploded like tiny gunshots.

"It's pretty cold to be working outside today," she said to Z, trying not to let her anger show.

"Oh, it's not too bad." Crouching, he moved along the framework he was building. In a minute, he'd stand up the portion of wall and nail it in place.

Molly watched for a few minutes. "I've never fired a nail gun. What's it feel like?"

"You want to try it?" Z asked in surprise.

She hesitated, then shrugged. "Yeah. I'm in the mood to kill a few boards." Stepping carefully, she crossed a gangplank laid down to span a gaping trench between the earth and the cement floor of the garage. "Show me how it works."

"You gotta be careful, Miss Stevens. A nail fired from a nail gun could go right through your foot."

"Don't worry. It's not me that I want to maim."

When Joe came outside twenty minutes later, she felt better. Until she remembered that she had to go back to the basement and face her computer and Jim Enders again. "I hope your day is going better than mine has so far."

"Every day is a good day, honey. You just have to look at the right things to see it sometimes."

"You really believe that, don't you?" she asked, lifting an eyebrow. "Now that I think about it, I've never heard you admit that you're having a bad day."

He pulled his hammer from his tool belt, tossed it in the air and caught it by the handle. "I'm showing off, honey. I hope you're paying attention."

"Oh, I am," she said, smiling in spite of herself.

"You let yourself have one bad day," he said, looking down at her, his blue eyes flashing with optimism, "then sure enough, that opens the door to another bad day. Pretty soon you start worrying about having bad days. And guess what? Then they happen. One after another. The same thing happens with good days. But, you see, the choice is mine. I can concentrate on something that makes for a bad day, or I can shift the focus a little and concentrate on whatever made it a good day." A grin widened his mouth and made his eyes sparkle. "Enough philosophizing—I need to get some pooches started on the foundation for your study."

"You're really a unique and special man, Joe Townsend," she said softly.

"You just keep thinking that," he said laughing.

Molly dragged her feet going back downstairs. She wasn't looking forward to working a few feet away from Jim Enders. Clenching her teeth, she swore she would ignore him.

But it didn't work that way. She had a feeling he'd been waiting for her to return.

"Can I talk to you for a minute?" he asked, climbing down off his ladder.

"Yes?" she said coolly, sitting down at her desk. "What is it?"

"Did you go up there and ask Joe to fire me off the job?"

Shock widened her eyes. "Of course not." She saw that her answer surprised him. "Look, Jim." Folding her hands on top of the desk, she considered what she would say. "Both of us care about Joe. So let's try to keep our differences between ourselves and not put Joe in the middle, agreed?"

He shrugged and spread his hands in a gesture that she took for assent.

"I'm curious about something," Molly said as he started back up the ladder. She might as well take this all the way. "Did Joe try to make trouble between you and Avis when you were dating?"

Jim scowled down at her. "I'm not trying to make trouble between you and Joe."

"Aren't you?" Turning her chair around, she faced her monitor and placed her fingertips on the keyboard. "It sure looks that way to me."

Leaning forward, she typed a line of nonsense words, pretending to work, but signaling to Jim that the conversation was over. She stayed at her desk long enough to appease her pride and long enough to be able to tell herself that Jim wasn't driving her away. Then she shut down her computer, and drove into town to buy some kitchen decorating magazines at Wiley Oats's grocery store.

JIM WAS WAITING in the back booth when Joe stopped by the Goosed Moose after work.

"You're keeping later hours than you used to," Jim mentioned when Joe slid into the booth and poured a glass of beer out of the pitcher Jim had waiting on the table.

"Yep. I've got a lady friend now." He shook his head at Bonnie when she started toward the booth. "Nothing for me, I already ate." Placing his hand on the back of his neck, he stretched his muscles. "We got a lot done today."

"Did Molly fix you dinner?"

"She's a good cook." He laughed. "Hell, if I'm not

careful, I'm going to start liking low-fat food. Somehow, she makes it taste good.'' Reaching, he pulled a notepad out of his jeans pocket. ''The electricians should be able to rig something so the oven and the burners don't trip the basement breakers.''

''Joe…did Molly say anything to you about me?''

He looked up. ''She said she gave you a list of catalog numbers for the rest of the faucet sets.''

''Yeah, she did.'' Jim frowned down at the glass of beer he turned between his fingers. ''I don't know what to make of her.''

''There's no mystery. She's a nice person who's had a hard time recently.''

Jim lifted his head. ''She's not our kind, Joe.''

He was tired and ready for bed. It had been a long day. ''What are you trying to say?''

Embarrassed, Jim looked toward the men sitting at the bar. ''You were supportive when Avis and I broke up, and I feel like I owe you.''

''You don't owe me anything.'' Joe looked aside, too. He and Jim didn't often discuss their feelings with each other.

''I just don't see how a relationship between you and a woman like Molly can work out, that's all. I mean, hell, Joe, she's famous. The thing is, I'd hate to see you go through what I went through when Avis dumped me. And Joe, you have to know that someday Molly is going back to New York. That's her world.''

''I know,'' he said quietly, taking a long swallow of beer.

''You know? And it doesn't bother you?''

''Sure, it bothers me.'' It bothered him a lot. Already he couldn't stand to think about losing her, and they hadn't even made love. Thinking about her leaving was going to get worse and feel worse after the upcoming weekend. ''If I avoided everything that might cause a little pain, then I'd also be avoiding a lot of things that might make me happy. And I'd have a lot fewer good memories.''

''Okay,'' Jim said, studying his expression. ''If that's

how you feel, then I'll back off and try to stop worrying
about you. I don't want it to look like I'm trying to make
trouble, because I'm not.''

"Jim, take my advice—'' Joe glanced at his watch and
stood ''—swallow your pride and go beat on Avis's door.
Tell her you're not leaving until she lets you inside. Then
tell her that you love her and you don't give a damn about
her age.'' He smiled. "It wouldn't hurt if you had a ring
in your pocket.'' Jim's expression made him laugh. "If you
get your own lady friend back, maybe you'll stop worrying
about mine.''

He was halfway to the door when Jim called his name
and he looked back.

"Have a nice weekend,'' Jim said solemnly. "Tell Molly
I said that, and I mean it.''

"Sure. Thanks.''

He had already packed and unpacked his overnight bag
three times. And he'd been to the liquor store twice, trying
to decide what kind of wine to buy for a very special weekend.

Nervous? No, not him.

Laughing, he opened the door of the pickup and fed
Aspen his burgers.

He would see Molly again in ten hours. Things must be
getting serious, because ten hours felt like a lifetime when
a man was counting the minutes.

Chapter Eight

"Excuse us for a minute, will you?" Joe took Molly's arm and led her down an aisle, away from the kitchen-cabinet salesman. "Honey, what are you doing?"

"Joe, those are the cabinets I want," she said, a mixture of relief and pleasure in her eyes. She had found what she wanted; they wouldn't have to look at more kitchens. "I love them. Look." Taking a picture out of her purse, she showed it to him. "I tore this out of one of those decorating magazines. Isn't it a beautiful kitchen? And the best part is, this place has the very same cabinets!" She gazed at him, unable to understand why he was so agitated. "We can order them right now."

Joe studied the magazine picture, then considered the displays of sample kitchens, his gaze fixing on the cabinets Molly had been raving about. "As usual, honey, you've zoomed right in on the most expensive items in the place. Listen. The bid allows eighteen thousand dollars for a kitchen. That's after my contractor's discount, and I figured that amount would include appliances." She watched him draw a long breath. "The cabinets you're looking at are going to run well over twenty thousand, closer to twenty-five. And that's *with* my discount and *before* you buy a single appliance."

Molly stepped back and frowned. "What are you saying? That I can't buy these cabinets?"

"I'm saying we should look around some more and see if we can't find something else you like that will fit your budget."

Exasperation sharpened her voice. "Not *my* budget, Joe. *Your* budget. For seven thousand dollars more, I can have the kitchen I want. Now does it seem reasonable to you that I should settle for something I *don't* want when I can afford to buy the kitchen I do want?"

"You still have to buy appliances." He followed her down another display aisle. "Honey, you don't need cherrywood or all the bells and whistles pictured in this magazine, do you? Look at this fluted decorator piece." He jabbed the magazine picture. "Do you know what each of those fluted froo-fras cost? Eighty bucks apiece. And for what? Sheer decoration. They don't do anything useful."

She turned on him, getting angry. "I don't care if the froo-fras cost two hundred dollars apiece. Joe, listen to me. I can afford this kitchen." She jerked the picture out of his hands. "Who is going to use this kitchen? Who's going to live with it? Who's going to pay for it? You or me?"

Tilting his head back, he glared at the ceiling. "I can't believe how badly I erred on the discretionary estimates."

"Joe, that isn't your fault. You bid an average kitchen, but it turns out that I don't want an average kitchen. I want this kitchen." She waved the picture. "I don't see any reason to waste time looking at more kitchens, when I know what I want right now, and I'm not going to change my mind. What's the point in waiting? We might as well order it right now."

"Give me a minute to cool off, honey." Turning abruptly, he stalked off down the aisle, taking long strides and shaking his head, muttering to himself.

Molly pushed a hand through her hair, released a breath, then walked in the opposite direction. It made her angry that Joe was putting her in a position where she sounded like a petulant child.

At the top of the aisle, she halted before a large display of drawer pulls and folded her arms across her chest, frowning. The disagreement between her and Joe could end in one of two ways. Either she put in the kitchen he wanted, or she put in the kitchen she wanted.

One of them was going to walk out of here upset. It was a hell of way to begin what they were both thinking of as a romantic weekend getaway.

A long sigh lifted her chest. Maybe the thing to do was to postpone this decision. They could have their romantic weekend, then, next weekend, they would return to the kitchen place and she'd buy the kitchen she wanted. Maybe it wouldn't matter so much then that Joe was going to be upset.

No, it would matter then, too.

Suddenly she remembered Joe saying they had to keep personal and professional issues separate. It occurred to her that if their personal chemistry hadn't been running in high gear, if they hadn't planned on leaving here and driving directly to Keystone, she wouldn't have thought twice about insisting on the kitchen she wanted. There was her answer. It was ridiculous to even consider settling for a kitchen she didn't want, simply to appease Joe's desire to meet an arbitrary budget.

Angry, frustrated, and feeling guilty that she was causing them both a problem, she stared at the stupid cabinet pulls. They should have known better than to combine kitchen shopping with a romantic weekend. The bathroom-fixture outing should have taught them a lesson.

"Honey?" Joe appeared beside her and touched her arm. "I'm sorry. I was out of line, and I apologize. It's your house, and you should have the kitchen you want, if you can afford it."

"Joe, I can afford it. Honest."

"Part of my job is to watch out for your money. I see it as my responsibility to bring this job in as close to the price you and I agreed on as I possibly can." He reached into his pocket and pulled out a thin slip of paper. "Remember this? It's the fortune I got the night we had Chinese. It says, 'Remember the bottom line.' Well, the bottom line is

that I want you to love the house I'm building for you."
He placed his hands on her shoulders and examined her
face. "I've done my part. I've pointed out that you're going
way overbudget. I've mentioned there are other choices."

"Joe..." She remembered her fortune, too. Follow your
heart. Her heart said buy this kitchen. It also said, Don't
mess up a fabulously romantic weekend.

"I know," he said, grinning down at her. "You want
this kitchen and you want Corian countertops. You probably want gold-plated hinges and drawer pulls. So, okay."
Leaning, he kissed the tip of her nose. "Let's go find the
salesman and make his day. Let's buy that fabulous
kitchen."

Molly gazed into his eyes and realized she didn't know
three other people who could have done the about-face that
Joe had just managed. There was no resentment in his gaze,
no anger, no upset. He'd thought about it, worked it out
with himself, and he was ready to buy the kitchen she
wanted. His mood had turned around, and he even sounded
enthusiastic.

"You know something?" she said slowly, studying his
handsome face. "You're a remarkable person in a lot of
ways."

"Thanks," he said absently, rolling up his sleeves, his
gaze fixed on the salesman. "Now the fun begins."

"What does that mean?" Molly asked, falling into step
beside him as they returned to the salesman's desk.

Joe's eyes twinkled down at her. "For the next two or
three hours, we're going to play musical cabinets on paper.
You and me and Mike," he said, nodding toward the salesman.

She halted in the aisle. "Two or three hours?" It was
almost noon already.

"And through it all, I'm going to be working on Mike
to bring down the cost." His chin came up, and a wicked
sparkle flashed in his eyes. This was the part he would most
enjoy. Riding in on his white horse to save her a bit more
money.

They were an hour into designing the kitchen layout before Molly realized two things. First, she had never suspected the intricacies of kitchen design, or how many different kinds of cabinets one could purchase. And second, delaying the drive to Keystone was a great relief.

In fact, her chest grew tighter and tenser as time wore on. Part of her looked at Joe's earnest and intent face and she couldn't wait to be alone with him, felt her cheeks grow hot with eager anticipation when she thought about the evening to come.

But she shrank in dread when she tried to imagine strapping on skis again. Now that Joe and Mike were talking about cabinet dimensions, she leaned back in her chair and withdrew from the discussion. Her mind leaped ahead to the moment when she would step off the lift at Keystone and look down at the snowy mountainside.

Suddenly, the memories of that terrible day a year ago were as fresh and immediate as this morning. She remembered inhaling the crisp, clean air that morning and feeling exhilarated, invulnerable. Remembered pushing herself to go faster, faster, zipping down the face of the mountain like a streak of blue lightning. And then the awful moment when she'd spotted the curve ahead and known she was flying out of control and couldn't make the turn.

She didn't actually remember sailing into space or hitting the tree. It must have been hideously frightening and excruciatingly painful. Painful enough that she only vaguely recalled the arrival of the ski patrol, followed by a helicopter that had taken her to the emergency room outside of Aspen. Her next real memory was of waking up in a hospital in Denver, with no idea how she'd gotten there. But after she touched the bandages wrapping her face, it hadn't mattered where she was. Nothing had mattered except the shocking realization that her life had changed irrevocably. Nothing was going to be the same as it had been before she sailed off the snowy edge of the trail's curve.

Leaning forward, she covered her face with both hands as a shudder convulsed her shoulders. It all might have happened yesterday. And her first horrified fear had been correct. Everything was different now.

"Honey?" Joe touched her hair, and she heard his concern. "Are you all right?"

"Yes," she said, her voice muffled in her hands. "Are you and Mike about finished?"

"Close. He's totaling up the order right now. In about two minutes, we'll have a hell of a fight. I'll shout and pound the desk and tell him that he's robbing us blind. He'll claim I'm trying to steal the cabinets and take food out of the mouths of his wife and babies. I'll sneer and swear I can buy the same cabinets down the street for fifteen percent less. He'll say that's a lie. We'll both threaten to walk away from the deal. Then we'll say, well, hell, we've got the whole thing worked out and put together, so you give a little and I'll give a little, we'll split the difference and everybody's happy. Then I'll give him a down payment so he can get the order going, and we're out of here."

Molly looked at him, knowing her face was white. "Would you mind if I stepped outside and waited for you there?"

"Honey, are you having second thoughts about the kitchen?"

"The kitchen?" She almost laughed. "No. I love the kitchen, Joe."

"Then…" His eyes darkened to a stormy navy color that Molly hadn't seen before. "Have you changed your mind about going to Keystone?"

She squeezed his arm. "I haven't changed my mind about us." That was what he was really asking. "But I keep thinking about skiing, and…"

He covered her hand with his own strong callused palm. "Skiing is an option. If you want to ski, fine. If you don't want to, that's fine, too. Don't put any pressure on this that doesn't exist."

But there was pressure, she thought, pacing the sidewalk

in front of the kitchen showroom. She wanted Joe to think well of her. She didn't want him to think she was a coward.

Jamming her hands in her pockets, her head down, she walked up and down the sidewalk, trying to swallow the sour taste of fear and dread. She could have said no to a skiing weekend. Joe hadn't pressured her; he would have understood if she'd said, "Some other time. Maybe next year."

But she hadn't really been thinking about skiing. She'd been thinking about her and Joe, alone in a warm, cozy condo, just the two of them, with nothing to do but enjoy being together. She'd been thinking about how he sometimes looked at her in a certain way and her stomach went clunk and dropped to her toes in a fiery free fall. And the way her knees started to crumple when he pulled her close to his body and she felt the solid, sexy heat of him.

She raised her head as he pushed out of the door, whistling happily, his step energetic and confident. There wasn't a whisper of his earlier upset or his difficulty with buying a kitchen that went over his budget. When Joe made a decision, he embraced it wholeheartedly and he didn't look back. He had jumped into buying Molly's kitchen as sincerely and completely as if that had been his choice all along. He truly was extraordinary.

"We're through working, honey," he announced cheerfully, slipping his arm through hers. "Now we can play." After helping her into the pickup, he jumped inside and backed out of the parking space. "We'll get there about five o'clock. Unpack, have a glass of wine. Then we'll have dinner beside the lake." He slid her a look. "There's a movie theater and several clubs, if you want to do something after dinner."

"Let's play it by ear, okay? See what we feel like doing." She liked him for being considerate, for trying so hard to make it seem that this weekend wasn't about going to bed together. And maybe it wasn't, she thought suddenly, frowning. It was also about skiing.

"Joe?" she said softly, determined not to think about

skis or slopes or face-wrecking trees. "Thanks for going along with the kitchen. For a minute there, I thought it was going to spoil our weekend. Thanks for not letting that happen."

He laughed, then grinned at her. "Honey, here's how it is. The project is going to come in over the bid. That is now a given, and I have to accept that." His gaze sobered. "But it's your house and your money. And you should choose the things that you want and are going to love. I apologize that I forgot that, even for a minute. Because you're right."

"I like what you said about watching out for my money. That's part of what makes you so good at your profession." She smiled. "I'll bet your clients appreciate that."

He laughed again and patted her knee. "Most of them. Occasionally I get one like you."

"Joe? Does it bother you that I have a lot of money put away?" she asked curiously. Suddenly, she wondered if he thought she was careless with money, or if he felt that she had extravagant preferences. In her opinion, neither was true. "Does it bother you that I can afford just about anything I want to buy?"

"Bother me? No." He drove for a mile without speaking further. "It bothers me that I misjudged things so badly. I think I was remembering you when we were growing up. Like you said, our families were in about the same economic situation. Sure, I read about the Apple Girl contract, along with most of America. But I guess the million dollars a year didn't register. Maybe it still doesn't." He took his eyes off the road long enough to study her for a minute. "You just don't seem like a person who has that kind of money."

She smiled. "Would my profligate ways seem more acceptable if I were draped in furs and diamonds?"

"Maybe," he said, laughing.

"Joe, that isn't me. I don't own any diamonds, and you know how I feel about fur. The money part of the Apple deal never mattered as much as being chosen did. That's what mattered. Being at the top of my profession. Sure, it feels good to be able to buy the kitchen I want or whatever else. But my tastes are pretty simple." She frowned, thinking about it. "In many ways, you're right. I'm still the person I used to be. I like nice clothes, and I've bought a few designer things, but I seem to always choose jeans and a sweater when I'm at home. I like to go out, but it doesn't have to be someplace fancy or expensive. I really enjoyed the welcome dinner and the square dancing. For me, the perfect evening is quiet. Maybe reading a good book. Or watching a great film on TV."

"Honey, what are you trying to say here?"

"I don't know," she said with a sigh. "I guess I'm trying to tell you that I don't spend money like it grows on trees. But when I really want something and it's important to me, then I do spend money. And this house has become very important to me."

"As long as we're talking about these things...does it bother you that I don't make as much money as you do? And never will?" he asked, keeping his gaze fixed on the highway.

"Hardly. In case you've forgotten, I'm currently unemployed."

"You know what I mean. Honey, you probably make more in interest and dividends than I make in a year."

"I stumbled into a profession where if you make it big, a lot of money comes with the fame. To make it big takes some skill and talent, and a whole lot of luck. I was lucky." She shrugged. "But most people will never make that kind of money. I sure wouldn't have if I hadn't fallen into it, and I'll never make that kind of money again. I'm straying from the question, aren't I?"

"I'm afraid so," he said with a smile.

"No. I don't care how much money you make. What I care about is the kind of person you are. Does it bother you that—"

"Oh, hell, no. I'm a modern kind of guy," he said, laughing. "I wish I made as much money as you did, but

I doubt that I ever will. I'm never going to be rich and famous, honey, but I'm going to be happy. I like where I live, like what I do, like the people in my life, like my dog and my girl…. That's what matters to me.''

"Speaking of your dog…where is Aspen this weekend?''

"Jim's keeping him for me. That reminds me. Jim asked me to be sure and tell you that he hopes we both have a great weekend.''

Molly sank back against the seat. Maybe it was good that she and Jim had cleared the air. It sounded as if he were sending her a message that declared a truce. She was glad.

"Honey, do you feel like we've been dancing around land mines all day?''

She burst into laughter and cast him an appreciative glance. "That's exactly how I feel. We've avoided an explosion, but sometimes it's felt like a near thing.''

"Yeah. Would you agree to putting any and all sensitive areas to one side for the remainder of the weekend? This is going to sound hopelessly romantic, but I'd like this weekend to be something we both remember happily.''

"I can live with hopelessly romantic,'' she said, smiling.

"Great.''

They gazed at each other long enough that Molly wondered how he kept from driving off the side of the road. And suddenly the chemistry was there again, as strong as powerfully attracting magnetic forces. She looked into Joe's eyes, and her mouth went dry and she clasped her hands to keep them from trembling. They had their differences, but they also had an electricity between them that fizzed and crackled and set her skin on fire.

"Are we almost there?'' she whispered.

"Almost.''

The look in his blue eyes promised more than a quick arrival.

MOST SKI AREAS reminded Molly of a Tyrolean Christmas, and so did Keystone. Tiny twinkle lights draped bare tree limbs, drifts of snow rolled back from shoveled walkways, marshmallow-perfect. This late in the season, with spring almost upon them, there were no overtly Christmasy items, but the twinkling lights and the heavy scent of pine and spruce made her think of holidays and high spirits.

Joe's condo faced the frozen lake, part of an older complex built of log and stone, with lots of glass open to the scenery. It was dark when they arrived, but during the day there would be spectacular views of the peaks. Inside were a galley kitchen, two bedrooms, and a large living area with inviting window seats and a massive stone fireplace.

"If you like this," Joe said, setting down their luggage, "you'll love my cabin in Vrain. There's a lot of common features."

Molly carried a bag of snacks, breakfast fixings and wine into the small kitchen. "It's a great place," she called. "Except for the kitchen. I don't see a single decorative froo-fra."

She smiled when she heard his outburst of deep, rumbling laughter. "You're a wicked, relentless woman," he said. When he returned from taking their luggage into one of the bedrooms, he drew her into his arms and ran his hands down her back, molding her against him. "You feel good. And you smell good, too, like spring lilacs."

"You feel good, too," she said, leaning into him and closing her eyes. His tall body was lean, but solid. He was all muscle and hard bone and heat. No matter how cold it was, Joe always seemed to radiate a high-energy heat that was enormously sexy. That heat enveloped her now and made her draw a sharp, soft breath.

"Why don't you freshen up, then we'll get something to eat," he murmured against her hair. "I'm starving."

Molly leaned back in his arms and smiled. "I'm starving, too," she whispered. They held each other's glances for a full minute, making promises with light touches and a long look, before Molly reluctantly broke away.

The bedroom was surprisingly spacious, with room for a

king-size bed, a couple of chairs and another window seat. Molly hung her clothing in the closet, then took her makeup items into the adjoining bathroom. Seeing Joe's shaving toiletries made her smile. There was something intimate and satisfying about setting out her things next to his. She hesitated a moment, then placed her red toothbrush next to his blue one. That, more than anything else, announced that they were a couple in her mind. For Joe, it had been taking her to the Goosed Moose. For her, it was seeing her perfume bottle sitting on the counter next to his cologne, and setting out their toothbrushes side by side.

After freshening her makeup, she tied her hair at the neck with a bow that matched her parka. Then she and Joe had a glass of wine, flirting with each other, before they left for dinner at a restaurant on the lake. From their table beside the window, they could watch ice-skaters twirling across the lake beneath the lights.

"It's lovely, isn't it?" Molly said, smiling through the pane at the skaters.

"You're lovely," Joe said huskily. "Every man in the place wishes he were me, sitting here with you."

"And all the women wish they were me, sitting here with you." He had changed into a turtleneck and sweater, and he looked devastatingly handsome in the candlelight. Molly had noticed more than a few women casting speculative glances in his direction. It pleased her enormously that Joe didn't seem to notice. He made it clear that the only woman he saw or cared about was her.

When the waitress appeared, she gave them a knowing smile. "Newlyweds, right?"

Joe and Molly looked at each other and burst into laughter. "Is it that obvious?" Joe asked, winking at Molly.

"I can always tell," the waitress said smugly. "We've got great hot buttered rum. And the special tonight is chicken Oscar. Sound good?"

They both nodded, absorbed in each other, not caring what they ate. One of the nice things about being twenty-eight and a little worldly, Molly thought, was that both of them understood that the lovemaking had already begun. Throughout dinner, they teased each other with long glances and lingering touches, with double entendres and lightly provocative remarks.

They talked about growing up and music and favorite books, discovering they enjoyed many of the same choices. They remembered incidents that reached back to high school, and they shared more recent experiences. Lingering over after-dinner drinks, drawing out the sexual heat building between them, they talked about things neither of them would be able to recall later.

When they left the restaurant to walk back to Joe's condo, they didn't wear their gloves, because they wanted to hold hands and feel each other's skin. It pleased them both that the people they passed smiled at them, as if everyone knew they would become lovers tonight and approved of their decision.

As if they had discussed it in advance, when they returned to the condo, Molly went into the kitchen to pour glasses of wine and arrange a platter of cheese, crackers and green grapes, while Joe built a fire in the fireplace and lit strategically placed candles. When she came into the living room, Joe took the platter from her hands and set it near the fire.

He took her into his arms, gently, tenderly. "Is this hopelessly romantic enough for you?" he asked, kissing her throat.

"Oh, yes," she murmured, closing her eyes in surrender. He had even spread a blanket in front of the fire and brought in their pillows. "It's perfect."

"Not yet," he whispered against her lips. "But it will be."

Slowly, he drew her sweater up and over her head, careful not to snag her hair. And she helped him out of his sweater and turtleneck. When she unhooked her bra and let it drop, Joe sucked in a sharp breath and stared at her.

"My God, but you are a beautiful woman!"

He was beautiful, too. Flickering light from the fireplace

played over his taut, heavily muscled chest, and slid over broad, well-developed shoulders. Dark hair sprinkled his chest, not too heavy, not too light. Just right, Molly thought, pressing the crisp springiness beneath her palm as Joe slid his hands up her ribs to the sides of her breasts.

Not hurrying, drawing out the delicious teasing of deliberate delay, they kissed and stroked, and Joe trailed hot kisses down her throat toward her breasts, which he cupped in his hands. She gasped when his mouth closed over her nipple and gently sucked, drawing the nipple into his mouth to explore with his tongue. It drove her wild and stirred the heat building in her lower stomach. Her hands moved over his bare chest and dropped to the belt at his waist, tugging, pushing, fumbling.

And then, eager to come to each other naked, they broke apart and finished undressing then looked at each other almost shyly in the warm light cast by candles and dancing flames. Molly reached a trembling hand and touched the tight, smooth skin curving over his hip.

"I like the look of you, Joe Townsend," she murmured hoarsely.

He framed her face between his rough palms and kissed her deeply, passionately. Then he untied the bow holding back her hair and buried his hands in the long, silky tumble. As they sank to their knees, Molly felt his heat in front of her, the heat from the fireplace warming her back.

Cupping her head, he gently laid her back on the blanket and pulled the pillow forward. And then he knelt beside her, looking at her in the firelight. When he touched her, she realized that his hands were shaking, too. She felt the trembling as he ran a hand from her throat to her breast, and slowly down her stomach. She felt the rough calluses on his palm against her smooth skin, and the eroticism of rough against smooth made her moan softly and call his name as she opened her arms to him.

With a groan, he came to her, his mouth hot and demanding on hers. Hours of teasing and calculated restraint ended as he stretched out beside her and Molly felt the thrilling electricity sizzling between them, felt their bodies ignite in feverish need. Locked together, pressing closer and closer in an urgent desire to meld and blend into each other, they kissed and touched and stroked and moved against each other until both of them were gasping and drenched in perspiration.

Only then, when Molly felt as if she would surely die if he didn't take her, did he guide her thighs apart and enter her with a small, quick intake of breath. For a moment, he held her without moving anything but his lips on her mouth. And then he stirred inside her, and they moved together as if they had made love a hundred times before, had danced before to primitive rhythms of deepening passion and urgency.

Afterward, they lay tangled in each other's arms, panting for breath. If it wouldn't have sounded like such a cliché, Molly would have told him that she had never experienced lovemaking like that, had never known that she was capable of soaring to such heights of pleasure.

By the time she'd decided to tell him anyway and let the clichés fall where they might, Joe leaned over her and kissed her breasts, then moved to her lips, kissing her deeply, and the wanting began again in the hot pit of her stomach.

This time they tortured each other by kissing each other all over, exploring with their tongues and hands and lips, delighting in each groan of pleasure, each tiny gasp of wondering discovery. They brought each other to ecstasies of release, again and again.

Near dawn, Joe carried her into the bedroom and curled his body protectively around hers, spooning her into a warm curve. Sated, exhausted, and thoroughly well loved, Molly fell asleep in less than a minute, a smile of drowsy contentment on her lips.

"RISE AND SHINE, honey. It's a beautiful day in the neighborhood."

She opened her eyes and stretched. "How can you pos-

sibly be so cheerful in the mornings?'' Sitting up and pulling the sheet over her naked breasts, she took the cup of
coffee Joe gave her, and smiled. He looked wonderful. His
hair was still damp from the shower, his blue eyes flashed
and sparkled with the joy of a new morning. ''I think tur-
tlenecks and sweaters suit you.''

''You think so? And all this time I thought I was making
a flannel fashion statement.'' He touched the rim of his
coffee cup to hers. ''You won't believe the dream I had
last night,'' he said, grinning at her.

Molly laughed. ''If it was anything like my dream, it
was fabulous.''

''I think I'm still having it. Or is there really a beautiful
naked woman in my bed?''

''Your naked dream woman is feeling slightly guilty at
still being in bed while you're up and dressed. What time
is it?''

He lifted a strand of her hair off the mounded pillows
and wound it loosely around his hand. ''Almost nine
o'clock. We're getting a late start. Why don't you get
dressed while I'm fixing breakfast, then we'll rent some
skis for you and hit the slopes? Sound like a plan to you?''

His words struck her like a blow. The wonder and beauty
of last night had completely made her forget about facing
the mountain. Now, the thought of it filled her chest with
panic, and her eyes widened.

Leaning over her, Joe kissed her forehead and her lips,
then he teased down the sheet and kissed both breasts.
''Good morning, good morning, good morning, good morning.'' Pulling the sheet to her knees, he kissed her lower
stomach. ''Good morning.'' Then, trying to make her
laugh, he grabbed pieces of furniture and pulled himself
toward the door, as if he were fighting a hurricane that tried
to blow him back into her bed. ''Whew. Almost didn't
make it,'' he said at the door, looking back at her. His gaze
drank in the sight of her. ''Breakfast in twenty minutes,
honey,'' he said in a husky voice. ''I hope you're noticing
the effort it takes to be a sensitive nineties guy.''

His comment did indeed make her laugh. Reaching, Molly twitched the sheet over her nakedness and smiled. "Your restraint is noted and appreciated."

"I'm guessing that, not being a morning person, you aren't too interested in morning, ah…you know." He gave her a charmingly appealing look. "I'm willing to be proven wrong," he added hopefully.

"Thanks for being understanding." Sex was the last thing on her mind right now.

"You know," he said, smiling at her. "It was so much easier on guys when we could just be pigs."

Laughing, she threw a pillow at him. "I like mine scrambled. And dry toast."

Ducking, he stepped into the hall, then poked his head back in the door with a wide grin. "I still respect you. You're beautiful. I'm wild about you. Did I forget anything?"

"You're seriously crazy, Joe Townsend. Now get out of here so I can get dressed."

The instant she heard him recede down the short hallway, whistling between his teeth, the smile faded from Molly's lips. Letting her head drop, she stared unseeing into her coffee cup.

She didn't think she could do this. If Joe hadn't been with her, she wouldn't even have attempted to ski. But her deepening feelings for Joe changed things. Ordinarily, she truly didn't care much what other people thought of her. But she cared a lot about what Joe thought. And she wanted him to admire her, to be proud of her. She didn't want him to think she was cowardly or afraid.

Wanting to appear in control got her through breakfast and almost through the process of renting skis. It wasn't until they were walking out of the rental shop, skis in their gloved hands, that she knew absolutely that she could not do it.

Stopping abruptly, she sat on a wooden bench and stared at brightly clad skiers zipping down the side of the mountain, their poles flashing in the dazzling sunlight.

"Honey?" Joe said beside her, facing her with a frown of concern. "Are you all right?"

"No," she whispered. "I'm sorry, Joe, but I can't do it." Small tremors rocked her body, and her hands were shaking. "I keep seeing the curve rushing toward me, keep remembering that terrible moment when I realized I couldn't slow down. I wasn't going to make the curve." She turned wide, moist eyes to him. "I'm not ready for this. I can't do it."

Slipping off a glove, he stroked warm fingertips down her cold cheek. "It's all right, honey. It's your decision. No one is pressuring you to do something you don't want to do."

"It isn't that I don't want to. I can't."

"No, Molly," he said gently, and she realized with a start that it was the first time he had called her by name. "You can do anything you want to. This just isn't the right time. But if you really wanted to ski…you'd find a way to do it."

"You think I'm lying to myself?"

"I don't know." Standing, he pulled his skis out of a snowbank and rested them on his shoulder. "I'll meet you back at the condo at three o'clock, okay?"

At first it startled her that he intended to ski without her. Then relief flooded her eyes. She would have felt guilty if her actions had cheated him out of his last chance to ski this season. Her guilt would have spoiled the day for both of them.

"Have some great runs," she said, gratitude in her gaze. "It's a beautiful day for it."

"See you at three."

Sitting on the bench, she watched him walk toward the lifts, smiling when she realized that his step was jaunty even in his awkward ski boots. Then she was alone.

For several minutes, she remained where she was, sitting in the sunshine, watching the skiers on the slopes, this time without her throat closing in panic. There was beauty in the forms traversing the mountainside, and she enjoyed watching them as she began to relax.

Sports had never figured prominently in Molly's life. She played a little golf, a little tennis, but she played neither game well, largely because she wasn't very interested. But she had loved to ski. Her parents had enrolled her in a ski school when she was eight. Perhaps that was the difference. She'd learned skiing young, and become an expert on the slopes by the time she finished high school. It had been "her" sport, the only sport she cared about.

Sighing, she stood and glanced over her shoulder at the rental shop. She might as well return the skis, poles and boots. But first, she decided impulsively, she'd have a cup of coffee at the warming house near the lifts. And she'd feel silly there without skis or wearing regular boots.

Ten minutes later, she stood outside the warming house, cradling a cup of hot coffee between her gloves, her gaze fixed on the skiers flying down the mountain.

And her private battle began in earnest.

JOE SAT ON A BENCH in the sun, watching her through dark glasses. Walking away from her had been hard. But he'd realized in the rental shop, as she grew more and more quiet and pale, that his presence acted as a pressure on her. He sensed that if he had stayed with her, she would eventually have agreed to face the slopes, out of pride, or possibly because she didn't want him to miss a day of skiing or whatever. She would have changed her mind a dozen times as she had done outside the rental shop, and he might easily have slipped into trying to second-guess and thereby pressuring her.

He didn't want to do that. Whether or not she ever skied again had to be totally her decision. And he wouldn't blame her if she chose not to. The last time she skied, her whole life had changed.

He also understood that there was more at stake than bad memories and a lost career. She had also lost faith in her own judgment that day. It didn't take a genius to figure out that that was where her difficulty with decision-making had originated. When she didn't think about making decisions, she made them easily, and with a quick, confident instinct that told him that was her natural characteristic. But when she knew in advance that a decision was coming, as she'd known she had to choose the faucets and kitchen cabinets, she worried the decision like a dog with a bone, swinging back and forth, and working herself into a state of anxiety.

As he watched her pace back and forth at the foot of the slope, his heart melted. She was so lovely, so unaware of the stares she elicited. He wondered absently if she was so accustomed to fame that she no longer noticed the attention she attracted, or if she didn't quite realize how famous she was. Maybe it was simply that her beauty had always drawn attention and she no longer noticed.

The thing was, she was so much more than her physical beauty. She was smart, funny, kind, giving. She was interested in new experiences, genuinely interested in other people. In books, a woman often became more beautiful the longer a man knew her. In Joe's case, Molly's outer beauty was becoming less noticeable as her inner beauty shone forth.

A year ago, a ski weekend had changed her life. This weekend had changed his.

Because he knew he loved her.

He also knew that her life would change again if she won the battle she was so obviously waging with herself as he watched. How, and in what ways, he couldn't predict. He only sensed that it would happen.

Standing for a better view, he watched her, and knew the instant she made up her mind. With mixed feelings, he waited as she pulled her skis out of the snow and stepped into them with a grim expression. Then she glided toward the puma that would take her the short distance to the top of the bunny slope. Following her bright red parka with his eyes, he saw her step smoothly off the puma and stand for a long time gazing down the gentle bunny slope.

Then, finally, she let herself slide forward, and he saw

at once by her grace and fluid ease that she was an expert skier, completely at home on the mountain. At the bottom of the slope, she bent over her skis and covered her face, shaking. And then she headed to the puma and skied down the gentle bunny slope again. And then again.

Joe didn't reveal himself until he saw her eyeing the lift carrying skiers up the mountain to more difficult slopes. When she walked toward it, he stepped into his own skis and moved forward, coming up beside her.

"I know a nice easy intermediate slope," he said, as if they'd been speaking only a minute before.

She put her gloved hand in his and looked up at him with shining eyes that reminded him of last night. She had looked at him like that then, too.

"Oh, Joe," she said softly, moisture brimming in her eyes. "It's going to be all right."

"I never doubted it," he said truthfully.

They leaned into one of the most awkward embraces he'd ever had, laughing when their skis and poles tangled. And then they let the lift sweep them off the ground and carry them on an exhilarating ride to the middle of the mountain.

She faltered for a moment when they glided off the lift, and raised wide eyes that begged for reassurance. Loving her, proud of what she was doing, he placed his hands on her shoulders and gazed into her eyes.

"We don't have to do this," he said softly. "We can ride the lift back down." He kissed her, tasting the warm sweetness of her mouth. "Or, since we're here, we can ski down."

"Joe?" she said, touching his cheek. "I'm going to remember this as one of the best and happiest weekends of my life. I…" But she hesitated, and didn't say whatever she had started to say.

Instead, she lowered her goggles and blew him a kiss. Then she pushed off, and flew away from him.

Chapter Nine

It had been a fabulous weekend, Molly thought dreamily. A Joe weekend. After a day of skiing, they had taken a sleigh ride up to a wonderful restaurant with a spectacular view of the Continental Divide. Molly had been ecstatic over conquering her fear of the slopes, and cuddling next to Joe beneath the sleigh blanket, listening to the gay tinkle of bells and harness, had sent the day over the top. After a wonderful dinner, they had returned to the condo for wine in front of the fireplace and an evening of slow, tender lovemaking.

Since the renovation project began, she had spent a lot of time with Joe. Not a day went by that he didn't call her upstairs two or three times to make a decision about something or other, or to solicit her opinion or approval. And he was constantly running downstairs to use the phone on her desk. Recently, they had started ending the day by having dinner together.

Even so, she had wondered how well they would mesh, spending twenty-four hours a day together. Somewhere at the back of her mind, their weekend had been a test of sorts. And they had passed the test with flying colors. At the end of the weekend, she had been as eager to be with him as when they drove away from her house. A man with Joe's cheerful vitality and interest in everything that occurred around him was a not a man that a woman grew tired of. She wanted more.

A crash sounded above her head, and Molly looked up at the ceiling. Pooches swarmed all over the house, finishing the framing, building the roof over the new kitchen and garage. The sounds of men's shouts, pounding music and hammering rang in Molly's ears. Outside, concrete trucks churned in the yard. But at least it wasn't as cold this week. She wore a turtleneck beneath a heavy sweater, but she wasn't trying to type while wearing a parka.

In fact, she wasn't doing much typing at all. She had daydreamed the week away, remembering the weekend with Joe.

Earlier in the week, she had actually believed that she might get some work done on the book, but Avis Morrison had dropped by to ask if Molly would like to make a contribution to a benefit fund for a family whose home had burned down shortly after Christmas. Molly had added fifty dollars to the town's collection, then offered Avis a cup of coffee and kept her talking until Molly could shift the conversation around to her parents.

"Touring the USA in an RV was my mother's idea," she'd said brightly. "Mom is six years older than my Dad, but he can hardly keep up with her."

Avis had seen right through her not-so-offhand comment. "Did Jim ask you to talk to me about age differences?" she'd asked suspiciously.

"No," Molly had admitted, feeling about as subtle as a sledgehammer. "This was my idea." Then they had talked, girl to girl, shouting to be heard over the noise surrounding them, about romance and men and other people's opinions and age differences. At the end of two hours, they hadn't solved anything, but Molly felt she'd made a friend.

Thirty minutes after Avis departed, Mr. Melvin had arrived, bringing his girlfriend, Gloria, who had been out of town at the time of the welcome dinner and square dance. "She wants to meet you, darling," he'd explained, introducing a good-natured blond with a stunning smile. "And

I want her to hear how you feel about borrowing earrings. And blouses. Tell her what you told me."

Molly had enjoyed the next two hours, but Mr. Melvin and Gloria had taken up the rest of yesterday.

Now here she was, watching today slip away, too, and not getting any work done. Sighing, she turned back to her computer. No sooner had she placed her fingertips on the keyboard than she heard a tremendous thunk and the ground shook beneath her feet. Gasping, she looked up in amazement as a rock the size of a chair flew past the basement window and landed with a jarring thud next to another chair-size rock that had not been there a minute ago.

"My God! Did you see that? Two big rocks just fell down here!" Joe said from the bottom of the stairs. He almost collided with Molly as they both rushed to the windows. "It's those damned Romaines!"

Molly blinked in disbelief at the large rocks now sitting on the patio. "They're throwing them now?"

"They're supposed to be doing the backfill on the garage and study." Jerking open the basement sliders, Joe ran out the door, yelling Toots's name. In a few minutes, both men returned to the patio and eyed the big rocks sitting in the center of cracks radiating through the concrete.

When she joined them, Toots tipped his cowboy hat to her. "Sorry, ma'am. Must of startled you some to see a couple of big rocks come flying past the window. I was trying to move them rocks away from the incline, but they got away from me."

"Don't you hate it when that happens?" Molly muttered, looking at the cracks in the concrete.

"Yes, ma'am, I surely do. Wouldn't have happened if we'd hauled them rocks out of here. Daddy said to tell you the offer's still open, but not for long."

Joe thrust his face up near Toots's. "You tell Daddy that we'll have to jackhammer this patio out and repour it, and I'm taking the cost of the repair off his bill, damn it."

"I have to get out of here," Molly whispered, more to herself than to anyone else. She nodded. "Yeah, I'm going to flip out if I don't get away from here for a few hours." Tossing back her hair, she narrowed her eyes on Toots and Joe. "Gentlemen? I'm going to town to do…something. When I return, I want those rocks off my patio. Got that?"

Joe and Toots stared at her, and then Joe grinned. "Yes, ma'am, boss lady."

"Good." She looked at the rocks, kicked one of them hard enough to feel the impact all the way up her leg, then grabbed her parka and car keys and headed to town.

She was on Main Street before she remembered that she'd forgotten to turn off her computer. Well, so what? If the electricians turned off the power and she lost every word of the stupid book, right now she didn't care. The book was a marble albatross hanging around her neck, pressing on her thoughts, causing a daily bout of panic. She wished she had never agreed to do it.

When she found a parking space in front of the drugstore, she pulled in, then sat in her car and tried to figure out what to do next. She didn't have any pressing errands, had nothing on her mind except flying rocks. She'd just needed to get away from noise and dirt and shouting men and ear-splitting music. Getting out of the car, she hesitated, then walked into the drugstore, sat down at the counter and ordered a cup of coffee.

The waitress slid a cup forward and frankly studied Molly's face. "Everybody's right. You can hardly see the scars. I tell you, you were screwed over. They shouldn't have fired you. The pharmacist and everybody who works here thinks you should sue Apple Cosmetics. Are you going to?"

Startled, Molly glanced at the waitress's name tag. "Well, thanks for your support, Wanda. But it was a contractual thing. I don't think a lawsuit is possible." It always surprised her to learn that people were talking about her and didn't mind letting her know their opinions about her life. She was going to have to get used to this, if she planned to stay in Vrain.

If? Now where had the qualifier come from?

Wanda poured herself a cup of coffee and brought it around the counter to sit beside Molly. "Did Elaine Gold call you?"

"The name doesn't ring a bell."

"Well, Elaine and me and Gloria—you met Gloria, she's Mr. Melvin's girlfriend—we were talking, see. And we wondered if you would be interested in giving some classes on makeup and fashion? You could make some real money doing that. I know a dozen women who would pay twenty bucks each to learn about makeup from you." Wanda leaned forward eagerly. "It would be just fabulous to have a real model, famous even, teach us about makeup and clothes!"

"Right now, I'm—"

"We know you're tied up with the house and your book right now. We were thinking about when the house is finished. Gloria said we could use her shop after hours for a place to meet. Would you be interested in doing something like that? God, Molly, we'd just love it!"

She thought a minute. It did sound like fun. "I might," she said, drawing the words out. And then she said, with conviction, "Sure, I'd like to do that. You set it up." The more she thought about the idea, the more appealing it became. She did know a few tricks and tips she could share, and it would be nice to shoptalk again. "Let's plan on meeting once a week for three weeks. Tell Gloria I'll meet with her after the house is finished and we'll figure out what supplies we need and how we'll structure the classes."

Wanda clasped her hands in front of her chest, and her eyes glowed. "Wow. Thanks a lot! I can't wait to tell everyone!"

Feeling better, Molly bought some Chap Stick, then left the drugstore. She stood on the sidewalk outside and scanned the storefronts, considered for a minute, then got into her car and drove out to the junction. Cal Dobie's Landscaping and Quarry Rock was right where Joe had said it would be. She parked, squared her shoulders and headed for the office.

A pleasant-looking woman glanced up from a littered desk and smiled. "Hi, Miss Stevens. Can I help you?"

"Is Cal Dobie in?"

"Sure is." She came around her desk, walked to the door of the office, leaned outside and screamed, "Cal, you got a famous visitor!" Returning to her desk, she smiled at Molly. "I'm glad you came in. If nobody else has told you yet, it isn't a rebound thing with Joe. He and Ellen O'Ryan weren't romantic, if you know what I mean. I thought you should know."

Molly had no idea how to respond. She cleared her throat and nodded. "I guessed that, but thanks for telling me."

"I'm Avis Morrison's cousin, by the way. Holly James. You probably heard that I ran off and married the oldest Van Tine girl's ex-husband, and that's true. Teddy drinks too much, but he's a good provider and it's working out."

"Oh. Well, I'm glad to hear that." She was also glad to see Cal Dobie walk into the office, wiping mud off his hands with a green towel. "Hi. I'm Molly Stevens, we've talked on the telephone. About the rocks out at my place?"

"Oh, yes." Cal Dobie smiled at her and waved a hand toward a chair. "I drove out to your place last weekend and took a look around."

"What I'd like to know is, are the rocks worth anything, or shall I let the Romaines haul them away? Daddy's offered me a good deal. He won't charge me to haul them off."

Cal Dobie blinked hard. Then he frowned, drew a breath and gave Molly a crash course in rocks, how they were used in landscaping, and what they would have cost her if she had to buy the rocks strewn around her yard. The rocks that Daddy Romaine wanted to do her the favor of hauling away were worth a small fortune.

By the time she returned to her house, men were pouring down off the roof and out the doors, heading toward pickup trucks, shouting plans to meet at the Goosed Moose for beers and burgers. Joe came up to her as she was getting out of her car.

He handed her his beer. "Want a taste?"

"What I want is a bite out of Daddy Romaine," she said angrily. Slamming the car door behind her, she waved a hand at the boulders stacked in a huge pile. "Head-size rocks are worth about a hundred dollars. Those mid-size ones go for about three hundred dollars. And the *big* rocks, and I've got dozens of those, would sell for one or two thousand dollars if you wanted to buy them for landscaping purposes." She glared at Joe. "And Daddy Romaine wants to haul them out of here as a favor to me! Like hell he does."

Joe grinned at her. "Honey, you're getting a tad bit obsessive about these rocks."

"Yeah, I am. Maybe it's because I just learned from Cal Dobie that I've got about forty thousand dollars' worth of rocks laying in my yard." Aspen came bounding up to them, tail wagging, his paws thick with mud. "A girl gets possessive about her rocks," Molly said, petting Aspen's head. "I'm not going to give them up. Cal Dobie is going to do some wonderful landscaping stuff with them."

Joe took off his baseball cap and wiped a sleeve across his forehead before he took back the beer she handed him. "What would you like to do this weekend, honey? Want to shop for lighting fixtures and carpet?"

She loved the way he assumed they would spend the weekend together, but the thought of making more decisions made her stomach cramp. "I know prowling around home showrooms is your ideal date," she said, teasing him, "but I'm not ready to even think about floors." She gave him her most dazzling smile. "Joe, could we just have a quiet weekend away from dust and debris and rocks and mud and—" she waved a hand at the house "—all this? Could we have a pajama party at your house, maybe? Someplace that's warm and clean and quiet?"

His deep, wonderful laughter rang across the sounds of pickups revving up and spinning mud behind their back tires. "You got it, honey. My place. Bring a slinky nightie."

IT WAS a wonderful weekend. One of the great things about Molly, Joe decided, was that she didn't require constant attention, didn't need to be entertained. On Saturday, while he caught up on his business ledger and a mountain of paperwork, she revised a few finished pages of her book. They grilled steaks for dinner, and cuddled together on the sofa afterward to watch old movies on TV. On Sunday, they both slept late, which meant he slept until six-thirty and she slept until ten, and then they worked the Sunday crossword puzzle together. In the afternoon they attended the April mud festival, held at the Vrain city park.

It surprised him to observe how many people Molly already knew. More rapidly than usually occurred in small towns, she was being assimilated into the community. Part of her swift acceptance could be attributed to the fact that her face was so familiar that people felt they knew her from the get-go. Part of it was that she was his girl and therefore accepted as he was accepted. But mostly Vrain claimed her as one of its own because of her open and friendly demeanor. She was a nice person, he thought, watching her buy a raffle ticket from Avis's daughter, Cheryl Morrison. She had the type of personality that fit in anywhere. Watching her, a person would swear she had lived in Vrain all of her life. He suspected he would have had the same impression if he had seen her on the streets of Paris or London or New York City. She adapted to her surroundings.

He slipped an arm around her waist and resisted an urge to kiss her on the neck. "How many raffle tickets did you buy?"

"Two for me and two for you," she said, sticking them in his shirt pocket.

"What are we hoping to win?"

"A microwave oven," she said, laughing, her blue eyes sparkling. "Come on. The mud race is about to start." Wrapping her arm around his waist, she hooked a finger in one of his belt loops and pulled him forward. "Could you believe it that Jim Enders's team won the tug of war?"

He laughed. "What I couldn't believe was watching Avis mop him off after they won." He slid her a look. "You and Avis spent a lot of time together last week. Would you have had a hand in that romance heating up again?"

"Maybe," she said, grinning up at him. "I like Avis a lot. We're having lunch next week. By the way, would you have a problem if Avis and I invite Ellen O'Ryan to join us?"

"Damn it, honey. I keep telling you, there was nothing romantic between me and Ellen."

She stepped in front of him, wrapped her arms around his waist and kissed him. Right there at the April mud festival. And Joe suddenly felt ten feet tall, the envy of every man.

"Joe," she said against his lips, not caring who watched, which was everyone. "After the mud races, I'm going to take you home and I'm going to take you to bed, and I promise to make you forget that you ever knew any woman but me."

He kissed her on the mouth. "How do you feel about mud races, honey? Do we really want to stay and see them?"

She laughed and pushed him forward. "Absolutely. How often does a person get to see people running a relay in ankle-deep mud?"

"Once a year. We can watch it next year." Would she be here next year? Please, God, let her be here next year. And the year after that, and forever.

Exactly as he had feared would happen, he didn't want a few weeks with Molly. He wanted more. He wanted to spend the rest of his life with her. That was what he had wanted from the first time he saw her, way back in junior high school, and that was what he still wanted.

He didn't remember the races, although he stood beside her and watched and cheered the mud racers. He remembered the sun shining in her wheat-blond hair, remembered her cheeks flushed with helpless laughter and the clean fresh scent of her perfume. He remembered pulling out his handkerchief and wiping splatters of mud off her cheeks and remembered her doing the same for him.

And he would never in his life forget the lovemaking later that night.

It began in the shower, with steam rising around their naked, glistening bodies. Soapy hands stroking and caressing. Lips seeking wet lips. He shampooed her wonderful hair, piling it in sudsy glory on top of her head, and she shampooed his hair and his chest. And they made love standing up, with the water cascading over them and shampoo bubbles sliding over her breasts and his torso.

Wrapped in towels, they moved to the living room and loved each other again before the fire in the grate, taking their time, delighting in the pleasure they could give each other.

After a dinner of blueberry hotcakes and bacon and juice and hot coffee, they went out on the deck and watched the stars through the telescope and searched for comets to wish on. Then, still hungry for each other, they made love again, as urgently as if they didn't know each other's bodies and had never been together before.

Finally, near midnight, he drove her home, with her head nestled on his shoulder and the fragrance of her hair in his nostrils. And he thought that he had never been happier.

The only thing needed for perfection was to be able to tell her that he loved her. But he couldn't let himself say the words. Not until she said them first. And he didn't know if that would ever happen.

"Thanks for a wonderful weekend, Joe," she said at the door, leaning her fabulous body against him, kissing him on the chin.

"If your intent was to make me forget ol' what's-her-name, it worked," he said, smiling, his lips against her forehead.

"I wish you'd stay over. What's the difference between

everyone in town knowing I spent the weekend at your cabin and you staying here with me?''

"This is the site, honey. Here, you're a client.''

She yawned and nuzzled his neck. "Speaking as a client, we're halfway through the project, aren't we?''

"About that, yes. Maybe a little more.''

"Good. Once we're finished, you can stay over with me.''

He didn't know what would happen once the project was finished. But for the first time in his professional life, he dreaded the end. Seeing her every day was what got him out of bed in the mornings, what filled his heart and made it sing.

"DADDY ROMAINE, you are just the person I want to see.''

Molly had carried a cup of coffee outside to enjoy the first truly warm day so far. Spring scented the air, the snow was off the ground, and the drifts were melting rapidly. Buds swelled on the limbs of aspens and old cottonwoods; the pastures wore a faint tint of green promise.

"Howdy,'' Daddy said, tipping his Stetson as he stepped out of his truck. Dumpling looked out the window, nodded to Molly, popped her gum, then went back to filing her nails. "Got most of the backfill done last week. Should finish digging the footings for the back deck today.'' Daddy rocked back on his heels, sucked in his cheeks, and studied a bright spring sky. "You given any more thought to my extremely generous offer to help you out and haul off them rocks for absolutely free?''

Molly gazed at him, thinking again how much he looked like Colonel Sanders. "Those rocks are worth a lot of money,'' she said. "I believe you intended to take advantage of me.''

"Well, hell—'scuse me—you done let that little landscaper pull the wool over your eyes.''

"You planned to haul off forty thousand dollars' worth of rocks...as a favor to me, so you claimed. Now just who do you think was trying to pull the wool over my eyes? And I'll give you a hint. It wasn't Cal Dobie.''

"Now, girl, you just get that look out of your eyes. There weren't no wrongdoing here. If a man sees an opportunity, he just naturally has to take it. That's good bidness.'' He grinned at her and dropped a hand on her shoulder. "Looks like you got a bidness head, too. I like that in a woman. So how much did that sissy flower boy give you for the rocks?''

"I'm going to keep them.''

"Well, it don't make sense to me, but if you want to keep thousands of dollars of rocks in your yard, I guess that's your bidness.''

"Yes, it is,'' Molly said pleasantly. For the first time, she felt as if she'd gotten the best of the Romaines, and it felt like a rite of passage. She would have laughed, except she spotted Jim Enders walking toward her, carrying an emerald-green toilet.

"I know you ordered biscuit,'' he said, giving her a hopeful look, "but they sent green. So, I was wondering…it's actually a good-looking green, don't you agree?''

She stared at the toilet in his arms. It was indeed a beautiful shade—if she didn't mind that it wouldn't match the biscuit spa tub, or anything else. "Sorry, Jim. Send it back and tell the vendor we want the biscuit color that we ordered.''

Feeling in control, she returned to the basement, sat at her desk and listened to the noise buzzing, whirring, hammering, banging and crashing inside the house and out. Walls were forming around her. Actual walls, not framing boards. There was a roof over the kitchen and garage now, and the new study was floored and framed, the roof going on. Miraculously, order was arising out of chaos.

She felt the same thing happening within herself.

Skiing again had settled something fluttery in her chest that had been there for almost a year. Silly as it seemed in retrospect, facing the mountain and giving herself to it had calmed some inner storm. She wouldn't have believed it, but somehow, skiing had made the house decisions easier. Not easy, but easier.

It was still crazy living on a construction site, still noisy and dirty and cold at night and inconvenient and aggravating. But she was coping much better now. She wasn't staying awake nights worrying that she was going to hate biscuit-colored fixtures, or feeling anxious about whether she would still like the kitchen cabinets when she saw them installed. Flashes of her previous confidence were appearing with greater frequency. And it felt so good.

When Joe came downstairs at the end of the day, she handed him a glass of wine and gave him a big smile.

"What's this?" he asked after tasting the wine. "Are we celebrating something?"

"Yes and no. I'm hopelessly behind on the book, and feeling guilty and rotten about it. So I phoned my editor today and asked her to extend the deadline. It's still panic time, but I've stopped thinking about sticking my head in the oven."

"Does that mean you can finish at your own pace?"

"I wish. No, it only means that tonight I'm not going to kick myself if I don't work on the stinking book." Smiling, she sat on his lap and wrapped her arms around his neck and gave him a kiss. "Hey, big boy, want to come upstairs with me and slide your tool belt under my bed? We can celebrate a condemned woman's temporary reprieve."

"Now that's an offer no red-blooded male could refuse." Standing, holding her in his arms, he grinned down at her, his blue eyes flashing sexy heat. "I'm about to find out if I can carry a skinny model up two flights of stairs. Think I can do it?"

"Tell you what," she said, laughing. "You carry me up the first flight, then I'll carry you up the second flight."

"You are in a good mood, honey."

That she was. She'd let Daddy Romaine know that she wasn't born yesterday, she'd received a bit of breathing room on the book, and she was with a man she was crazy about. She threw back the bedspread, then tossed off her clothes and opened her arms. "If you aren't too exhausted from staggering up all those stairs, come over here."

"I'll show you how exhausted I am," Joe said, grinning and throwing his clothes every which way. "Move over, honey, and give me some room to work."

Later, lying in his arms, watching moonlight stream through the window, Molly laughed softly.

"What's funny?" Joe asked drowsily. His arms tightened around her. "Can you see the clock? I have to go home, shower and shave, and get back here before the pooches arrive."

"I was laughing because I'm happy," Molly murmured, pressing her cheek against his bare shoulder. "The construction project has been crazy, aggravating, infuriating, and some days I want to scream and tell everyone to get out of here. But it's also been fascinating, interesting, and fun."

"You forgot to mention expensive," he said, smothering a yawn against her tangled hair. "I don't think you've stayed within the budget on a single item."

"Joe?" Tilting her head back, she gazed into his eyes. "I…" She longed to tell him that she loved him, that she couldn't imagine the end of the project or a time when she wouldn't see him every day or hear his voice shouting on the floor above her. She wanted to tell him that life would be a pale thing without him.

But he hadn't said anything about love.

"I like you so much," she whispered. "I like being with you."

He framed her face between his callused hands and gazed into her eyes. "I like you, too."

It wasn't enough for either of them.

THE WEEKS FLEW BY. Molly hung her parka in the hall closet and didn't expect to wear it again until next autumn. Green flowed down the mountain sides and spilled wildflowers onto the roadsides. Drifts of dandelions draped a yellow carpet across the pastures and valleys.

Decisions came hard and fast now, but they didn't seem as difficult as before. Every weekend, she and Joe drove to Denver to select and buy something that had to be purchased immediately, as the schedule accelerated and the pooches raced to finish the project.

"Hi, honey," Joe called, coming down to the basement to have his coffee break with her. "Next week the painters will come in and stain the baseboards and woodwork, and then they'll shoot the walls and ceilings." He leaned across her desk to kiss her, then smiled. "You might want to consider staying at my place for a couple of days while they shoot the paint."

"I could make that sacrifice," she said, giving him a flirtatious glance.

"Great. Aspen and I will count on it."

"Joe, the project is almost finished, isn't it?" she asked, studying his profile. She loved the look of him. His nose was straight and true, his jawline firm and strong. Smiling, she noticed that he needed a haircut again, and his tan was deepening.

"We're getting there. A couple more weeks..."

"What's next for you?"

"Didn't I tell you? I meant to. I won the bid on the Henderson job." Looking pleased, he smiled broadly. "It's new construction, not a rebuild. I'm planning to break ground the third week in June. Thanks to your suggestions, I went back and increased the estimate on all the budget items."

Falling silent, Molly tried to imagine her house after all the workmen departed. At this point, the pooches felt like old friends. She knew about Coke's troubles with his girlfriend, about Al and Z taking college classes at night. Jim Enders was becoming a friend, and she knew each of the electricians' quirks. The roofers had given her a ficus plant as a housewarming gift. She'd thrown an impromptu party when the drywallers finished her walls, and it had felt like a party for people she had known most of her life.

Most of all, she would desperately miss Joe, from his

hearty "Rise and shine, honey" in the mornings to the deeply passionate kisses stolen throughout the day. She couldn't imagine what it was going to be like not seeing him several times a day. He had become such a familiar and welcome presence in her daily life that his absence would leave huge, gaping empty spaces.

Abruptly it occurred to her that her newly remodeled house was going to be gorgeous and wonderful. And very, very quiet. And lonely, without all the people she was accustomed to seeing every day.

"Joe, when you start the Henderson job…when will we see each other?" Eyes filled with concern and alarm, she peered at him. He'd become so much a part of her life that she couldn't imagine a day without him.

"What do you mean?"

"Well, you'll be on the new site every day, and most weekends you'll be in Denver with the Hendersons, picking out things for their house, like we've been doing."

He gave her a sheepish smile and lowered his coffee cup. "Honey, I'm about to make a confession. You're the first client I've accompanied to Denver. Usually I give the client a list of places where I receive a contractor's discount, and they go by themselves, then tell me what they picked out, and I order it by phone."

Molly stared at him, then burst into laughter. "I'm deeply flattered." And his confession told her a lot about his feelings. "But you know what? I'm grateful that you came with me, because I loved the time with you, and because I didn't know anything about most of this stuff. Your ideas and guidance were invaluable."

He rolled his eyes and grinned. "I don't think you took my advice even one single time."

"Maybe not," she admitted cheerfully. "But thanks to you, I made informed decisions. Actually, it's a bit of a shame that you don't go on these excursions with all your clients. I think it would be equally as helpful to them as it was for me."

He nodded, his expression turning serious. "Actually,

you're probably right. But think about it, honey. I can't go during the week, because that would mean leaving the site unsupervised. And I'm not wild about giving up my weekends for work, unless the client is you. If I ever get that secretary I need to hire someday, one of her duties will be to take the person making the decisions around to the fixture places and the kitchen showrooms and, and, and... She could do it during the week.''

''That's a good idea,'' Molly said thoughtfully. ''If she knew what she was doing, it would be a fun job.''

''You're kidding!''

''Come on, admit it,'' she said, blowing him a kiss across the desk. ''It really was fun. And it would be more fun if the choices weren't so important, if it was someone else picking out things for *their* house. I'll bet shopping with the client will turn out to be your someday-secretary's favorite part of the job.''

''If you say so, honey. But unless you're the client, it's never going to be *my* idea of fun to follow some woman around, hoping she'll make up her mind in my lifetime.'' He laughed. ''And praying that she'll stay within her budget.''

After Joe went back to work, Molly thought about the conversation and fell into a dreamy fantasy state. In her daydream, she and Joe worked together, Joe on the construction end of things, Molly on the decorative side. She could imagine herself escorting a client to Hardbaugh's and sharing her own hard-won knowledge, helping the client unravel the mysteries of faucets and fixtures. Could see herself guiding clients through the maze of tile and carpet choices. Actually, she thought she might be good at such a job and enjoy it enormously.

She was still playing with the idea that weekend when Joe picked her up. But Saturday passed so quickly that she didn't find a chance to talk about it again. ''Better hurry,'' she called to Joe, poking her head in his office door. ''Did you forget? We're meeting Jim and Avis for dinner at Ma and Pa's Café tonight. In about thirty minutes.''

Joe leaned back from his computer and stretched. "Damn. I was planning on steaks on the grill and an evening in. Maybe we could ask for a rain check?" he suggested hopefully.

"Nope. When Avis called, she hinted there was something they wanted to tell us." Molly sat on his lap and wrapped her arms around his neck.

"Gee, I wonder what that could be," Joe said, laughing. He kissed her on the nose, then nibbled her ear.

"According to Wanda at the drugstore, two of the electricians and Bonnie at the Goosed Moose, Jim bought a ring in Longmont and planned to propose last night." She pressed her face against his neck, inhaling the good male scent of his skin.

"I have it direct from the mayor, Toots Romaine and Bernie Schadler, that Jim planned to take Avis to dinner at the Chateau in Boulder and pop the question over dessert." His hands roamed teasingly from her waist to her breasts.

Molly slipped her hands inside his flannel shirt. "Good grief. Does anyone in Vrain ever keep a secret?"

"Not a chance." He kissed her on the mouth, then looked deeply into her eyes with a smile. "You haven't told anyone any secrets, have you?"

"No." She hadn't told a soul how much she loved him. "Much as I'd like to stay here and keep doing what we're doing, we need to get a move on." Sliding off his lap, she pulled him to his feet, then leaned against him, pressing her cheek against his chest. In Joe's arms, she felt safe and secure and happy.

But loving him with all her heart was still her secret.

Chapter Ten

Ma and Pa's Café reminded Molly of an old-fashioned diner. The decor was bright and slightly deco, and the menu was brief and simple, a collection of favorite old standbys enlivened by a daily special. As this was where locals came to grab a cup of great coffee and a slice of homemade pie or a quick good meal, or to catch up on the current gossip, a steady stream of people moved past the booth where the four of them sat.

Everyone stopped to congratulate Jim and a beaming Avis and to ooh and ah over Avis's new engagement ring. They winked and said things like "Now you raise him up right, Avis." Or "Like Ben Franklin said, older women are grateful if you treat 'em right, so you treat 'er right, Jim." But it was all in good fun, and clearly everyone was happy to have an upcoming wedding to celebrate. Things had changed between Jim and Avis to the extent that age-related teasing didn't dent their happiness and obvious delight in each other.

Molly smiled until her cheeks ached and talked to everyone who stopped by their table, and she must have wished Jim and Avis a happy future a dozen times. She tried to resist the impulse to hide her own left hand when people automatically looked from Avis's hand to hers.

It was an odd, bittersweet evening. She was genuinely happy for Jim and Avis, but sharing their engagement made her acutely aware that she was twenty-eight and still alone. Throughout the evening, she found herself sliding speculative peeks at Joe, wondering where their relationship was going, and trying to imagine how she would have felt if they'd been celebrating a ring on her finger tonight.

As Jim and Avis chattered away about their plans and dreams for the future, Molly's mind drifted. Tonight it seemed as if everyone had exciting impending plans except her. She couldn't see her own future past the end of the remodel project. Joe and the pooches would eagerly move on to the Henderson project, and after their departure her house would settle into a deep quiet. With no distractions, she would finish the book, please God. But then what? How would she fill her days? What would she do with herself?

Everyone she knew was moving on with their lives. But her future was shrouded in fog that she couldn't penetrate. The remodel project had diverted her for several months, but it was almost finished, and she was moving closer to the question that had brought her to Vrain. What was she going to do with the rest of her life? In her heart, she knew the answer depended on Joe.

"Molly?"

She emerged from an unsettling reverie with a start, surprised to see that Avis was standing at the diner's counter, showing her ring to Ma Callahan, and Joe had slid into a booth next to Mr. Henderson, at the far end of the café. He was talking and drawing something on a napkin.

She blinked at Jim. "I'm sorry. I was daydreaming."

"I want to apologize for the things I said to you that day in the basement." A rush of color warmed his cheeks. "I was out of line, and I said things I regret. I think I was jealous that Joe had found you and I'd lost Avis. Anyway, I was rude, and I guess I sounded like I didn't like you. That isn't true, Molly." He lifted his head and looked into her eyes. "I owe you a lot. I really appreciate how you've helped Avis deal with the age issue. She told me how you helped her think it through and decide that the difference in our ages didn't matter."

"You and Avis are great together."

"So are you and Joe," he said. "Joe loves you, Molly."

"I…" She stopped and bit her tongue. "I'm glad." Jim was so obviously biting his tongue, too, that she laughed and reached across the table to pat his hand. "I'm going to try like hell not to break his heart, okay?" Jim grinned at her, relief in his eyes. "Tell Joe to try like hell not to break mine."

"Count on it," he said softly as Joe and Avis returned to the table.

"Count on what?" Joe asked, sliding in beside Molly. He smiled into her eyes and draped a possessive arm around her shoulders.

She wished he would tell her that he loved her. Or was he waiting for her to say the words first? "Count on it that this place has the best mud pie in town," she said lightly.

"Mud!" Avis groaned. "I'm so sick of mud. Is it ever going to dry out?"

"Did you hear that Toots Romaine was missing for three days?" Joe asked, a wicked twinkle in his eyes. "His dozer sank in the mud and just kept sinking until Toots and the dozer disappeared. By the time Daddy and Gene found him and dug him out, two of Toots's ex-wives had maimed each other and the third wife was fighting with his current wife and it was all about who got to be the chief mourner at his funeral."

"You made that up," Molly accused, laughing as the mud jokes began.

She didn't notice that she was stroking her empty ring finger instead of the tiny scar above her lip as she usually did.

USUALLY Joe didn't have difficulty falling asleep. But tonight, he folded his arms behind his head and stared up at the dark ceiling, listening to Molly's even breathing.

She had become such a large part of his life. He didn't sleep as well during the week when she wasn't with him. A burger at the Goosed Moose no longer felt like a real meal. A real meal was sitting down to something he and Molly had prepared together. And they were slowly blending their lives. She kept an extra bathrobe at his place. He kept a toilet kit at her place. She had started buying dog food for Aspen and keeping it at her house. He had started keeping her favorite snacks at his house. They did laundry together, shopped for groceries together. Their lives were blending, and that was what he wanted. The only way he could have been happier was if he came home to her every night, instead of just on the weekends.

Molly murmured in her sleep and snuggled closer to him. Smiling, he dropped an arm around her and gently kissed the top of her bright head. Neither of them had mentioned the word *love*. But he knew he loved her. And he was beginning to believe that she loved him, too.

Holding her close, staring at the ceiling, he thought about Jim and Avis and how they had worked out their problems. He and Molly had a few differences, too, but they could work them out, just as Jim and Avis had.

If he slipped a ring on Molly's finger, then he'd stop worrying about her leaving Vrain and him. And he would be the happiest man alive.

His chest swelled with love for her, and he wanted to wake her up and tell her that he loved her and couldn't imagine a life without her. He wanted to ask her right now if she would marry him, beg her if he had to. He'd never wanted anything as deeply as he wanted Molly to be his wife and share her life with him.

He had turned toward her on the pillow before he stopped himself. No, a man with any sense didn't wake his beloved out of a sound sleep to talk about something as serious as forever. He had to give this some thought. He had to do it right. He had to make sure she said yes.

MOLLY LOOKED UP from her desk and sucked in a breath. One of the painters—Bill, she thought his name was—stood at the bottom of the stairs. His face was cherry red, his chest was puffed out, and he looked as if he were about to explode. Uneasy, she rose behind her desk.

"Yes?"

"I don't have to put up with this, and by God I *won't* put up with this! It's not my job to make the damn drywallers look good! If they would do their job like they are supposed to, *my* job would be a lot easier! A man has to draw the line somewhere, and I have had it!" Hauling back his arm, he hurled a paint rag to the floor.

"Ah, Bill?" His face was now a dark plum color, and she was worried that he was going to have a heart attack right in front of her. "What are you talking about?"

"The boogers, that's what I'm talking about!"

"Boogers?" Molly frowned. "What is a booger?"

He threw out his hands and craned his head to look at the new basement walls. "There! See that drip of texture? That's a booger."

Molly walked to the wall and inspected the little dots of texture. Using her fingernail, she scraped one off. "They come off pretty easily."

"That isn't the point!" Crimson pulsed along the veins bulging in his temple. "It's not my job to flick boogers! The drywallers are supposed to do it. *That's* the point! But if I don't clean up all the boogers, then you'll have guests, and sure as hell, they'll be standing next to a wall and they'll flick off a booger and it won't be painted behind it. It's always the painter who gets blamed for that!"

"Bill? Why don't you sit down a minute and take a couple of deep breaths? I'll find Joe."

Backing out of the room, she whirled and ran up the stairs, calling Joe's name. When she found him, she gripped his arm and drew a breath herself.

"Listen the painter is having a meltdown in my office. He's on a tangent about, about—" She couldn't help it. Suddenly, it struck her as hysterically funny that a grown man was furious over who was supposed to flick paint boogers off the wall. A giggle bubbled up from her chest. "About—" A guffaw doubled her over. Laughing hysterically and holding her side, she shouted the last word. "Boogers!"

"Boogers?" It wasn't funny to Joe. He walked over to a wall and leaned close. Then he checked another wall before he scowled and headed for the basement steps.

Molly followed him downstairs, fighting to compose herself.

"You got a problem with flicking a few boogers?" Joe demanded, walking up to Bill.

Bill jumped to his feet. He stood four inches taller than Joe, and he was red-faced angry. But Joe didn't step back.

"I don't mind flicking boogers if there's only a few of them. But that's not the case here, damn it. The texture guys did a poor job. So you get them back in here to flick those boogers, because I'm not going to do it!"

"The texture crew came out of Longmont, and I'm sure as hell not to going to pay travel time and overtime for them to come back here, when you can flick as you go." Joe's lip pulled back from his teeth. "All painters flick boogers. What are you trying to pull?"

"I'm sick of those texture cretins taking advantage of me." His face flushed a deeper scarlet, and the spit flew from his lips. "If you don't want to call them back, then put your crew on it."

Joe leaned up and forward, his nose inches from Bill's. "I'm not pulling my pooches off their job to do your job!"

"It's not my job!"

It was Molly who exploded. Two grown men were standing in front of her screaming at each other about whose job it was to flick boogers. It was so bizarre, so crazy, that she fell over her desktop gasping in hysterical laughter.

Joe and Bill stopped shouting and stared at her.

"That's it," Bill yelled. "I quit!"

"You can't walk off the job!" Joe shouted. "You're under contract!"

"Call my boss and tell him to send someone else out here, but it won't be me!" Bill stormed up the stairs, Joe right behind him.

By the time Molly got hold of herself and wiped the tears of helpless laughter out of her eyes, she heard more yelling upstairs, then the sound of slamming doors. Twenty minutes later, Joe stamped downstairs and pulled her desk phone in front of him, and another shouted booger discussion ensued with Bill's boss. At the end of it, Joe slammed down the telephone and threw himself in the chair across from Molly. His throat was as angry red as Bill's had been. "Wes says he stands behind his painters."

"So what do we do now?"

Joe stood up, putting his hands on his hips. "Right now, I'm going to the Goosed Moose to have a few beers and cool off. I'm not good company tonight, honey. So I'll see you tomorrow."

He gave her a distracted kiss and bounded up the stairs. In a minute, she heard the door bang shut upstairs and the house was suddenly quiet.

It took her a few minutes to grasp what had occurred and, more important, what was going to happen. Tomorrow a new crew of painters would appear, and they were going to paint over the boogers. And as sure as sunrise, everyone who visited her house would find the little dried drips irresistible, and they would flick at them and reveal an unpainted dot underneath.

Concerned, Molly walked through the house, inspecting all the walls for boogers. Bill was right. There were a lot. Frowning, she considered the problem. Everyone was gone for the day. The painters would arrive at seven in the morning—to paint over the boogers. Unless someone flicked them off between now and then.

"And guess who that someone has to be?" she said aloud, making a face.

She started scraping boogers in the basement and worked her way upward. At eight o'clock, all the breakers blew, and nothing she did restored the power. But she didn't let a lack of electricity stop her. Holding a flashlight between her chin and her chest, she kept after the boogers until two in the morning. She didn't get them all, but she got them as high as she could reach.

Someday, she thought as she stomped upstairs to fall into bed, the great booger fight would seem funny again. But right now she was amazed that it had turned out that flicking boogers was her job. Who would have guessed?

Before she fell asleep, she burst into helpless laughter. Since Joe whirled into her life like a tornado, every day had been exciting and interesting.

How would she bear it when he took his pooches and moved on?

To her surprise, she found herself unable to go to sleep, because she was thinking about the Henderson job. Wanting to be part of it, as she wanted to be part of everything in Joe's life.

"RISE AND SHINE, honey." Joe sat on the edge of her bed and waved a coffee cup under her nose. Aspen jumped up beside her legs and thumped his tail on the bedspread.

Molly opened one eye to look at them. "Is it morning already?" Then she sat bolt upright, so abruptly that she almost knocked the coffee cup out of his hand. "What happened to your face?" A purplish bruise spread over one cheek, his chin was scraped, and he had a black eye.

A sheepish grin curved his lips. "Remember when I left here last night? I was going to the Goosed Moose? Well, me and a few pooches ran into Bill and a few painters."

"You got into a fight?" She accepted the cup of coffee and tasted it, not taking her eyes off his.

"More like a brawl, I guess you could say." He laughed. "Before Matt Anderson broke it up, I think everyone at the Goosed Moose had chosen sides and was getting a few licks in."

"Joe, that's terrible!"

"Naw, honey, it was great." His eyes danced and twinkled and flashed as if he were telling her about a wonderful vacation. "Cleared the air. Bill's coming back on the job, and the painters agreed to flick the boogers." He lifted an eyebrow. "Except all the boogers below model height are already flicked. I don't suppose you know anything about that?"

She kept staring at his bruised face. "The elves must have come in the night, done the job, and vanished with the dawn."

He raised his cup of scalding coffee in a toast. "If you see those elves again, thank them, but tell them it wasn't necessary. Your contractor is always on the job, and he took care of the problem."

"Do the other pooches look as bruised and battered as you do?"

His laugh made her smile. "Everybody got a little dented." After glancing at his watch, he leaned forward and kissed her soundly, then stood. "Better get a move on, honey. We're taking all the doors off today to stain them. That includes all the bathroom doors, so if you want privacy while you're in the shower, you'd better be finished in the next twenty minutes."

She blinked. "How long will be the doors be off?"

"A couple of days."

"Days?"

"The prep work will finish today, and the painters will shoot tomorrow. You're coming to stay with me, remember? All you have to do is get through today without bathroom doors."

Molly thought about that after Joe bounded off. She leaned down to scratch behind Aspen's ears, and smiled when the dog sighed with bliss. She was going to miss seeing Aspen every day, too. Then she glanced at the clock, finished her coffee and jumped out of bed to use the shower while she still had a door to close.

But after she was dressed, she didn't hurry down to her office. She lingered upstairs, pretending to enjoy the view out of her new windows, while pooches and painters arrived. And she tried not to laugh or gasp in dismay when she saw the black eyes and bruised faces. To her astonishment, everyone was in an exceptionally cheerful mood.

Pooches and painters greeted each other like the best of buddies.

Shaking her head and deciding that men were alien creatures, Molly went downstairs to labor in the word jungle. After reading what she had written last week, she sighed heavily, and decided that happy lives were boring lives.

"No one is going to want to read this book," she said morosely when Ellen O'Ryan and Avis dropped by to ask if she wanted to go with them to Boulder to shop.

"Aren't you being a little hard on yourself?" Ellen asked, sympathetically.

"I don't think so," Molly said, after pouring coffee for everyone. She sat down at her desk and waved a hand at her computer. "I hate doing this. Every word is a chore. And I don't know what to say or the best way to say it."

"What you need is a day off," Avis said firmly.

"I'm so far behind, I can't possibly take a day off."

"If you're that far behind, what would another day matter?" Ellen asked. "Come with us. We're going to look at bridal gowns, and we'd love to have your advice. We'll have fun."

"Thanks for including me, but I'd better take a rain check. I've *got* to make some progress on this lousy book." And looking at bridal gowns with two prospective brides didn't really appeal to her, but she didn't tell them that. She also didn't tell them that when she looked at them, what she saw was their diamond rings. She didn't tell them, because she didn't understand her own confusing feelings. "Excuse me a sec," she said when the phone rang.

"Molly? It's Addie Madson."

"Addie? How nice to hear from you."

Avis and Ellen gazed into their coffee cups, smiled and tried to look as if they were not listening to Molly's conversation, even though she was sitting across the desk, not three feet away from them.

"I have great news!" Excitement bubbled in Addie's voice, and she wasn't the type to get excited very often.

"Wonderful. I can always use some great news. What is it?"

"Remember when we sent out the test shots?"

Molly frowned. "To be honest, I'd forgotten all about the test shots. Things have been hectic here, and there's the book…"

"Molly, I've received fantastic response. Offers are pouring in."

She sat up straight and blinked. "You're kidding! Offers from whom?"

Addie laughed. "Chanel in Paris would like to sign you exclusively as a walking advertisement. And you'll love this, absolutely love it. They'd like you to live and play in Europe and wear their designs all year around." Molly heard papers rustling at Addie's end of the phone. "We also have a *very* lucrative offer from Couture Cosmetics, who want a single Couture Femme to put in direct competition against the new Apple Girl. They love the idea of you being the Couture Femme, and they're already kicking around publicity concepts that will make mincemeat out of Apple for firing you. And there's another interesting offer from…"

Dazed, Molly listened as Addie detailed one plum opportunity after another, each one a dream offer. She couldn't believe what she was hearing. "But why?" she whispered, her fingertips moving over her upper lip. "Addie, you saw those photos. The scars show up in the black and whites. Even corrective makeup can't hide them."

"Honey, Couture Cosmetics intends to capitalize on those scars. They're talking about a campaign based around someone the public can identify with. Slogans like 'You don't have to be flawless to be beautiful.' 'Our makeup doesn't hide your individuality.' And so on. Can't you see it? Couture is going to make the new Apple Girl look so damned bland and inaccessible by comparison. They are going to tout you as Everywoman. Don't strive to be perfect, strive to be the perfect you! It's brilliant!"

"My God," Molly whispered, releasing a breath she

hadn't realized she had been holding. "Maybe I'm not a has-been after all."

"A has-been?" A burst of excited laughter erupted in her ear. "Hardly! The top accounts are begging for you. All it took was a little hype, a few suggestions, and the photos to show them that whatever they'd heard about you was wrong. Molly, you can pick and choose. You can write your own ticket. Honey, you're back! And you're back on top!"

"Addie, I don't know what to say." Tears sparkled in her eyes, and she dashed them away with the back of her hand. "How can I ever thank you?"

Addie's laughter sang in her ears. "By getting on a plane and coming to New York immediately. We need to sit down and go over these offers, talk about what you want and what's best for your career. When can you get here?"

Suddenly, Molly heard pooches voices calling all over the house, heard music blaring somewhere upstairs. Jim was working in the bathroom behind her, the electricians were installing the foyer lights today. Deliverymen tramped around upstairs, carrying in the wood that would become the floor in her kitchen and foyer.

"Wait." Shuffling through the papers on her desk, she found her calendar and pulled it toward her. "I can't possibly leave until the house is finished. The major decisions are made, but there are little things that come up every day. Let's see." She stared at the calendar, thought a minute. "Addie, can you put everyone on hold for two weeks? Everything's moving fast now. The house should be finished in about two weeks."

"We'd have done that anyway," Addie said promptly. "We don't want anyone to think we're too eager. But we do need to go over these offers in detail. If you're absolutely certain that you can't get here sooner, we'll try to do some of this by phone."

"That's great. Look, I need some time to digest this wonderful news. Let me think about everything we've discussed, and I'll call you in three or four days. Could you

FedEx summaries of the deals you think are the most interesting? We'll discuss them next week.''

''Excellent. I'll put something together today and send it out to you tomorrow.''

''Oh, wait. I won't be here tomorrow. Let me give you the address where I'll be staying.'' Drawing a deep breath, she gave Addie Joe's address then hung up the telephone, a dazed look on her face.

Joe. How was she going to tell Joe about this?

Avis and Ellen both cleared their throats and glanced at each other self-consciously. They stood at the same time. ''I guess you won't be coming shopping with us,'' Avis said. ''There's the book, and you have a lot to think about.''

''We couldn't help overhearing,'' Ellen said apologetically. ''Congratulations.''

She heard Joe at the top of the stairs, instructing a set of deliverymen to put the rolls of carpet in the recently completed garage until the carpet layer was ready for them.

Joe.

Her heart rolled in her chest as she stood and tried to focus on Avis and Ellen. ''I'm sorry,'' she said, spreading her hands and giving them both a smile of regret. ''Thanks for being understanding. Perhaps we can go shopping another time.'' She heard Joe coming down the stairs, his step distinctive from all the other steps that ran up and down the basement stairs all day.

''Hi, honeys,'' he said, appearing at the bottom of the stairs. ''I thought I smelled a whiff of orange blossoms coming from down here.'' A grin widened his lips. ''Here come the brides.''

''And here go the brides,'' Avis said, stepping past him. She didn't meet his eyes.

''Hi, Joe. Bye, Joe.'' Ellen hurried past, too. She didn't meet Joe's eyes either.

He didn't seem to notice. The minute Avis and Ellen disappeared up the staircase, Joe strode forward, took Molly in his arms and kissed her, passionately, deeply. A kiss so emotionally intense that Molly felt stunned when he released her.

"What was that about?" she whispered, staring at him. It was the first time he had kissed her when pooches were close enough to catch them.

"Come outside with me," he said, opening the slider onto the back patio. Bowing, making a flourish with his hand, he smiled at her. He was so handsome, so filled with happiness and good cheer, so bursting with something he wanted to tell her.

Molly stepped past him into the warm sunshine flooding the patio. She lifted a puzzled eyebrow. "What's happened?" The rocks that had fallen on the patio were long gone, so that wasn't it. "Did the Romaines cut their bill in half? Bill hasn't found any boogers? You won the lottery?"

"I decided I can't wait another day, not another minute. I want to do this now, but suddenly I don't know how."

"Do what?" she asked, frowning.

He laughed and pushed a hand through the dark curls falling forward on his forehead. "I would have sworn there wasn't a shy bone in my body."

"I would agree with that," Molly said, smiling. God, she loved the look of him, even with his black eye and bruised cheek. His low-slung jeans, the tool belt hanging off his hips. She even liked his flannel shirts, and especially the tanned arrow of skin at his opened collar. He was so energetic, so full of life and zest, so handsome, that he took her breath away.

"Okay," he said, regarding her with blue, blue eyes that sparkled and flashed with amusement at himself, and heat when he looked at her. "I got to thinking about Avis and Ellen coming by, and wondered if you were blinded by diamond rings." Taking her left hand, he raised it to his chest, his fingers stroking her ring finger.

"Joe?" She tried to read the mixture of tenderness and passion in his eyes. "What's...?"

But suddenly she knew. Impulsively she lifted her other

hand to cover his lips, but he caught it and brought that hand too to his chest.

"Molly," he said softly, raising his gaze from her mouth to her eyes. "I love you. I planned to tell you over candle-light and wine tonight. But I don't want to wait. I want to tell you now. Right now. I love you. I've probably loved you since the eighth grade," he admitted with a low chuckle. "I know I never forgot you. All these years, you have been here." He pressed her hands against his heart. "Now fate has brought you to Vrain and to me, and I don't want to ever let you go again."

"Oh, Joe."

"Molly? Can I hope that you care about me too?"

"You wonderful idiot! I love you, too." It was the truth. She loved him more every day. "But, Joe—"

"Oh, my God!" He pulled her into his arms in a fierce embrace. "You've made me the happiest man on earth!" He held her so tightly that she thought her bones would crack before he released her. "Honey, my brain is working in overdrive, thinking about our future. That's why I wanted to tell you here, on the site." He covered her face with kisses. "We could be so great together! I've been thinking about what you said."

"What I said?" Her mind was whirling. She had to tell him about Addie's phone call.

"About someone going with the clients to help them select all the items for their house, and how you thought that would be a fun job." Throwing back his head, he laughed, happiness bubbling up from his chest. "That could be your job. What do you think? You and me together, partners. I'll handle the on-site work, and you handle the off-site work. I've seen what great taste you have. You'd be a natural. Best of all, we'd work the business together. And, honey, this is something you could do even after the babies start to come."

"You're way ahead of me," she said weakly, over-whelmed by his happiness.

He took her by the shoulders and grinned down at her.

"I guess I missed the part about us getting married and living happily ever after, huh? The part about a diamond ring for you, too." He kissed her exuberantly, then lifted her and swung her in a circle. "Honey, my mind is going a mile a minute. We have so much to talk about! I'd love to send everyone home right now and cancel my appointment with Frank Henderson tonight."

"We've got—"

"I know," he said, cutting off her words with a kiss. "We've got the rest of our lives to talk." He pulled her into his arms. "I love you. Tell me again that you love me."

"I love you," she murmured against his shoulder, glad that he couldn't see the sudden confusion filling her eyes.

"Look, here's what we'll do. The painters are masking off now, so there's no doubt they'll shoot tomorrow. You pack a bag and drive over to my place. Build a fire and put on something sexy." He kissed her again. "And plan to stay up all night making love and talking about the future. Tonight is very special for us."

Coke stuck his head out of the sliding doors. "Hey, boss? The carpet's unloaded in the garage. The delivery guys want you to sign off the paperwork." He smiled at Molly. "I've got a date with Margie on Saturday. Things are working out."

"I'm glad," she said, looking at the cut on his chin and the bandage across his knuckles. Right now, she didn't want to think about Coke's love life. Her own had just gotten amazingly complicated.

"Tell them I'm coming right upstairs," Joe said. He ran the back of his hand down Molly's cheek. "Things are working out with me and my girl, too," he said gruffly. "Henderson's going to get short shrift tonight. I think I'll dash into the Goosed Moose, tell him we'll have to talk some other time, then run home to you." Tenderness softened his gaze. "I want to spend the rest of my life coming home to you. I like the sound of that."

Molly stayed on the patio after Joe left, looking at the

far mountain peaks and the snow that still capped them. A multitude of conflicting emotions warred in her chest, and what should have been one of the happiest days in her life became one of the most confusing.

In the span of an hour, she had gone from having no discernible future to having two possible futures, each wonderful, each something she wanted with all her heart. And each incompatible with the other.

Frowning, she leaned against the post that supported the upper deck running along the back of the house.

Joe loved her, and she loved him. Somehow they would work this out.

He was right. They had a lot to talk about.

Chapter Eleven

Molly had been charmed by Joe's cabin from the first time she stepped inside, but back then, the log cabin had undeniably been a bachelor's residence. Now the spare, male aspects had softened. One of her sweaters hung on the pegs beside the door, her mud boots sat in a line with his. She kept a second set of cosmetics in his bathroom. Over the weeks, she had added a vase of silk flowers to his mantel, and scented candles. She had purchased new towels and a throw rug for the loft. A stack of her books waited on the floor beside the sofa, where she had left them a few days ago. Joe had subscribed to the Sunday *New York Times* so that she could have the puzzle, and he'd stocked the fridge with her favorite snacks and foods.

Already their lives had started to merge.

But there were so many questions. Pausing in the middle of making a salad, Molly gazed out the window above the sink. The most important question on her mind right now was how to tell Joe about Addie's call. And what would his reaction be?

All afternoon she'd been thinking about the offer from Chanel—she didn't see how she could even consider that opportunity, as running around Europe wouldn't mesh with her and Joe—and the offer from Couture Cosmetics. Couture's offer was the one that made her heart beat a little faster. The campaign Couture had outlined to Addie was an exciting new concept, and Molly could visualize the buzz it would cause in the industry. The concept was so innovative and so good that she knew Couture would pursue it with or without Molly Stevens. Whoever they chose as their representative of perfect imperfection, that model would be assured of top dollar, and she would find herself at the very pinnacle of the modeling profession. She would make history. There would be television and talk-show exposure, a chance to promote the idea that a lived-in face could be beautiful. There would be endorsements. The sky was the limit.

Dazzled by the prospects, the possibilities, the opportunities, Molly lost herself in daydreams, rousing herself only when she heard the chime of Joe's mantel clock. With a guilty start, she glanced at the dial, then frowned.

She'd expected Joe to arrive at least forty-five minutes ago.

Concerned, she went to the front windows and breathed a sigh of relief when she saw his headlights coming down the drive. Quickly she checked her appearance in the mirror, smoothing down the filmy folds of a silk robe that covered an emerald silk nightgown that she hoped was as sexy as Joe had fantasized for tonight. She, too, wanted tonight to be wonderful and special. In fact, she hadn't decided yet whether she would mention Addie's call tonight or wait until tomorrow.

He didn't come inside immediately, and that surprised her. And it surprised her again that he didn't kiss her when he finally did walk through the door. To hide a moment of awkwardness, she bent to let Aspen lick her face and smiled at his enthusiastic welcome.

"At least someone is glad to see me," she said lightly, standing and smiling at Joe. When she saw his expression, her smile faded, and she suddenly felt very uncomfortable wearing a negligee and silk robe. At once she understood that everything had changed.

He looked at her for a long moment, then hung his cap and jacket on the wall pegs. "You might have told me about your agent's call before you let me make a fool of myself.'' Striding past her, he went into the kitchen, glanced at her half-made salad, then took a beer out of the refrigerator and pulled the tab.

"You heard,'' Molly said, sliding onto a stool before the kitchen counter. Damn small towns, anyway. They might have let her tell him in her own way.

"Oh, yeah. I heard,'' he said grimly. Tilting his head back, he took another long swallow of beer, then stared at her. "At first I didn't believe it. I thought it was a joke the guys at the Goosed Moose had cooked up. I couldn't get it through my head that everyone in town except me knew that you'd been offered a fabulous new contract and were leaving for Manhattan in two weeks.''

Molly dropped her head and closed her eyes. "Good Lord. What did Avis and Ellen do? Get on the phone and call everyone they know?''

"What on earth were you thinking when I was going on and on about how we could work together? Were you too embarrassed for me to say anything?'' He crushed the beer can and flung it at the trash receptacle, then raked a hand through his hair. "How did you keep from bursting out laughing when I was talking about you taking my clients shopping in Denver? God, what an idiot I am. To think for even a minute that someone like you would be satisfied hauling clients around to look at faucets and toilets! I must have lost my mind.''

"Joe, please.'' She gazed at him, a plea in her eyes. "Don't do this.''

"Don't do what? Don't feel like an idiot? Don't feel embarrassed about forgetting who you are? And who I am?'' Leaning a hip against the kitchen counter, he folded his arms over his chest. "Why didn't you tell me immediately, instead of letting me run off at the mouth?''

Standing, Molly came around the counter and stood in front of him. "I wanted to tell you about Addie's call immediately, but you kept cutting me off.''

"Yeah," he said, staring at her. "I was trying to propose."

She drew a breath and tried again. "Then the moment passed and it wasn't the right time. I thought we could sit down tonight and talk. I'm sorry you heard about my private business at the Goosed Moose. That wasn't fair, and I apologize. If I'd remembered how fast news travels in this town, if I'd recalled that no one respects privacy, I'd have asked to speak to you alone before the workday ended."

He studied her expression. "There's no point getting angry about gossip, honey. That's how it is. But you're right. You should have remembered."

"I should have remembered?" Anger crept into her voice. "This is our private business, not the town's." But it had hurt him to learn her news from others, instead of her. He'd been embarrassed at the Goosed Moose. She touched his arm, feeling his tense muscles, trying to control her irritation. "Look, I'm sorry I didn't tell you myself."

"I'm sorry, too. We would have gotten through this easier if I hadn't made that stupid speech on your back patio."

Molly jerked her hand back as if his touch scalded her. "Telling me that you loved me was stupid? You regret talking about love and marriage and...and babies?"

He stared into her eyes, keeping his gaze well above the plunging neckline of her negligee. "If I'd kept my mouth shut, I might have come out of this with some pride." He stepped around her and walked to the sliders that opened to the balcony, staring outside. "Damn it. I always knew you'd leave. I knew you weren't small-town material. What the hell was I thinking of?"

Molly stood in the kitchen, watching the muscles swell along his shoulders and back. Anger heated her skin. "Is your pride the only thing that matters? Have you asked yourself what Addie's call meant to me? Have you tried, even for a few minutes, to look at this from my point of view?"

"I know your point of view," he snapped, not looking at her. "You believed you were washed up, a has-been.

That thought eroded your confidence, left you floundering. Now you have a chance to climb back on top.''

"Yes," she said, her voice as sharp as his.

"Remodeling your grandparents' place started merely as something to occupy your thoughts, something to do while you were waiting to get your head together. The project grew as you became more interested in it, and gradually you started thinking of the place as a home, not just a project. How am I doing so far?" he asked, turning to look at her across the room, his face tight and his eyes narrowed.

"You're right on target." Her cheeks felt hot, and she flattened her palms on the countertop so that he wouldn't see the trembling in her fingers. "Maybe you do understand."

He nodded. "Damned right I do. I think you tried, honey. I think you made an effort to meet people, make some friends. I think you really tried to see yourself living in Vrain, maybe with me." His gaze held hers. "What you and I both lost sight of is that there's nothing here for you."

"Damn it, that's not true, Joe."

"Isn't it?" A challenge lifted his chin. "Then why didn't you tell Addie no? Or even that you needed to think about those fabulous offers? But that isn't what happened, is it? You pulled out your calendar and said you'd be in Manhattan on such and such a date to choose the best of the bunch." He stared at her. "You didn't need to think it over. In less than five minutes, you'd made your decision. You'd decided it was bye-bye Vrain, hello New York City." He shoved a hand through his hair and shook his head. "Then I came running downstairs, talking about love and working together and..." Swearing softly, he turned back to look out of the balcony windows. "I wish I'd kept my mouth shut."

"Are you finished?" Molly asked angrily. "Because, if you are, I have a few things to say."

He finally turned around, facing her with his swollen eye, bruised cheek and scraped chin. And a glare. "Go ahead. Say your piece."

"I'm sorry you heard about all this at the Goosed Moose. But you've made up your mind about a lot of things that aren't true, and I'm angry about that. I wish you'd waited until we'd had a chance to talk before you decided you were a fool to say you loved me." Her eyes flashed. "I haven't made any decisions, except to sit down with my agent and discuss some very good business offers. I owe Addie that, and I owe it to myself to at least look at the offers. I thought you and I would sit down and calmly discuss how these opportunities might affect our future. I thought we'd explore the possibilities and perhaps reach a decision together."

"Go on," he said when she stopped abruptly.

Her chin rose. "All right, I will. You seem to be looking at this situation solely from the viewpoint of your pride. Your pride can handle a declaration of love to someone who's washed up, as you put it. But your pride apparently can't handle mentioning love to someone with a lucrative offer on the table. Why is that, Joe? Didn't you tell me that you could care less how much money I made?"

"Come on, Molly. This isn't about money, it never has been. This is about your leaving." He strode toward her, stopping at the countertop, keeping it between them. "Vrain never had anything to offer you. I was stupid to think it did. Stupid to think that maybe I had something to offer you."

She hated this, absolutely hated it that they were shouting at each other and letting things get so twisted around. "So that's it? We're finished? I'm leaving and you're stupid, and there's nothing else to talk about?"

His eyes were hard. "I'd say that about covers it."

"What happened to you loving me and me loving you?" Molly shouted. Unable to stand in one spot, she paced up and down along the counter. "People who love each other try to find ways to work out their problems!"

"People who love each other don't live in separate states!"

"All right, let's talk about this." Spinning in a swirl of

silk, she stared at him. "Suppose for a minute, just one minute, that I take one of the job offers. Could we at least discuss the possibility of you moving to New York with me?"

He covered his face with a hand. "Déjà vu. I knew this is what would happen."

"What?"

He let a silence develop before he answered. "Molly, I don't live here because I'm running away or because I'm whiling away the time waiting for something better to come along. I live in Vrain by choice. I've made a life here, and this is where I want to be. I have good friends, and a successful business. I like being able to walk a few steps from my back door and drop a fishing line in the creek. I like breathing clean, fresh air." He spread his hands. "I'd be miserable living in Manhattan. What would I do there? How would I make a living?"

She couldn't stand the way this was going. Hot tears clogged her throat. "You could take your time making that decision. The truth is, you wouldn't have to support us. Couture Cosmetics is offering—"

He threw up a hand. "Don't even tell me. I'm right on the edge of taking that comment as an insult. But there's something you need to understand, and I don't want you to forget it. I don't care if you make a billion dollars a year. If that happens, great. Good for you. But the day I let a woman support me, that's the day hell freezes over! It's never going to happen."

"Joe—"

He touched the tool belt still hanging around his hips, and his eyes flashed. "This is who I am, honey. What I do. I build houses."

She spread her hands, feeling the tears creep up her throat and sting her eyes. "They build houses in New York, Joe."

"So I should leave a successful business and move to a huge metropolis where no one knows Joe Townsend's work? And start all over? Just fire my pooches and go?"

He shook his head. "Once upon a time, you said it must feel good to drive by the homes I'd built. You're right. It does. It feels even better to know the people who live in the homes I built. To run into them in Wiley's grocery store, to watch their kids perform in the school plays or on the school football field. To see them at the town meetings, to call them friends. Would that happen in Manhattan? I don't think so. No, Molly. I belong here, and this is where I'm going to stay."

"Joe, please." She looked at him across the countertop, through the tears glistening in her eyes. "There's another possibility. I could turn down the offers."

Finally the stiffness flowed out of his shoulders and a glimmer of softness returned to his gaze. "Now you're the one who's talking dumb. You'd have to be an idiot to turn down a million dollars a year and all the perks that go with it. Your face in TV and print commercials. The travel, the attention. The success and recognition. You told me that you got into the modeling business through luck. But you didn't stay there and become a huge success because of luck. You reached the top of your field with sacrifice and hard work. It took commitment and a love of what you were doing. Are you going to give up all of that to bury yourself in a tiny town that none of your New York friends have ever heard of? Oh, sure. That makes sense. Manhattan can't compete with Vrain's mud festival or our potluck dinners." An expression of disgust twisted his lips.

Molly sank down on one of the kitchen bar stools. "So where does that leave us? What are you saying?" she whispered, feeling the blood drain out of her face.

He studied her expression. "I don't know."

"I love you and you love me," she said, feeling a sharp pain in her chest. "There must be a middle road, some kind of compromise that you and I can both live with." It broke her heart to look at his face and read what she saw there.

"What would that be? Do we try to maintain a relationship while you live in New York and I live in Colorado? You fly here on odd-numbered weekends, and I fly there on even-numbered weekends? How long do you think it would be before you said, 'Joe I can't come this weekend, I have to fly to Europe to be at a shoot on Monday'? Or before I said, 'Honey I can't come this weekend because I have to baby-sit a client who can't pick out cabinets without me being with her'? How long before one of us starts to resent flying halfway across the continent to discover that the other has a list of unavoidable business commitments for the weekend? As for the weeknights...how lonely do we get before we say, this isn't working?''

He looked at her with such sadness in his eyes that Molly wanted to throw herself in his arms and burst into hysterical tears. ''Being a model and all that went with it was the life you were missing and regretted losing when you came here. You looked in the mirror and saw two tiny scars and told yourself that your career and a way of life was gone forever, so you tried to adjust and settle for something else. Something less. Now you discover that you didn't lose everything. Your career is alive and well and it's waiting for you to reclaim it. And the offers are bigger and better than what you thought you lost. If you're honest with yourself, Molly, that's what you want.''

There was no argument Molly could offer, because everything he said was true. She did want to be back on top again. If Addie had called her three months ago, instead of today, she wouldn't have hesitated for a heartbeat. In a blaze of relief and happiness, she would have caught the next flight to New York City and she would have spent a triumphant few days reviewing the offers and deciding which she would accept.

Three months ago, she had been attracted to Joe, but she hadn't yet recognized that she loved him. She hadn't known that he loved her, or that a wonderful future was possible right here in Vrain. Three months ago, she wouldn't have dreamed that she'd be so conflicted about getting everything she had believed she wanted.

''Oh, Joe.'' Dropping her head, she covered her eyes

with a shaking hand. A tense silence opened up before she could speak again. "I wish I could be two people."

He came around the counter then and finally drew her into his arms. Wrapping her arms around his neck, she pressed against the muscled length of him, leaning on his strength and solidity. "What are we going to do?" she whispered against his throat.

Reaching down, he unhooked his tool belt and dropped it on the countertop so that he could hold her closer. Then he buried his face in her hair. "Sometimes problems can't be fixed, Molly. Sometimes things just don't work out. It's nobody's fault. It just happens that way." He held her so tightly that she could hardly breathe. "So, what we do is enjoy the time we have left together."

How could she do that, when her heart was breaking?

Leaning back in his arms, she looked up at him. "I love you, Joe. I do love you," she said. Then she burst into tears and ran into the bedroom. She hoped he would follow, hoped he would say something to make everything right. But he didn't.

After a while, she blew out the candles surrounding the bed, then crawled inside the covers, wrapped her silk negligee around her and cried herself to sleep.

JOE LOOKED IN ON HER a few hours later, then quietly left the bedroom. He expected Aspen to follow, but Aspen remained on the bottom of the bed, draped across Molly's feet. Each of them saw it as his job to protect her. Unfortunately, Aspen was doing a better job of it than he was.

Opening the slider, he stepped outside onto the moon-washed balcony and leaned his forearms on the railing. He could hear water tumbling over rocks in the creek bed, heard the rustle of a small animal moving through the dark underbrush. Tonight the sky was spangled with bright stars, and he could see the broad sweep of the Milky Way, unobscured by any haze of city lights. The fragrance of pine scented every breath, along with the fresh smell of spring earth.

He couldn't give this up for the blare of traffic and the stink of exhaust fumes. He couldn't live in a cramped condo high above a stream of cabs and buses and automobiles. He didn't want to live where his dog couldn't run and the nearest patch of green was in a park several blocks away. And how did people raise families in Manhattan? Where did the children play hide-and-seek on a warm summer evening? Where did they fish? Where did they play? And with whom? How did a man make a living competing against millions of others just like him? If he didn't think he could be especially successful in Denver, how could he possibly hope for success in New York City?

Dropping his head, he pressed his fingertips against his forehead. He'd known this would happen. He had foreseen this dilemma. Exactly as he'd predicted, Molly had asked him to follow her to New York, and he felt guilty about not being able to do that. And he felt certain that she felt guilty about not being able to stay here with him. Guilty and sad and angry and frustrated.

If only he hadn't told her that he loved her. If only she hadn't told him. Then they could have pretended that it didn't hurt to go their separate ways. He could have pretended to be happy about her renewed career. It wouldn't have been too hard, because he truly was happy for her. He loved her enough to want her to have her dreams and her world. It hurt only when he thought about losing her. Losing her devastated him.

The crazy part was that he didn't doubt that she loved him. He saw it in her eyes, felt it in her touch. Leaving him would cause her the same pain he was feeling. But he also didn't doubt that she *would* leave. How could his small world compete with the exciting glitter and glamour of her universe? It couldn't.

He couldn't offer her fame or fortune or international recognition. He couldn't promise her excitement or travel to exotic locales. Hell, he couldn't even promise her special status in Vrain. Already the townsfolk had begun to accept her as one of themselves, and few continued to treat her as a renowned celebrity. She was a local now, Joe's girl, a friend. No one asked for her autograph or granted her special favors. She waited in line at the post office like anyone else. He didn't get quicker or better service at the Goosed Moose because Molly Stevens was on his arm.

She was no longer a celebrity, cloaked in glamour and unapproachable mystery. She was someone the men had danced with and the women had told their secrets to. People in Vrain had shared parts of their lives with her. They had taken her to their hearts and claimed her as one of their own.

But they were wrong. Molly Stevens belonged to the world, not just this small corner of it.

When Aspen pattered onto the deck and nosed Joe's hand, he knew she was standing in the slider door.

"Joe? Couldn't you sleep?" she asked in a voice that was soft and worried.

He knew what she would look like even before he turned around. Moonlight burnished her loose hair to a silvery sheen. Beneath the silk negligee, her legs were long and pale and shapely. He knew the slender curves beneath her nightgown as well as he knew the lines in his own palm.

"You are the most beautiful woman I have ever seen," he whispered. "What makes you such a miracle is that you're as lovely inside as you are on the outside."

"Joe, now that we're both a little calmer, can we talk?"

"No," he said in a hoarse voice, staring at her in the moonlight. "I have something to say to you, but I can't put it in words."

He strode toward her and caught her around the waist, pulling her roughly against his body, holding her so firmly and tightly that the veins stood up in his arm. She gasped softly and looked up at him, wide-eyed, while he memorized the oval shape of her face and the pliant curves yielding against his chest and hips.

Stepping forward, almost as if they were dancing, he backed her against the outside wall of the cabin, placed his hands against the logs and leaned into her. Gazing into her eyes, his mouth an inch from hers, he almost kissed her, but didn't. He let their breath mingle as he slowly moved his hips against hers, letting her feel the rock-hard power of his arousal and how much he wanted her. Her eyelids fluttered and her body arched to meet his, and she tried to catch his lips, but he didn't kiss her. Not yet.

One hand dropped to slide the tiny strap of her negligee off her shoulder, and he ran his callused palm over her smooth, polished shoulders, his touch almost worshipful. Staring into her eyes, his lips an inch from hers, he traced the lace bodice of the negligee, following the lush curve of her breasts. Then he placed both hands on her waist and slid them up until the weight of her breasts rested on top of his hands. He wanted to remember that he could span her waist with his two large hands, wanted to remember the erotic heaviness of her breasts and the silky smoothness of her warm skin.

Sliding his hands back down, he curved over her waist, cupped her hips, then slid his hands behind and over her slender buttocks, pressing her hard against him. She moaned his name and rocked against an aching erection that felt as if it would explode from his jeans.

Finally, he buried his hands in her silky, moon-bright hair and kissed her as he had kissed no other woman, deeply, passionately, urgently. Because words would never be adequate, he tried to tell her with his lips and his body that he loved her with a passion and depth that would never diminish. He tried to tell her that she was his heart, his center, the missing piece of himself that he had searched for and had despaired of finding.

And he tried to tell her that his love for her was true enough and deep enough to let her return to the world that made her happy, and that he would make her choice as easy for her as he could.

It was a lot to ask of one kiss, but he must have succeeded, or at least come close, because when he opened his eyes he saw moonlight glistening in the tears spilling down her cheeks. He brushed her tears away with shaking fingertips. Then he slid the other strap of her negligee off her shoulder and eased the silk nightgown down over her breasts and hips and thighs until it whispered to the floor of the balcony in a filmy puddle.

When she stood naked and trembling in the moonlight, he began kissing her at her throat, brushing his lips across the pulse pounding in the hollow between her delicate bones. Then he brought one beautiful breast to his lips and made love to the milky smoothness, caressing the nipple with his tongue, sucking gently, licking and tasting, before he turned his attention to her other breast.

Molly trembled and moaned softly, her eyelids flickering. But when she tried to touch him, he gently moved her hands away. He didn't want to be distracted from what he was trying to tell her with his hands and lips in the only way he knew how.

Dropping to his knees, he trailed his fingertips down to her navel and across her stomach, then to her thighs, gently spreading her legs. The night air was chilly, but her skin was as hot as his, covered with a light dew of perspiration, as his was, also. His arms went around her body, and for a moment, he just held her. He knelt before her, his face pressed to her naked stomach, his eyes closed, and he held her, inhaling the scent of her skin, feeling the softness of her stomach against his cheeks and lips. He would never forget the fragrance and the feel of this woman.

And then he kissed her. He kissed her waist and hips and stomach, kissed her thighs and tasted the honey-sweetness of her center. He branded the taste and scent and feel of her on his memory.

"Oh, God, Joe. I'm weak and shaking all over. My legs won't support me," she whispered, her fingers in his hair. "What you're doing...I've never..."

Standing, he caught her in his arms and held her tightly when she rocked hard against him, her hands flying over his hair, his face, his shoulders. And she caught his lips and kissed him until his body burned and shook and he needed to be inside her with the same urgency as he needed air to breathe. Lifting her, he carried her inside, back to the bedroom. And he made love to her, passionately, wildly, out of control and holding nothing back. And before either of them had caught their breath, he came to her again, this time slowly, tenderly, thoroughly, completely, until they were both drenched in sweat and gasping each other's names.

He gave her the one thing he could give that she wouldn't find in her New York world. Himself.

Afterward, he held her nestled in his arms, his cheek against her wild, tousled hair, and he listened to the ticking of the bedside clock.

The countdown had begun.

"I REVIEWED the material you sent," Molly said into the telephone, pulling her notes in front of her. "And basically I agree with your comments. The Chanel position would be great fun, but it wouldn't really promote my career. What Chanel is actually seeking, I think, is a socialite willing to be a walking mannequin. The job is too unstructured, too nebulous."

"What on earth is all that noise?" Addie asked. "I can hardly hear you."

"Just a minute." Covering the receiver with one hand, Molly glared at Jim. "Must you pound on those pipes right next to my desk?"

"If you want your kitchen sink to drain," he said shortly, "then yes, I need to fit these pipes."

They both looked toward the staircase as Joe strode into the basement. "Honey, are you going to be on the phone very long? Mike sent us the wrong front for the dishwasher, and one of the cabinets is the wrong size, not what you ordered. I need to call him."

"Can you give me another thirty minutes?" she asked. The bruise on his cheek had faded to pale yellow now, and nothing remained of his black eye but a blue crescent beneath his lower lashes. When she looked at him, his high-energy virility stopped her breath for a moment. There was something about a man wearing low-slung jeans and a tool belt... And if he was heart-stoppingly handsome to begin with... Molly swallowed and gazed up at him. "Give me a few more minutes."

"Okay." Frowning, he looked up at the ceiling, and then at Jim. "Get a move on, honey. We need to button up this lid. Are you running the kitchen plumbing or the pipes for the back bathroom?"

"This is the kitchen line," Jim said. "I'll finish today. Then all I have to do is plumb in the sink and the ice maker and I'm outa here. *Finis*. The end. Pay me."

"You got it." Joe considered the ceiling again. "I'll get a pooch down here tomorrow and we'll close and finish the ceiling." He gave Molly a smile and a wave. "Back in thirty minutes, honey."

For an instant, Jim and Molly contemplated each other. Then she turned away and spoke into the phone. "Addie? Are you still there?"

"If this isn't a good time..."

Molly summoned up a smile. "You wouldn't believe the frenzy of the last few days. This week has been chaos. The painters have been here finishing the stain and trim work, and painting the outside of the house. The plumber is here now, running the last of the waterlines. The hardwood floors went down a few days ago. The kitchen is being installed even as we speak." She paused and lowered her head, rubbing the bridge of her nose. "Everything will be finished next week except the final walk-through."

"I'll bet you'll be so glad. I don't know how you've kept your sanity through all that's been going on around you. By the way, how's the book progressing?"

"Not you, too," Molly groaned. "My editor is phoning weekly, and I dread her calls." She glanced at her computer screen. "I'm going to have to ask for another deadline extension. I hate to do it, but there's no way I can finish on time."

"I've been thinking...if you accept the Couture offer, we could coordinate the release of the book with the launch of the Couture campaign. It could be good for everyone involved. Let me make a reminder note. You *are* leaning toward the Couture deal, aren't you? Or am I getting a wrong impression?''

Molly hesitated, then drew a deep breath. ''On the face of it, Couture is offering the best package. But I don't want to make any decision until we have a chance to sit down and look at each offer in depth. Addie? There's something... It appears from your notes that the preparation for Couture's launch would be all-encompassing. Am I correct?''

''Lord, yes. They'll work your tail off, darlin'. Nights, weekends... I hope you finish the book before the craziness begins, because you aren't going to have two minutes to spare once they start preparing for the launch.'' She laughed. ''When you're in the thick of it, remind yourself how much they're paying you.''

Molly rolled a pencil back and forth beneath her fingertips. A headache pounded at her temples ''There won't be any free weekends...?''

''Not for a very long time. By the way, how's your weight?''

''I've gained a few pounds since I've been in Colorado,'' she admitted, frowning. ''But they're coming off fast. I'm back on a regimen of rabbit food.'' No more greasy cheeseburgers for her. No more of Ma Callahan's fabulous mud pie.

Addie laughed. ''Good. Now let's get back to work. Take a look at page four in the material I sent you. Find it?''

''Addie, the contractor needs to use this phone. I'm in a pocket where cell phones don't work. Could we postpone further discussion until I see you next week?''

''Hmm... All right, if that's what works best for you. I've cleared my schedule for Thursday and Friday of next week. You get in Wednesday night, right? We'll get an early start on Thursday. Fine, that works. I'll see you then.''

Molly hung up the telephone, acutely aware that Jim En-

ders had overheard her conversation. Sighing, she turned
her head and watched him standing on the ladder, working
on a line of pipe in the ceiling.

"Jim? You can say 'I told you so' to me, but please
don't hit Joe with it, okay?"

He lowered his arms and looked down at her. "I won't,
but others might."

She nodded and looked away from him. "What are they
saying in town?"

"Everyone's happy for you. We all thought the Apple
people did you dirty. They shouldn't have fired you. But a
lot of people are disappointed, Molly. Wanda and her group
of friends were really looking forward to the makeup
classes you were going to teach. Cal Dobie was counting
on working with the rocks and doing some showcase landscaping out here. The Vrain Ladies Society hoped you'd
join their group." He shrugged. "I could go on, but you
get the drift."

"I might still do the landscape project," she said in a
low voice.

"Why would you? How much time are you really going
to spend here? Enough to justify that kind of expense?
Mayor Castle hoped you would ride in his convertible in
the July Fourth parade. Avis wanted to ask you to be in
our wedding. Everyone who worked on your house has
chipped in to buy a gift for you that they planned to present
at the end-of-project party, but I guess there won't be a
party now. The Vrain Ladies Society intended to invite you
to be on the planning committee for next year's mud festival." He spread his hands. "Don't get me wrong. No one
blames you for choosing to be rich and famous. Hell, there
isn't a woman in the county who wouldn't trade places with
you that fast." He snapped his fingers.

"But?"

"But you made friends here, Molly. Maybe you don't
believe it right now, but I'm one of them. And we'll miss
you. You could have had a life here. A good life. 'Course,

it wouldn't have been the kind of life you'll have in New York City.''

She looked down at the pencil she was still rolling beneath her fingertip. "Joe and I are looking for a way that we can have it all. Don't give up on us yet.''

Jim made a snorting sound. "Maybe you're still looking for an impossible solution, but Joe isn't.''

Her head snapped up and she frowned. "What are you saying?''

"Joe knows that when he puts you on that plane for Manhattan, you aren't coming back. He's always known that loving you was a recipe for heartache. He knew it the night he took you to the Goosed Moose that first time.'' He stared at her. "He'll let you go, Molly. And he'll suck up the I-told-you-sos. He'll take the pity. And he'll smile at the jokes about being footloose and fancy-free again. But he'll be hurting.''

She looked at him.

"But you'll never know it, I can promise you that. Because Joe isn't that kind of man. He won't beg you to come back. He won't put any guilts on you. He'll wish you happiness and success, and he'll mean it.''

Molly nodded. Joe hadn't said another word about diamond rings or marriage or babies. When she tried to talk about the future, he assured her that she was going to fulfill all of Couture's expectations and then some. She was going to take the world by storm. He didn't speak of his future.

She and Jim fell silent when they heard Joe's step on the staircase. He bounded into the room, charging it with his own brand of energy and electricity. Stopping short, he gave them both a mock glare, his eyes sparkling. "Is it quitting time and I didn't notice?" he said, a grin in his voice. "Honey, my client isn't paying you to stand on a ladder and gab. Get back to those pipes. And, honey—" this time he spoke to Molly "—why aren't you writing that book of yours?"

Striding forward, he turned her phone to face him and

punched in a number. "Is this Mike? Honey, we got a couple of problems on the Stevens job."

Molly listened to him, thinking that Joe Townsend was absolutely unique. For the rest of her life, every time she heard someone use the word *honey,* she would think of Joe. When she saw a tool belt or a flannel shirt, she would remember Joe. When someone mentioned building or remodeling, whenever she passed a kitchen or plumbing supply showroom, every time she spotted a booger on a wall, she would think of Joe.

She would remember him when she climbed into her bed in the New York condo. Alone. He would haunt her memory every time she saw lovers walking hand in hand, or watched a long, passionate kiss on a film screen. She would imagine him inside every green pickup, and she would see him whenever she saw a man and a dog.

Lifting eyes brimming with tears, she stared at him in mute anguish. He stretched out a hand and gently brushed the tears off her cheek.

"Don't," he said softly.

"I want it all, Joe," she whispered. "I want the Couture deal, and I want you, too."

"You have to follow your dream." Then he laughed and spoke into the phone. "Not you, honey. I'm talking to a different honey." He listened a minute, then laughed again before he looked at Molly with teasing eyes. "Mike says to tell the other honey that he's in favor of following dreams, too." Then he spoke into the phone again. "This honey's dream is to have her kitchen match and to have all her cabinets. So when can you get the missing pieces up here? We're supposed to be outa here on Friday, final walk-through on Monday."

Jim was right, Molly thought, lowering her head. Joe was going to make it as easy as possible for her to break both their hearts. He'd thought about it, he'd come to terms with the impossibility of a shared future, and now he was dealing with it. Better than she was.

As far as Molly could tell, he was as cheerful, as energetic, as quick to laugh, as he always had been. He still brought her morning coffee with a shouted "Rise and shine, honey," as if a wonderful day waited for them both. He kissed her every night and made love to her as if they held forever within their grasp, as if loving her didn't hurt.

He held his pain inside, and didn't let her see it or be wounded by it.

A tear dropped on her hand.

Chapter Twelve

At three o'clock on Friday, Al, Coke, Trey and Z carried Molly's desk and computer equipment upstairs to her new study. They moved her bedroom furniture out of the guest room on the second floor and reassembled everything in the new master bedroom. Then they shook Molly's hand, gazed around with pride, and walked out of her front door. They jumped in their pickups and raced down her drive for the last time.

The house was finished.

Joe stood in the living room, thumbs hooked in his back pockets as he turned in a slow circle. "This is a great house," he commented softly, smiling. "The design is open, all the wood gives it a warm feeling. This would be a good family house." He nodded, pride and satisfaction glowing in his eyes.

In his opinion, all houses had personalities. When he began this project, the Stevens house had been feeling its age, sad and neglected. He and the pooches had given it a face-lift and a tummy tuck and a cosmetic fix. They had flushed out old pipes, added new pipes, plumped out the sides and added space. Throughout the renovations, Joe had imagined the old house shedding years, standing taller and prouder. Now it was beautiful again, warm and welcoming, shining with renewed youth and vigor. Now it waited expectantly for someone to make it into a home.

He wondered if Molly would ever bother to furnish the empty rooms, wondered if she would ever live in the house he had built for her.

She turned away from the kitchen window where she had been standing, watching the pooches drive away. Frowning, she ran her hand along the smooth Corian countertop. "I feel bad that there won't be an end-of-the-project celebration party." She bit her lower lip. "Daddy Romaine wanted barbecue."

Joe walked across the plush Berber carpet. "Most people don't have parties for the pooches," he said lightly. "It's nice when it happens, but it isn't expected."

"I wanted a long weekend with you. Then I'll be packing for New York." She shrugged, her frown deepening. "Still, I'm sorry now that I didn't try to throw something together." Her gaze slid to the green marble bookends the pooches had chipped in to buy her as a housewarming gift. "They gave *me* a gift."

Joe picked up the card lying on the countertop beside the bookends. Nearly sixty men had worked on her house, and Mr. Melvin had tracked them all down and asked them to sign the card. It was a nice gesture. So were the bookends.

"If you want to give the pooches a party, you could do it later in the summer. No one expects you to host a party before you've even moved in."

It was a meaningless statement, intended to take them past this moment, and he suspected Molly recognized it as such. By the end of the summer, she would be spending every minute at Couture's direction, excitedly preparing for her launch as the Couture Femme. Long before August, she would have forgotten the faces and names of the men who had signed her card and contributed to the purchase of the bookends. By then, she wouldn't remember how she was feeling right now.

Picking up his clipboard, he scanned the punch list. "I believe we've completed everything on this list. There's no sense waiting until Monday to do the final walk-through.

Unless you have something planned for the rest of the afternoon, would you like to do it now?''

"We might as well," she said in an oddly listless voice. Moving to the new refrigerator, she opened the door and stared at the empty shelves inside. "I wish I'd thought to buy a bottle of champagne or some great wine. Something to celebrate this moment."

"Let's start in the basement," he suggested, walking toward the door. How many times had he run up and down these stairs, and stopped in wonder when he reached the bottom and saw her sitting at her desk? An image flashed into his mind, and he remembered her hunched over her keyboard, wearing her parka and blowing warm breath on her fingers. Even cold and miserable, she'd been beautiful.

He continued past the area where her desk had been, remembering the plastic canopy he'd nailed above her to catch the dirt and loose nails and chips of drywall falling down from above. She had gazed at him with gratitude, her eyes shining, as if he were her hero.

Lifting the clipboard, he peered at his list, then waved her into the new basement bathroom. "Turn on the shower, if you would. Flush the toilet and check the faucets."

Silently she did as he'd requested, then nodded, and he placed checkmarks on his list. "If you see anything that isn't exactly right, that isn't exactly as you wanted it, tell me, honey."

They walked around the basement recreation room, and Joe tested the electrical outlets, examined the new ceiling. He eyed the walls, proud that they were straight and true.

"Remember when the rocks came flying down on the patio?" Molly laughed softly, looking toward the new sliders leading outside. "That was a crazy day."

"Let's check the bedrooms down here." He opened closet doors for her, waited while she gave the rods a cursory look. He asked her to make sure the windows opened easily.

When they finished in the basement, he followed her up the stairs, his eyes fixed on her provocative fanny. She had filled out a little during her stay in Vrain, and he'd liked that. But in the past week, she hadn't eaten enough to keep a bird alive, as his mother used to say. He didn't need to ask what that meant.

"Upstairs next," he suggested. "We'll do the ground floor last."

There wasn't a trace of the old chimney chase upstairs. The pooches had done an especially fine finish in the area where the chase had been. He ticked it off his list. Then he asked Molly to test the new bathroom fixtures, waiting while she tried the faucets.

"Remember the day you took off the bathroom door to stain it?" she asked, smiling. "Longest day of my life."

Joe glanced toward the bedroom where he had brought her morning coffee for so many weeks. "We didn't do anything in the bedroom except give it new carpet." Turning, he led the way back down the stairs. "Okay, let's start with your study." It was new construction; he didn't anticipate any glitches, and there weren't any.

"This is a bigger room than I pictured," Molly commented. "My desk is lost in here." She scanned the room. "I like the bookcases. They came out well, don't you think?" She smiled. "Oh Joe. Remember Bill the painter? And the great booger brawl?"

"Make sure the switch on the gas fireplace works." After she tested it, he checked that item off his list.

The living room, dining room, laundry room and guest bath went quickly. So did the pantry.

"I love this kitchen," Molly said quietly, looking around her. "Even you have to admit that it's beautiful."

"Even me?" he said with a laugh. "Honey, I never fought you on the looks of it. Just the price of it." He scanned the cabinets, the decorative fluted pieces. "I was wrong about the foo-fras. They pull the whole thing together." He checked his list. "You have pullout shelving. Let's check each shelf to make sure the rollers move smoothly."

It truly was a wonderful kitchen. The cabinets were

warm cherry. The countertops were emerald green. Two people could work together without stumbling over each other. He didn't let himself wonder if she would ever cook a meal here.

"Good," he said after she'd rolled out every shelf. "Now the appliances. The fan on the Jenn-Air gave us a little trouble. Would you check that?"

"Perfect," she said, turning it on and off. "Remember the day we bought the kitchen? That was the day I admitted to myself that I loved you."

"My lucky day," he said, grinning at her, hoping to relieve some of the tension he felt stretching between them.

Her fingertips wandered over the sink faucet and rested lightly on the decorator tiles forming the splash block. "I had such an awful time making up my mind about the tiles. They look nice, don't they?"

"You made an excellent choice, Miss Stevens," he said, smiling. Remembering that he had laid a row of tiles out on the showroom floor so that she could see how the assembled result would look. They had been silly that day, competing to see who could find the worst or most tasteless tiles. Intoxicated with each other, playing with the tiles, they had laughed until their sides ached. "We're almost finished. So far so good."

He walked into the master bedroom, glanced at her bed, then continued into the master bathroom, lifting his clipboard. "You want to check out your million-dollar bathroom?" he asked, trying to make her smile.

She touched the crystal and gold-plated fixtures on the home spa tub. "We went out for Chinese food that night. Your fortune said you should remember the bottom line. Mine told me to follow my heart."

He hadn't forgotten. He remembered every moment with her. And he was doing his damnedest to remember the bottom line. The bottom line was that he wanted her to be happy. If she couldn't be happy in Vrain with him, then he loved her enough to wish her happiness without him, wherever she wanted to be, doing whatever she wanted to do.

"Two more items and we're finished. Test the switch for the gas fireplace." He watched her flick the switch and glance at the flames in the fireplace. "Good. Now, if you okay the closet, that's it."

"The closet is great," she said, not bothering to look at it. "Joe? Does it make you happy or sad to finish a project?"

"A little of both," he replied truthfully. Walking away from a house he had built was like leaving a friend he knew inside and out. But by the time he reached the final punch list, his thoughts were moving onward toward the next project. Tonight he would close out the books on the Stevens project, and Monday he would schedule the Romaines for the excavation on the Henderson foundation.

Her eyes fixed on his, Molly lifted her hands and pulled out the pins that held her hair wrapped in a coil on top of her head, letting it spill down her back in a pale, silky waterfall. As he stared at her, she unbuttoned her oversize shirt and dropped it on the carpet. She wasn't wearing a bra, and he sucked in a breath at the sight of her small, perfect breasts. She unzipped her jeans.

"Joe?" she whispered. "Make love to me. Please?"

He tossed the clipboard on the bureau and unbuckled his tool belt.

AFTER HE LEFT, Molly put on her oldest, most comfortable robe and the slippers that were falling apart but that she couldn't bear to part with. She walked through the house again, this time alone, trailing her fingers over smooth wood, opening doors, flicking switches, looking at everything.

It was a wonderful house, she thought, moisture glistening in her eyes. Late-afternoon sunlight flooded the rooms, streaming through the new banks of windows. There was a feeling of spaciousness and air and light.

Molly wasn't usually a fanciful type, but she imagined a sense of expectation, as if the house were waiting impatiently for the door to burst open and children to run laugh-

ing inside. As if the kitchen beckoned her to scent the air
with the smell of baking cookies, and the master bath
awaited the arrival of two toothbrushes, placed side by side.

With a start, she suddenly realized that this was not a
house for one person. Joe had built her a home that needed
a family to fill the spacious rooms. This was a home created
for Thanksgiving dinners and tall Christmas trees, a home
that wanted ponies in the pastures outside, and children
running in the door. It was a home that needed clutter and
happy noise, a home to celebrate love and joy, a home that
would cushion life's small sorrows. It was a safe place, a
haven.

Turning, she fixed her eyes on the front door, holding
her breath and waiting for the door to open. The children
would have Joe's sparkling electric-blue eyes, and maybe
her wheat-colored hair. They would be noisy and full of
their father's vitality and their mother's impish humor.
They would love animals and skiing and fishing in the summers. They would be tall and beautiful and secure in the
knowledge of their parent's love.

Molly stared at the closed door with tears running down
her cheeks and the silence ringing in her ears.

THEY SPENT the weekend and Monday and Tuesday at Joe's
cabin. There was no furniture in Molly's newly finished
house, and it didn't make sense to stock the fridge, since
she was leaving and didn't know when she would return.
Or even if she would return.

Their last days together might have been a disaster of
recriminations or a sad awareness of "This is the last time
that we'll…" But Joe didn't let either possibility happen.
To Molly's relief, he behaved as if there were nothing out
of the ordinary about these last days together.

On Friday night, he closed out his files on her house
while she washed their dinner dishes. Then they popped
popcorn and watched television. After he finished the paperwork on her renovation, Joe staggered into the living
room and pretended to faint on the sofa next to her. Clasp-

ing his heart, he told her the final amount by which she had exceeded the bid. Molly grinned, clapped a hand on his fevered brow, then made him forget about overruns by taking him to bed and making love to him until streaks of pearly pink lightened the eastern sky.

On Saturday, they slept in, then spent a lazy day doing things around the cabin, walked in the pine forest behind Joe's cabin and watched videos of favorite old movies.

Sunday, they hiked up to an icy creek swollen with spring melt that rushed down from the high mountain valleys. Breathing in the scent of pine and early wildflowers, they ate a picnic lunch and relaxed in the sunshine.

"It's so quiet here," Molly said. Joe had his head in her lap, and she let her fingers play in his dark hair.

"Not really," he murmured lazily. "It just seems that way to a girl with city ears."

There was so much they should have talked about but didn't. She didn't ask why he had never mentioned marriage again. He didn't ask when she would return. They made no plans past Wednesday, when Joe would drive her to DIA, outside Denver, and put her on the plane to New York City.

Sighing softly, Molly leaned against the white trunk of a leafy aspen and gazed at the water tumbling down the mountainside. "Joe?" she said quietly. "Give me a year. Let me be the Couture Femme for a year. I want to be on top again. I want to retire when I'm ready, not because of a stupid accident." When she looked down at his head in her lap, she discovered he'd been gazing up at her.

"No strings, Molly, no time limits," he said, speaking as quietly as she had. "No promises."

"What are you saying?"

"You'll need all your energy focused on the preparations for the campaign launch. I don't want you looking at your watch in the middle of a late shoot or at a party and thinking, 'Damn, I've got to get to a phone and call Joe because it's Friday night and we always talk on Friday night.' And I don't want to phone you at ten because we've agreed we'll talk every night at ten, and then you're not there and I drive myself crazy with worry or jealousy. I don't want us setting up a weekend-visit schedule that we might not be able to keep. And I don't want you to limit your career by placing a time limit on it. You don't know where the Couture deal might take you, honey. Maybe it will lead to even bigger opportunities. Leave that door open for yourself.''

"So…what? Our relationship is over?'' She stared down at him.

"Sometimes loving isn't enough to make a relationship work," he said, speaking slowly in a way that told her he had thought this through. "Every person has the right to pursue her dream. But, Molly, honey, sometimes people's dreams conflict. I don't have the right to ask you to abandon your dream any more than you have the right to ask me to give up my dreams. If either of us abandoned our dreams, it would only lead to resentment and eventual bitterness." He sat up beside her and took her hand. "The sad truth is that people can recover from a love that doesn't work out. But people don't recover from shattered dreams.''

"I don't want to recover from loving you!" Tears glistened in her eyes. "Oh, Joe. I'm so confused and upset and frustrated. I keep thinking that sometime soon Apple is going to launch their new Apple Girl and that makes me want the Couture deal so badly I can taste it. But I want us, too.'' She struck the ground with her fist, then angrily brushed at the tears on her lashes.

He took her face between his hands. "We've had more than a lot of people ever do. We've had a window of time together, and it's been wonderful. We've laughed and loved, argued and compromised. We've worked together and seen each other at our best and at our worst. Don't let the fact that we can't have more spoil what we did have. Don't do that, Molly. Don't feel guilty or angry or upset. And there's nothing to feel confused about. It just didn't work out for us." He shrugged. "For a brief time, our worlds touched and meshed. Now our worlds are moving apart again. I'm just grateful that we had this time together. I'll never forget you. Part of me will always love you, and I hope that part of you will always love me.''

"My God," she whispered, pulling away from his hands and struggling to her feet. "You're saying goodbye." She stared at him, then spun and ran back toward the cabin, blinded by tears.

After that, a gulf opened between them. They both tried to ignore those moments beside the creek, but a distance had developed and they couldn't bridge it. Even their love-making was slightly awkward and self-conscious. And for the first time since they had known each other, uncomfortable silences stretched between them. Every time the phone rang, and it rang frequently, it was almost a relief.

"It's for you again," Joe said on Monday afternoon.

He brushed a kiss across her cheek as she passed him to take the call.

"Hi, it's Wanda at the drugstore. I just wanted to wish you good luck in New York. We all know you're going to show those Apple people how wrong they were to fire you!"

"Thank you," Molly murmured, wrapping the phone cord around her finger. "I appreciate your support." She hesitated. "I'm sorry the makeup classes didn't work out."

"Oh, your career is a lot more important than some silly classes.''

Silly classes. She remembered how Wanda's eyes had glowed with excitement and anticipation when Molly agreed to the classes. She pressed her forehead against the wall and closed her eyes. "It's nice of you to be so understanding."

By Tuesday, she was half convinced that everyone in town had called to wish her a safe trip or to congratulate her on her good career news or to tell her that she would be missed.

"Even Bill the painter called," she told Joe as he drove her back to her house to pack. "And Cal Dobie was so disappointed that I had to postpone the landscaping project. I didn't expect him to wish me good luck, but he did.'' She thought a minute then laughed. ''And Dumpling called, did I tell you? No good-luck wishes there. She said I owed her and Daddy some barbecue. I'd mentioned an end-of-the-project party and promised to serve barbecue, and she and Daddy were holding me to it.'' They both knew this was Dumpling's way. In her own fashion, Dumpling had been saying the same thing as everyone else.

Joe grinned at her. ''What did you say?''

''I told her I hadn't forgotten. I'm thinking about sending Daddy some barbecue from New York. Sort of a joke. He thinks I'm crazy anyway.'' She smiled, thinking about it, hoping she remembered to do it. ''Dumpling said that Daddy and the boys are going to decorate the bulldozer and drive it in the Fourth of July parade.''

''They usually do. They fill the scoop with candy and Dumpling rides there and throws the candy to the kids along the parade route.''

Molly could picture it. Already everyone was talking about their plans for the parade. Mr. Melvin would have a float, and so would Wiley's grocery store, and several of the high school classes. Sandy and Bonnie were planning something special for the Goosed Moose's float, but no one could pry the secret out of them. The volunteer fire department had shined up the fire engine, and Matt Anderson had made the town pay for a new paint job on his police cruiser just for the parade. Jim and Avis were organizing the town picnic, scheduled to begin after the parade.

''I'm sorry I'll miss it,'' Molly said, looking down at her hands.

''I'm sorry, too,'' Joe said lightly. ''We could have used a pretty girl in a convertible. Guess we'll have to make do with the Van Tine twins again.'' When she didn't speak, he glanced at her. ''The parade doesn't amount to much. It has to go around the block three times just to seem like a real parade. You won't be missing anything. The whole deal is over in about twenty minutes.''

They turned down the driveway, and Molly looked out the windshield at her house. Her grandparents wouldn't have recognized it, but she believed they would have approved. "Thank you, Joe, for giving me this wonderful house."

He came around the pickup and opened the door for her. "Sorry," she said, smiling up at him. "I was daydreaming."

"Thinking about packing?"

"No, I was thinking the house looks vacant without drapes at the windows." It looked vacant because it was. She still had that peculiar feeling of expectation every time she looked at the house, as if it were eagerly waiting for its family to arrive. "There's still a lot to do," she said after a minute, trying to shake off fanciful thoughts. "Drapes, wallpaper, furniture." Pictures for the walls. Throw rugs. Decorator towels and sheets. Vases and flowers. All the items that transformed a house into a home. Unfortunately, she didn't know when she'd get to those things.

She started walking toward the front door, then realized Joe wasn't behind her. She stopped and looked back. "Aren't you coming?"

"I don't think so," he said, his gaze on the house.

Her breath stopped and her chest tightened. "Joe...it's our last night. We don't know when we'll be together again."

He hooked his fingers in his back pockets, and finally he looked at her. There was no sparkle or flash in his eyes. Just an intense sadness. "I don't want to spend the evening thinking this is our last meal together. The last time I'll hold you in my arms. The last time we'll make love. That would be too hard, and it would put too much pressure on both of us." He seemed to consider for a minute. Then he nodded shortly and jerked open the door of the pickup. "I'll pick you up tomorrow morning, honey."

Stunned, she stood at the foot of the porch and watched him drive away.

At first she was angry, then hurt, that they wouldn't be together tonight, and finally she understood. She sat on the edge of her bed, staring at her suitcases, and listening to the deep, lonely quiet around her.

He was hurting. He'd tried not to let her see it. He'd tried to keep their last days together light and amusing and loving. But he couldn't pretend anymore. And maybe she couldn't, either, she thought, burying her face in her hands. The past couple of days had been a strain. It would almost be a relief to leave.

That thought shocked her, then broke her heart. Throwing herself across the bed, she burst into a storm of weeping.

"THERE ARE SO MANY THINGS I want to say to you," Molly whispered. Stepping forward, she dropped her head and pressed her forehead against his chest. "Oh, Joe."

They stood at the gate, waiting for her flight to be called, as awkward with each other as they had been during the mostly silent drive to Denver and the airport.

"You'll never know what our ski weekend did for me," she said, pressing her hand flat on his chest, feeling the steady thump of his heart against her palm. Her own heart was cracking, little pieces falling off. "Everything started to turn around for me after that weekend."

"I'm glad, honey." He patted her back awkwardly, then gently tugged on her braid.

"Oh, Joe." Tears swam in her eyes when she looked up at him. "Talk to me. We've never had trouble talking before. Why is it so hard now?"

Tilting her face up to him, he gazed into her eyes. "We've said it all," he said in a gruff voice. "There's nothing left except to tell you how grateful I am for the time we had together. But you know that already." Swallowing hard, he glanced toward a woman standing beside the door to the jetway. "Honey," he said in a strained voice. "They just called your row for boarding."

"I love you. I didn't want—"

"I know," he said softly, placing a finger over her lips.

She kissed his finger, then pulled his hand away from her mouth. "We've both been behaving as if I've already accepted Couture's offer. But I haven't," she said, hearing the desperation in her voice. "I might not."

He gazed into her eyes and gripped her shoulders. "We both know it's what you want. Don't do something you'll regret, Molly." He glanced toward the jetway again and clenched his teeth. Knots appeared along his jawline. "Honey? It's time. You need to go."

She shot a glance toward the people leaving the waiting area. "I'll call you tonight."

Stepping back from her, Joe pushed his hands in his pockets and looked at her lips. "I won't be home."

"Oh?" She couldn't stand this. It hurt too much. There were so many things she wanted to say, things she needed to hear him say. "Do you have a date?"

"A date?" He laughed, and a couple walking past them looked at him and smiled. "I guess you could say that. I'm meeting Jim and Avis at the Goosed Moose." The laughter faded from his eyes. "The three of us are going to sit in the back booth and drink a hundred pitchers of beer. I intend to get as drunk as I've ever been in my life."

"Oh, Joe." She covered her face with her hands and struggled against the huge lump in her throat. When she could, she dropped her hands and gazed at him with pleading eyes. "It isn't that I don't love you. You know that, don't you? You have to know it. I love you so much."

"Honey, this is killing me," he whispered, staring at her. "You have to go now. They're waiting for you."

Then he stepped forward and crushed her against his body. He kissed her so hard that Molly knew her lips would be bruised. Clinging to him, her hands moving frantically over his face, his hair, his shoulders, she pressed tightly against him, wanting to melt into his heat and strength and solid frame. When he released her, she was gasping, and her knees felt weak.

He stared down at her for a long moment, and gently he

touched her cheek with trembling fingertips. "I hope it's everything you want it to be, Molly. Be happy."

His fingers moved to brush her lips, lingering for a brief instant, and then he turned and walked away from her. Shaking, Molly stood still, raising a hand to her lips, waiting to see if he would look back. But he didn't.

Finally, she dashed a hand across her eyes, picked up her makeup case and stumbled toward the woman waiting to take her ticket. The woman studied her as if trying to place where she might have seen Molly before. "Great-looking guy," she said, taking Molly's ticket. She tore off the stub and handed it back. "It's hard to say goodbye, isn't it?"

Molly looked at her, unable to speak, then ran down the jetway and onto the plane.

IT WAS SIX O'CLOCK by the time she collected her luggage and hailed a cab to take her into the city. But it didn't feel that late. Her system was still on Colorado time and it was light out, a soft June evening stretching before her. By this time next month, the city would be sweltering in heat and humidity, but tonight was pleasant, warmer than it had been in Colorado.

As the cabdriver didn't speak easily understandable English, Molly didn't attempt to converse. She leaned back and watched flashes of graffiti speed past, noticed the thickening traffic. The air inside the cab smelled of stale smoke and a woman's heavy perfume, so she opened the window, but doing so only added the odor of exhaust fumes. With every passing minute, it became harder to recall the fragrance of the pine forest behind Joe's cabin, or the new-house scents of fresh paint and carpet.

But there was something else in the city air that she chose to concentrate on, and that was the excitement, the electric scent of success. When she left here, she'd done so like a whipped dog, with her head down and her tail between her legs, running away from sensational tabloid headlines that claimed she was horribly disfigured, her career in ruins.

And now, a few hectic months later, she was returning in triumph, with her career restored and a half-dozen wonderful offers to consider. Thinking about it, she laughed aloud.

She was still smiling when she stepped out of the cab in front of her building. Three years ago, she had paid a bucket of money for a condominium in a secure building at a good address in the east fifties. There were trees along the sidewalk, and there was a Korean deli on the corner. The Metropolitan Museum was within walking distance, and so was the Park. But it was odd that she had forgotten how small the lobby was and that the building was showing its age so badly.

"Good evening, Miss Stevens."

She nodded and smiled at the doorman, who helped her inside with her luggage, then pressed the elevator call button for her. "It's a lovely evening, isn't it, Mr. Polanski?"

"A nice long spring, this year. Hope you enjoyed your trip," he said as she stepped into the elevator.

Her trip? The phrase was a catchall that could cover a lot of possibilities, but the implication was that she had been away for a weekend, not for several months. A light frown puckered her forehead as she wondered if it was possible that Mr. Polanski didn't realize how long she had been gone. Or care. But then, that was one of things about the city that she liked, wasn't it? Her business was her own. She didn't inquire into the doorman's life, and he didn't ask about hers. Still, it seemed that he might have noticed she had been away for several months.

Suddenly she realized that she didn't know Mr. Polanski's first name. Strange that she could know a man for three years and not know his first name or anything about him.

Shaking off the peculiarity of this thought, she jiggled her key in the door lock, then carried her luggage inside a tiny, dimly lit foyer. She was home. But, good heavens, home was small. And dark. She had forgotten the perpetual gloom of north-facing windows, and only three of them, at that.

Walking through a small living room crowded with too much furniture, she opened the windows to air out the place, then slowly looked around her, seeing her condo from a new perspective.

From the first, she had known it needed renovation, but she hadn't found the right moment to begin remodeling, and she hadn't spent much time here, anyway. During the week, she'd been working, and on the weekends there had been errands to run, things to do. Or perhaps she had sensed it would be depressing to spend too much time in these small, oppressive rooms.

Frowning, she imagined what Joe's impressions would be if he ever visited. He'd feel claustrophobic. There was no deck to step out onto, nothing to see but the facing building even if there was a balcony. He'd probably want to tinker with the tiny fireplace and see if he could get it to work.

The kitchen, she thought, moving to the doorway, was a disaster. First, it was tiny and airless, with no window. The scratched countertop was Formica, she knew that now, but in a burnt-orange color that hadn't been popular since the early seventies. The cabinets had been painted so many times that one could only guess what kind of wood might be hidden beneath the heavy layers. A steady leak had produced a rust stain around the base of a cheap nickel faucet.

The rest of the small unit was no better. The bathroom had been updated before Molly bought the place, but with her newly acquired knowledge, she now noticed that the faucets were plain-Janes and the toilet and tub were definitely on the low end of the fixtures scale. Her bedroom and closet shocked her by how small they were.

Sitting on the edge of the bed, she gave her head a shake and smiled at the craziness of life's twists and turns. She owned a beautiful new home two thousand miles away that was airy and bright and spacious. There were gold-and-crystal faucet sets in her master bathroom, for heaven's sake, and a fabulous spa tub that she hadn't yet sampled. She had soaring ceilings and a fabulous kitchen. Tall windows, decks, and a breathtaking view.

She had begun to think of it as home, a safe nest where she could settle in. Long before the house was finished, she'd known she would love it. She'd known she would be happy there.

But Addie's phone call had changed everything. The house outside Vrain wasn't home, this was home. Her tiny, dim condo, with a half-dozen locks on the door. Her fixer-upper that would have kept Joe occupied for a couple of months. She sighed, letting her shoulders rise and drop.

She hadn't been here an hour, but already she knew the condo wouldn't work for her anymore. Even if she tore out the kitchen and redid it, and put Berber on the floor, and replaced all the faucets and fixtures, even if she installed a working gas model where the old fireplace was...the place would still be small, poorly lit, and claustrophobic.

How had she managed to forget about the cramped rooms and tight spaces? Gazing around her, she tried to decide where she would set up her computer to finish the book. There really wasn't room for a computer and printer. Well, she had a few days to think about it, a few days before the computer would arrive. She hoped it survived shipping. Or maybe she didn't hope that. She had begun to hate the computer, because it represented her struggles with the damned book. Which she did not want to think about right now.

She wanted to change her clothes and shower, send out for something to eat, then daydream about her triumphant return as the Couture Femme.

But she discovered that she couldn't concentrate on what lay ahead, because she kept thinking about what she'd left behind.

Near midnight, she gave in to impulse, reached for the bedside telephone and dialed Joe's number. The phone rang and rang before she remembered that he would be with Jim and Avis and the Goosed Moose regulars.

After hanging up, she leaned back against a mound of pillows and imagined them ordering the usual cheesy burgers dripping grease, and fat, salty french fries, washed down with pitchers of icy Coors. They would be sitting in the last booth near the fireplace and, because the nights were still chilly in Colorado, Sandy the bartender would have a low fire crackling in the grate.

Wiley Oats would be at one end of the bar, and Bernie Schadler would be holding down a stool at the other end. Maybe Dumpling and the Romaines had arrived by this time. And maybe Matt Anderson, who would be off duty by now but still wearing his police uniform, had stopped in.

They would all commiserate with Joe and buy him a drink. They would tell him that he'd been a damned fool to fall for a big-city model. They would pat him on the back and say, "I told you so" in a voice that also said, "I'm sorry it worked out like this." Avis would tactfully hide her engagement ring beneath the edge of the table, and Jim would tell jokes in an attempt to make Joe laugh.

Molly wished that she, too, was with friends tonight, with people who understood that she was hurting, and would try to make her laugh and feel better.

But she was alone. And missing Joe. And feeling utterly miserable.

Chapter Thirteen

"All right," Addie said at the end of the day, her brisk voice ringing with satisfaction. "By Jove, I think we've got it!" She laughed, then smiled at the collection of scattered files littering the conference table. "I knew you'd take the Couture deal. It's far and away the best opportunity, the best career move."

Molly leaned back in her chair, her mind reeling with comparison figures and confusing clauses. "Do you think Couture will give in on the contract points we want changed?"

Addie tossed back a wave of perfectly coiffed silver hair. "You have them in the palm of your hand, Molly. They don't want just any model with some kind of small imperfection, they want *you*. They want to exploit the furor over Apple's decision to replace you with a new Apple Girl." Standing, she stretched, then ran her hands down her slim black sheath. "Apple is going to launch their new Apple Girl this weekend, by the way. I hope you won't let the campaign upset you. Believe me, the Couture deal is going to be bigger and splashier." She studied Molly's expression. "But there will be comparisons between Kelly Amstutz and you. Your name will come up in the trade reviews. You should be prepared for a rehash of the accident, your various surgeries, the eventual termination."

"It's all right." Standing, Molly also stretched, then

walked around the conference room to work out the kinks from sitting for so many hours. Large photos of the agency's most successful models lined the walls, including two shots of her. Pausing, she studied one of them, focusing on her upper lip and left eyebrow. To her surprise, the perfection of line and features struck her as rather bland and flat. A hand wandered to the small scar above her lip. Couture was correct. Her face was more interesting now. Being able to realize that told her how far she had come in the past year.

"Remember, the Couture deal is hush-hush," Addie cautioned. She pressed a button on the conference table that would summon her assistant. "So far no one knows that you are about to make a fabulous comeback. When your name is mentioned this weekend, and believe me, it will be, it will be mentioned in the context of tragedy. Top model horribly scarred, blah, blah and more blah. Since you wouldn't permit any photographs after the accident, no one in the industry knows that you're still beautiful and marketable." She waved a hand across the paper blizzard on the table. "Except these few accounts who saw Apple's test shots."

"Seriously, Addie, I'm all right with it. Now that we have a new deal, the announcement of a new Apple Girl doesn't bother me."

Addie stared at her. "What on earth are you doing?"

Molly laughed and looked at the wall, then down at her fingernail. "I just flicked a booger."

"I beg your pardon?"

"You had a paint booger on the wall, here by the light switch."

"Darling, I don't have a clue as to what you're talking about."

"Never mind. It isn't important." But she noticed that Bill the painter was right. Flicking the booger had exposed a tiny unpainted dot. For some reason, it pleased her that she'd known it would.

"Ah, finally," Addie said when her assistant knocked

politely, then opened the door of the conference room. "Please bring champagne, and enough glasses for the staff. We want to drink a toast to the success of our new Couture Femme."

Molly smiled. "How long will this remain a secret if everyone on your staff knows about it?"

Addie gave her a sly wink and lifted one perfectly arched eyebrow. "Now wouldn't it be oh-so-terrible if the news leaked out? Especially while we're in the midst of contract negotiations? Why, Couture might think we're trying to exert a little pressure." She blinked innocently, then laughed. "It's business, darling."

Molly smiled, remembering Daddy Romaine. "Just bidness," she said lightly.

Addie's staff gathered in the conference room—some of whom Molly knew—most of them she didn't—and Addie's assistant poured flutes of champagne and everyone toasted Molly and predicted great things ahead for her and for the agency.

Then Addie glanced at her slim gold watch and announced the end of the day. "A very successful day, I might add," she said, smiling at Molly while her assistant gathered up the files on the table. "We'll send a decline to Chanel and the others, and I'll meet with our attorney tomorrow and go over new wording for the clauses we want changed in Couture's contract."

She walked through the suite of offices with Molly, escorting her to the door. "Couture will undoubtedly request changes to our changes, but I'd guess that we'll have the contract firmed up within three months, probably less. That should give you time to finish your book. Couture loved the idea of coordinating the launch with the book's release, by the way."

At the gold-embossed glass doors, Molly stopped and clasped Addie's hand. "I don't know how to thank you. You made this happen, Addie. You didn't give up on me, you didn't stop believing in me. When your call came, I was floundering. I didn't know what I was going to do with the rest of my life.''

Was that true? When she first arrived in Vrain, yes, it would have been true. But at the time Addie called? That was the day Joe had told her that he loved her. Eyes sparkling and flashing, he had swung her in a circle and talked about marriage and babies and a future that might have swept her breath away. If Addie hadn't just told her about the flood of career offers.

Addie pressed her hand. ''No thanks are necessary. You deserve a second chance, Molly. You're one of the best.'' She opened the door. ''Now go out tonight with your friends and celebrate. Have a good time and enjoy your success.''

Flying high on champagne and triumph, Molly floated down the elevator to the street and hailed a cab. Addie was right, a celebration was just the thing. She'd go home and call…who?

For a moment she drew a blank, then a few names floated to the front of her mind. She could call Darcy. But Darcy would bring her wonderful Bruce along, and they would want to tell her all about their wedding and their future plans. Frowning, Molly rubbed her ring finger. Right now, she didn't really want to hear about weddings. And the models she knew wouldn't be enthusiastic about celebrating on a weeknight, when most of them would be facing an early wake-up. She didn't know how happy they would be for her, anyway, when they learned of the plum she was celebrating.

Idly nibbling her thumbnail, Molly gazed out the cab window, trying to think who would understand what the Couture deal meant to her, and who would drop whatever they were doing to celebrate on a weeknight, and who she really cared about seeing.

Joe.

Sighing, she stepped out of the taxi and entered her building. Already her buoyant mood had started to deflate. And it didn't help to notice that there were no messages on her phone machine. Well, why would there be? No one knew she was back in town. She would have to change that.

After pouring a glass of wine, she sat down at the phone and pulled out her address book. Two hours later, she leaned back in her chair and stared out the window at the face of the building across the street.

Everyone she phoned had seemed happy to hear that she was back in Manhattan, although some of them hadn't appeared to realize that she'd been gone and the others had laughed and said they couldn't believe she'd been gone for months, they would have sworn it was only weeks. When she announced that she had agreed to a wonderful new contract, everyone, without exception had said, "That's great!" Then they'd immediately gone on to tell her their own news, about how busy they were, and yes, we really should get together soon. But tonight? Oh, sorry, not tonight, couldn't possibly.

Couture's hope for secrecy had not been compromised. In the end, Molly had not divulged anything about the be-the-perfect-you concept, had not mentioned her selection as the Couture Femme.

And now it was too late to put together an impromptu celebration party, even if she'd found enough people without other plans to do it.

After pouring another glass of wine, Molly wandered around her small condo, feeling penned in. And she wondered about the quality of her friendships, something she'd never thought about before. Her friends were ambitious young professionals with busy lives and not much time to cultivate relationships that were much more than superficial at best. There were exceptions, of course, like Darcy and a few others. But the sobering truth was that Molly knew more about Mr. Melvin's personal life than she knew about the life of Janie Robinson, the last person she had talked to on the telephone. The realization shocked her.

Feeling lonely and a little cheated because there would be no celebration, she changed into her bathrobe and slippers, then drew a long breath and did what she'd been wanting to do ever since she arrived in New York. She telephoned Joe.

"Hi. This is Joe Townsend speaking," his deep voice said in her ear. "If this is a business call, please phone again before seven tomorrow or leave your number." There was a pause in the message. "If this is a certain leggy model checking in from the big city, call the Goosed Moose, honey." He repeated the phone number just before the beep.

Smiling, Molly hung up and redialed.

"Goosed Moose. Who ya calling for?"

"Sandy? It's Molly Stevens," she said, listening to the noise in the bar. "Is Joe there?"

"Molly! Hi. How's the big city treating you?" Sandy asked.

Molly said, "fine," and waited for a break in his conversation to ask about Joe again.

"Oh, yeah. You didn't call to talk to me," Sandy said, laughing. "Hey, Joe! I got a beautiful babe here who wants to talk to you."

But before Joe could get to the phone, Bonnie came on the line to say hello and pass along the news that Ellen O'Ryan and Don White had moved up the date of their wedding.

Then Daddy Romaine took the phone. "Damned— 'scuse me—shame about the end-of-the-project party, girl. We were all looking forward to it. Joe says you're going to send us some New York barbecue. Is that true? Never had any New York barbecue before."

Molly smiled, and scribbled a reminder on her notepad. "Sure is."

"Dumpling is standing right here beside me, and she says New York barbecue ain't nothing but crap, but we'll try it." He paused, and Molly heard him conferring with Dumpling. Then he laughed. "We want to know if there's any of them queen flies in New York City."

"This time I'm looking for the queen cockroach." It was a joke that only a fellow New Yorker could really appreciate, but Daddy laughed anyway.

"Molly? Hi, it's Jim. Avis wants me to ask if you could possibly fly back here to be in the wedding. We've decided on September sixth. We'll understand if you're too busy, but we'd both like you and Joe to stand up with us."

She scribbled another note. "I'll be there," she promised. Somehow. She'd just have to tell the Couture people that it was a commitment too important to cancel.

"Well, my God." Joe's voice boomed in her ear. "I had to elbow my way to the front of the line." He drew a breath. "Hi, honey. How are you?"

"Missing you," she said softly. She could picture him, standing against the wall at the west end of the bar, wearing jeans and a flannel work shirt, his hair tumbled across his forehead. "How did the first day go on the Henderson job? I forgot to ask Daddy if he and Toots started the excavation."

"Yeah, they broke ground. And guess what they're pulling out of the foundation hole?" A grin spread through his voice.

"Let's see. Let me think. Could it be, oh…rocks, maybe? Big rocks?" she asked, laughing.

She heard someone in the background shout, "Joe, you dumb pooch. She's calling long-distance! Ask her about the modeling deal! Did she take the Couture offer?"

Someone else yelled, "The Chanel deal was the best offer!"

And someone disagreed: "No, it wasn't. We're talking comeback, and that has to be the Couture deal."

Joe lowered the phone and shouted. "If all you barflies would hold it down, maybe I could hear what happened at the agency today. Honey? Are you still there?"

"I'm here, Joe." Blinking at the wall, midway between tears and laughter.

"I guess you heard. Everybody in the Moose wants to know what happened."

"We're going to accept the Couture offer." She waited while he told everyone and a cheer went up in the background. "Now tell me what's happening on your end."

"Oh, no, you don't, honey. We want details. Wait a min-

ute. I've got a list of questions I'm supposed to ask. Okay.''
He shouted behind him again. "Who the hell was rude
enough to put in this question about money? I'm not going
to ask her that. Honey? What happens next? How soon do
you start shooting? Where will the shots take place? Will
you have to go to Europe? How soon will the campaign
launch? And where should we look for your picture? In
what magazines or on what commercials?''

"They really want to know all that?" When he assured
her that everyone wanted to know, she answered the questions, with several pauses so that Joe could relay the infor-
mation. And it was wonderfully satisfying, to talk about it,
to let her excitement and enthusiasm bubble up.

"Wait a minute, honey. Sandy's pouring free champagne
to celebrate. And… What? Okay. Honey? Get ready, I'm
going to hold the phone out so you can hear.''

A tear slipped down Molly's cheek, and she frowned and
dashed it away. A blast of noise sounded in her ear. "Hip,
hip, hooray! Hip, hip, hooray!'' And then shouts of "Congratulations'' and "Good Luck'' and "We knew you could
do it.'' Someone shouted "Screw Apple Cosmetics,'' and
Molly laughed, wiping tears from her lashes.

"All right,'' Joe shouted over the tumult, "now get away
from the phone and give a man some privacy, will you?''
Molly heard a few protests, and then Joe must have moved
around the corner, because the background noise faded
somewhat. "Honey? I'm so proud of you. Congratulations.''

"Oh, Joe,'' she whispered. "I miss you so much. I miss
everyone.''

A hole opened in her heart, and she pressed a hand
against her chest and closed her eyes. Suddenly it didn't
make any sense, none at all, that she was here and he was
there.

"It's great that you called,'' he said. "I didn't really
expect that you would. We all figured it would go well for
you today, and I just assumed you'd be at some fancy restaurant tonight, celebrating with your friends.''

"I wanted to talk to you."

He was silent for a full minute. "Did you happen to watch any of the pooches when they were sawing lumber for the framing?"

"What?"

"If you cut a two-by-four halfway through, it breaks off in splinters and it can't be used. But if you saw it quick and clean, you get a straight, smooth cut and a good board. Molly, do you understand what I'm saying?"

"My mother said it a different way," she whispered. "She used to say a quick, clean cut hurts the least."

He was silent again, and then he said, "Molly, you have wonderful things ahead for you. You're going to take the advertising world by storm and break new ground. If you thought you were famous as the Apple Girl, wait until you see what happens with Couture. It wouldn't surprise anyone if you get a film deal out of this. Or...who knows? We're all going to say we knew you when."

She dropped her head and covered her eyes. He was making it sound as if they didn't know each other well, as if he were no different from Sandy or Jim or Daddy Romaine. A good friend who wished her well.

He came on the line again when the silence became uncomfortable. "Bonnie says my cheeseburger is getting cold, and one of the electricians is standing here saying he needs to call home. Congratulations again."

"Thanks." She watched a tear fall on her notepad.

This should have been one of the happiest days of her life. So why did she hurt so much and feel so awful?

JOE HUNG UP THE TELEPHONE and squared his shoulders. He'd lied to her about someone wanting to use the phone, and about a cheeseburger waiting for him. He'd wanted to get off the telephone, because it hurt too much hearing her voice and knowing he couldn't reach out and touch her or hold her or kiss her.

There was something else he had lied to her about. He'd

lied when he told her that people recovered from loving someone.

He could break off the relationship and withdraw from her life so that he wouldn't hold her back, but he couldn't stop loving her. He had always loved her and he always would.

Instead of returning to the cheerful noise in the bar, he picked up Aspen's burgers, then pushed out the door and walked to his pickup. Swinging inside, he gave Aspen his supper, then reached into his pocket and withdrew a thin slip of paper and rubbed it between his fingers.

Remember the bottom line.

He was trying to keep it in mind, but damn, it was hard. The bottom line was that he and Molly hadn't worked out. The bottom line was that her world and his didn't mesh. The bottom line was that he had to let her go, had to set her free to ride her ambition as high as it would take her. The bottom line was that she didn't want him or his way of life.

"That's a lot of bottom lines, and I hate all of them," he said to Aspen. Aspen looked at the empty passenger seat, then back up at Joe. "I know," he said, stroking the dog's head. "You miss her, too."

He slammed the truck into gear and burned out of the parking lot.

LOW IN SPIRITS and feeling out of sorts, Molly decided to spend Friday reading the finished chapters of her book. It annoyed her that her living room was so dim that she had to turn on a light to read. If she'd been at her new house, she wouldn't have had to turn on a light at nine in the morning. And she would have had a decent cup of coffee, because she would have made it in Joe's battered old pot, which, though she didn't understand why, made the best coffee she had ever tasted.

Two hours later, she set her manuscript pages aside and swore softly. The chapters were about her and about people she loved and knew. And they bored her half to death. If what she had written bored *her*, heaven help the poor reader who tried to wade through this. Who besides a devoted family member would possibly care about her childhood? Or that she had met a boy named Joe Townsend in the eighth grade?

She crossed her ankles on the ottoman, tented her fingers beneath her chin and stared at her bare toes.

The book was a mistake. She should never have agreed to attempt it.

The reason she'd agreed, she remembered, was that she had needed something to fill the gap after Apple Cosmetics fired her. Renovating the house had quickly filled that gap, and the book had been a struggle ever since. Worse, the struggle had yielded sentimental remembrances of no interest to anyone. Not even her. Therefore, what was the point in continuing?

She pondered that question for another two hours, then sighed and reached for the telephone. It was time, past time, to correct the mistakes she'd made.

"Debbie?" she said when her editor came on the line. "I can't do this. I don't want to write this book." She drew a breath. "Aside from the fact that the book is dull and boring, twenty-eight is too young for an autobiography." She cut off Debbie's protests. "My life is just beginning. And, Debbie, it's going to be more than the Apple Girl experience, so much more. Someday I'm going to look back and recognize that the Apple Girl experience was fun and lucrative and exciting for a while. But it wasn't the high point of my life." For an instant, she considered telling her editor about the Couture deal, but something stopped her.

Debbie talked for twenty minutes, asking her to reconsider, but Molly firmly repeated that there was nothing to think about. Her decision was made. Finally, reluctantly, her editor sighed and agreed. There would be no book. She was free.

Immediately Molly felt as if an enormous weight had been lifted from her shoulders. Her first impulse was to reach for the phone and call Joe. He would tease her about the time she had spent agonizing over sentences and trying to write under the worst of circumstances. He would also support her decision and understand her reasoning. But Joe would be at the Henderson site, striding around the foundation, shouting at the Romaines, with Aspen at his heels.

Slowly she withdrew her hand from the telephone and leaned back in her chair, looking at the television and then up at the ceiling. There were paint boogers on her ceilings. Seeing them made her smile. The last time she looked at her ceiling, she hadn't known about things like paint boogers.

Eventually she wrenched her mind away from remembering the vivid experience of remodeling her Colorado house, and she thought about something she had said to Debbie.

If the Apple Girl experience hadn't been the high point of her life, then what would be? Becoming the Couture Femme? If she took a hard look at what lay ahead, how would the Couture experience be all that different from the Apple experience?

Couture had offered more money, but she didn't need more money. The exposure with Couture would be more intense and comprehensive, but so what? Would her life be better if she was more famous? She didn't think so. Was she going to love returning to an early-to-bed-and-early-to-rise schedule? Yuck. Did she really welcome the idea of never eating another cheeseburger or basket of fries?

What exactly had she enjoyed so much about being the Apple Girl? Or even about modeling, for that matter? The success had felt good. But what else?

She couldn't think of anything. But she remembered now that she had gone into modeling for something to do while she was waiting for her "real" life to begin. And real life was a man who loved her and a family and a dog and a home of her own.

In short, everything she had walked away from so that she could be here in a cramped condo that she didn't like, waiting for the phone to ring so that she could talk to someone she knew only slightly, while she marked time until she began a new job that would require her to work like a dog, keep terrible hours, give her no time for a social life and make her famous enough that she'd be afraid to appear in public for fear that a tabloid photographer would snap her in an awkward moment.

Had she lost her mind?

Feeling low and dispirited, she wandered around the condo, then dialed out for Chinese. When the cartons arrived, she arranged them around her chair and clicked on the television, looking for the early news.

A few minutes later, she dropped her chopsticks and sat up straight, staring at the television screen. Reaching for the remote control, she turned up the sound and watched the new commercial for Apple Cosmetics. Kelly Amstutz's lovely, perfect face smiled at her, while a voice-over extolled Kelly's matte cheeks and glowing lipstick.

How many rolls of film had they shot to get Kelly's expression of luminous delight? How many times had Kelly smiled for the camera? Or changed her costume? Or begged for a ten-minute rest break? Molly remembered how it had been. The heat under the lights. The people beaming at her, murmuring outrageous compliments. The long hours and hard work that hopefully wouldn't show in the final commercial.

"Oh, my God."

She looked at Kelly, the new Apple Girl…and she didn't care. She didn't care that it wasn't her face in the commercial. She absolutely did not care.

Why had she ever imagined that she would?

The following commercial was for frozen egg rolls. Molly watched and then laughed out loud. What a fool she had been. Smiling, she cracked open the fortune cookie that had been delivered with the cartons of takeout. And her eyes widened in disbelief.

Follow your heart.

Good grief. This was the third time that she had received

the same fortune. What were the odds of that happening? And when was she going to start paying attention to the best advice she'd ever received?

Everyone, including her, had talked about following dreams. But the message in the fortune cookie was right. It was her heart she should be following. If she had listened to her heart, she wouldn't be sitting here now, alone and miserable. She would be in Vrain, starting her real life, the life she had been waiting for for so many years.

Reaching for the phone, she dialed a number, and her face lit with radiance when she heard the voice on the other end of the line.

"Addie? I'm sorry to call you so late, and at home. And I hope you're sitting down, because I have something to tell you that you aren't going to want to hear. But I'm fixing mistakes today." She drew a long, joyful breath. "I'm following my heart."

JOE STOOD at the edge of the foundation, watching Toots Romaine maneuver the scoop of the backhoe, trying to rock out a boulder the size of a Volkswagen.

"Remember when we pulled out that big-mama rock over at the Stevens place?" Daddy Romaine said beside him. "Remember her expression when she saw it?"

"It's time to break for lunch," Joe said, glancing at his watch.

"I miss that little gal. She was crazy as a caterpillar, but she paid her bills on time. Had a good head for bidness, too. I like that in a woman."

Joe didn't want to talk about Molly, but everyone in town assumed that he did. They thought it would help if he talked about her, but it didn't. Talking about her only kept the wound raw. Turning away from Daddy Romaine, he looked down the Henderson driveway and frowned.

"You know anybody who drives a brand-new Dodge Ram? Dealer plates still on it?"

"Looks like it belongs to you, son," Daddy said, squinting toward the road.

The pickup bounced around a curve, and now he saw a hand-lettered sign taped to the side of the passenger door. *Townsend and Associates Construction Company.*

"What the hell?" Joe muttered, stepping forward. "Is this some kind of joke?"

He tried to see the driver, but the sun was in his eyes. All he could tell was that the driver wore a cowboy hat and a red flannel shirt. And then... No, it couldn't be. It wasn't possible.

But she braked in front of him, spinning up dust, then popped out of the pickup door and lifted her hat. A silky sheet of wheat-colored hair dropped almost to her waist. She grinned at Joe, and her eyes sparkled. Then she pointed a finger at Daddy Romaine.

"You're just the guy I came to see. Come over here." Beckoning him forward, she walked around to the back of the pickup and let down the gate.

"Honey?" He couldn't move, couldn't believe his eyes. It was her. And unless he was going blind, she was wearing a tool belt around the waist of her jeans. Aside from the shock of it, he couldn't imagine where she'd found a tool belt small enough to fit her. "Honey?" he said again, forcing his legs to move. He followed her around the pickup.

She slid a look toward him, then waved her hand over a truck bed filled with picnic baskets and smiled at Daddy Romaine. "Barbecue," she said, her chin coming up like a challenge. "Delivered in person. All debts paid. Until the party. Which will be in August, at my house."

Daddy lifted the cover over one of the baskets. "New York barbecue?" he asked suspiciously.

Joe stared at them in amazement. Daddy didn't seem remotely surprised that Molly had driven out of nowhere to deliver his lunch in person. When she ought to be a world away.

"These two baskets are from New York. The others are from the Rib Shack in Longmont. You decide which is best. Hi, Toots."

"How do, Molly? Welcome home." Toots thumbed

back his hat and grinned at her. "Good thing we have a lot of pooches out here. You brought enough to feed the whole county."

Leaning around the side of the truck, Molly waved to the pooches drifting toward the pickup. Then she turned to Joe and he remembered to close his mouth. She put her hat back on her head and thrust out a hip. "Aren't you going to say anything, honey?"

Everything exploded inside him. He couldn't speak, because of the fireworks going on inside his chest, but he could move again. Striding forward, he caught her in his arms and swung her around in a circle, then crushed her against his body. He kissed her like he was a dying man and she was breath, and he didn't even notice her tool belt digging into his waist.

"God, I'm glad to see you! What the hell are you doing here?"

"Things didn't work out in the big city, so I'm looking for a job, trying to impress a potential employer," she said, laughing up at him. "The 'Associates' on the sign? That's me, if the offer is still open. But I'm not going to get a tattoo on my arm, and I'm not going to call everyone 'honey.' Just you."

He drank in the sight of her. Her hat had spun off in the dirt, and sunshine glowed in her hair like a halo. What she did for a flannel shirt and a tool belt ought to be outlawed. He knew every man on the site was staring at her.

"You're hired. Even though I notice you've promoted yourself to an associate. But what happened? The Couture deal, taking the world by storm, your comeback…?"

She stroked his cheek, and his skin burned under her fingertips. She set his body on fire, and his mind whirled with questions, with wanting her, with trying to guess why she had come back.

Lifting up on tiptoe, she kissed him, and the questions faded from his thoughts. She was here in his arms, where she belonged, and that was all that mattered. He'd been a damned fool to think she might belong anywhere else.

"You're always talking about the bottom line. Well, the bottom line is that you love me and I love you. The bottom line is that we belong together. The bottom line," she said, gazing into his eyes, smiling, letting him see her love for him, "is that you and I are real, Joe, and nothing else is."

"But your dream…" She fit against him like they'd been made for each other, like she was the missing piece that would make him whole.

"My dream is you," she whispered. "This is where my heart led me."

"Damn—'scuse me—this is mighty fine barbecue! Toots, get on the cell phone and tell Dumpling to come on out here."

Joe looked up and saw the Romaines and the pooches eating barbecue, standing in a semicircle watching him and Molly with big smiles on their faces. "Gentlemen…let me introduce my new associate, the soon-to-be Mrs. Joe Townsend." While the crew cheered, he whispered in Molly's ear. "Am I right about that?"

"You better be," she said, laughing and winding her arms around his neck, "since we're going to have a baby."

"What?" He blinked at her, and his mouth fell open. "Honey, are you pregnant?"

"Not yet," she said with a grin. "But I hope to be by tomorrow." She clapped a hand over her mouth, and her eyes sparkled. "Oh, no. By tomorrow, everyone in town is going to know I said that."

"Reckon so," Daddy agreed. "Boy, if that gal wants to be pregnant by tomorrow, you better get busy. I know how you feel about leaving the site, but a higher duty calls." He elbowed a grinning Toots in the ribs. "If I was you, boy, I'd take that gal over to her brand-new house and I'd get to work."

Joe laughed, gazing into Molly's glowing eyes. Then he picked her up and carried her over to his green pickup and tossed her inside. Aspen jumped up beside her, and he followed.

Before he laid down some dust and burned up the roads

to the nearest king-size bed, he pulled her into his arms and kissed her just to make sure he wasn't dreaming.

"Are you going to regret this decision?" he whispered against her lips. "When you're showing clients fixtures and faucets, are you going to think, 'I could have been the Couture Femme'?"

"Sure, I might think that," she said, nuzzling his throat. "But regrets? Never." Leaning back in his arms, she gazed into his eyes. "Regret would have been looking into a camera and thinking, 'I could have been Joe's girl.' That's real, Joe. And that's what I want to be. I want to be with you. I want to ride in the Vrain parade and help plan next year's mud festival. I want to work on your next construction project, and the one after that. I want to make a potluck dish to welcome the next new resident. I want to join the PTA, and lead a scout troop. That's the life I want. And someday I want to show our children my scrapbook and tell them how I was once a famous model while I was waiting for you to find me."

"Oh, God, I love you, honey!"

"Then take me home, and you better hurry," she murmured huskily, one hand on the buckle of his jeans, the other fumbling with the buttons running down his shirt. "Or you're going to scandalize the town by driving down Main as naked as a jaybird."

Laughing, he slammed the truck in gear and floored the gas pedal. When a beautiful woman said she wanted to get pregnant, a man had to follow his heart and do what he could to build a baby.

That was the bottom line.